Vampire Sovereigns
Book One

Kendrai Meeks
& Killian McRae

VENICE DUSK

© 2020 Tulipe Noire Press

Kendrai Meeks, Killian McRae

VENICE DUSK

All rights reserved. No part of this publication may be reproduced, stored in a retrieval system or transmitted in any form or by any means, electronic, mechanical, photocopying, recording or otherwise without the prior permission of the publisher or in accordance with the provisions of the Copyright, Designs and Patents Act 1988 or under the terms of any license permitting limited copying issued by the Copyright Licensing Agency.

Published by: Tulipe Noire Press
Visit our website at tulipenoirepress.com.

Text Design by: The Last TK.

Cover Design by: The Last TK

Edited by: Rebecca Hodgkins; Chantell Ried

First Edition: September 2020

ONE

Bells rang the hour from high atop the *Campanile*, but it was the arrival of the mysterious stranger and his silver-tipped cane to the Piazza San Marco that signaled the time.

Portia hadn't been so infatuated since middle school. Twenty-five years later, she found herself using the same tactics she had with Billy Martin in seventh grade: observe from afar, quickly avert your gaze when he turned your way, and practice writing Mrs. Billy Martin in the back of your notebook. Except that she wasn't thirteen anymore. The act she had undertaken for the last three weeks had a name: *stalking*. She didn't need to fake disinterest, because the sex-on-a-stick man *never* looked at her. At least, not after that first day. And as for writing Missus anything in her sketchbook? She'd need to know his name first.

Which was why she was sketching his portrait instead, because that was the refined, *adult* way of living out your romantic daydreams. Also, not a bad way to spend a six-week stay in Venice celebrating the anniversary of your debilitating divorce. From a distance, *Il Reboundo* (as her best friend had christened him from afar) could be anyone she imagined. Why ruin her fantasies by getting to know him? One of the best ways to be disappointed was to hold expectations. If you never expected anything, you were never let down.

Yes, six weeks stalking handsome Italian men and sketching their portraits without their knowledge like a foreign weirdo was just what the doctor ordered.

Oh, she did *other* things in the ancient city, too. Days passed in the museums or seated with a view of one of the city's bridges and a cup of espresso or gelato in hand. But one evening, as she drank tea like a proper citizen of the Realm and watched Americans, Germans, and Chinese tourists let the omnipresent pigeons in the piazza crawl all over them, she'd seen *him*. The gentleman. It was really the only way to describe him because he wasn't a tourist, and he certainly wasn't something as common as a waiter or a store clerk. Not that there was anything wrong with being either of those things, just... *He* couldn't be.

He walks with a motherfricking cane. Not because he was old or feeble, but because it increased the sexy. That's what she attributed it to, anyways.

The gentleman appeared each evening without fail, entering the square from the far end, under an archway housing the tourist-trap shops, before strolling at a leisurely pace down the center, as though waiting for the fall of shadows cast as the sun set to proceed him like some kind of majestic, moonlit carpet unfurling. *Like royalty.* Women (and some men) gawked, and it hadn't slipped Portia's notice that she wasn't the only repeat attendee to his daily performance. The fact that he looked like he'd just walked out of the opera, wearing a full suit, silver tie, and a finely tailored, heavy wool coat meant he didn't exactly blend in among the tourists with their selfie sticks, gelato served in a cone (an abomination, if ever there was one), and blue jeans. One time, Portia watched with amusement as two young women proved bold enough to broker an approach. One look and half-cocked smile had sent them into hysterics, however, and the photo they'd probably been hoping to get never came about.

Portia was *not* bold, but she was an opportunist. She wasn't about to let a male muse keep vigil through the middle of her evening routine and let it go to waste.

Their eyes had met that first night and only that first night, and when they did... Wow. Over the eight years of her marriage to Richard, not a single thing they'd done in or out of the bedroom had quaked her knees in quite the same way. *Il Reboundo* hadn't smiled or made any gesture to encourage her then. Portia only had herself to blame for the obsession she'd developed, because he certainly hadn't acknowledged her existence since.

Her pencil went to work the moment he stepped into view. The majority of the sketch was finished, but the eyes and the shape of his mouth still gave her trouble. They held a quality difficult to render in two dimensions. As her Nana might have said, *Il Reboun-*

do had the eyes of an old soul, ones which had witnessed both joy and sorrow beyond their years. Then again, Nana had also claimed that Portia had such eyes. Richard had scoffed. "I don't know, Port. They look like plain old brown to me."

The trench coat brushed the sides of his legs as he promenaded, eyes forward, silky ebony curls jostled by both his gait and the salty breeze coming in off the sea at dusk. The omnipresent pigeons flew from his path, adding to the façade of his bigger-than-life presence. As typical, women old enough to recognize the appeal swooned as the statue of Adonis-brought-to-life passed, a modern masterpiece of genetics.

Portia wondered what it may be like to eat gelato off *him.*

The pencil made way for her eraser. *Again.* The cheekbones—high, but not as symmetrical as she'd first drawn them. She looked down, correcting the mistake, even though it meant she'd miss his exit under the arches of the basilica, and... Wow, if he was pleasant to look at from the front, he was twice as nice from the rear. The coat hid some of the view, but its swish and sway allowed one to take in the defined outlines.

Her pencil leapt all over the page, scratching memory made graphite. Portia set down her tools after a few more minutes of work and held up the piece for closer inspection.

"As the locals say... *è perfetto.*"

The beauty of her sketch lay not on the talent of the artist but in the magnificence of the inspiration behind it. When she'd leave Italy in two more weeks *"Gentleman in Piazza San Marco"* would go with her, an eternal reminder of this glorious time in her life, when she'd left it all behind and had run off to Italy for a season like she'd always dreamed.

But as her stomach rumbled, Portia reminded herself that, even when living one of your life-long dreams, reality required a budget. Venice came with a price tag. The café had a great view, but her daily cup of latte was really the only thing her pocketbook allowed. Time to get back to the flat and yet another bowl of homemade minestrone. Portia stowed the sketchpad in her side bag and left a few euro to cover the bill, just as she'd done every evening for the past month.

She'd only gotten six steps from the table when someone called out behind her. "*Signora*, you forgot this."

She spun, already taking a mental inventory of what it was she could have left, when every cell in her body electrified.

It was *him*. But how? He'd already passed through the far end of the square and out of sight. How could he have had time to... Why was he grinning? Was he speaking? Yes, his lips were definitely moving.

His lips... *mmmm*.

"Signora?" His eyebrows rose as he jerked his hand before her, drawing her attention down. "Your pencil?"

Portia let out a huff and reached out. "Oh, yeah, thanks. I must have... I use it to write. A lot, actually. Hard to pencil without that, isn't it?"

Pencil without...? When had she forgotten how to speak English?

Il Reboundo grinned. "Indeed."

Jesus, Mary, and Joseph, she was going to melt on the spot. *Those cheekbones... Those eyes.* Nope, her sketch was *not* done. She'd gotten it wrong. All of it, so, so wrong.

He a hand into his pants pocket as his paused to survey the square at leisure.

Lucky hand.

"What is it you draw here each night? San Marco? The palazzo or the *Campanile*?" He motioned at the former home of the Doge of Venice and the three-hundred-foot-tall red brick clocktower that dominated not only the piazza, but defined the Venice skyline, as far as there was one, in turn. "Or perhaps it is our overly-friendly pigeons?"

"The pigeons are pretty fascinating, but..." She clutched her side bag a little harder. "It's the people, actually."

A dimple on one side of his face got her full attention as it blossomed into being. How did she not pick up on that before? Oh, that's right, because he'd never smiled. He'd never even *looked* at her but once. Well, he was looking now, his eyes slightly narrowed but his eyebrows still a little raised. Like he was trying to figure her out. Trying to inspect her for some hidden quirk.

"Indeed, Signora. I find the people... irresistible as well."

God, that accent. Definitely local. Combined with those broad shoulders, silky hair, dark eyes, and godlike features, she was about to combust on the spot. Good thing there was a church just a few hundred meters away, because Portia might need to make confession before long.

"May I see them?"

Portia's toes curled in her boots. "Sorry, who?"

"The pictures of whomever it is you've been sketching for the last few weeks." His gaze landed on the bag at her side, the one that suddenly felt like it weighed three times as much.

"It's not any one particular person. It's an amalgamation..." Her head cocked to the side and she realized that her five-dollar word must have outpriced his lexicon. Only then did she realize that he had a lexicon. "Wait, how did you know I spoke English?"

"Your mouth looks..." His head tilted as he focused. "British. But if you prefer another language? French, perhaps?"

Her cheeks reddened as her gaze fell to the ground. "Sorry, no. Learned some in primary school but it's slipped away through the years unless it's something that appears on a traffic sign or a fast-food menu. Anglican? What do you mean by that? What makes it look English?"

"Not English. English-speaking." He shrugged as he turned his gaze across the square, taking in a survey of distant thoughts. "When you've lived in this city as long as I have and have seen so many, you come to recognize it." Suddenly, he conjured his smile and turned back to her, tipping an imaginary hat. "Signora, I've enjoyed meeting you. Be careful in the city after dark, no? I know it feels safe, but..."

She nodded, her smile fading. "Yes, I heard about that."

Her best friend Mae had called all the way from Victoria, B.C., within an hour of the dispatch coming over the *local* television news in Venice. How she'd learned about the mugging and murder of two American college students half a world away, Portia had no idea, but Mae was satisfied that Portia couldn't possibly be the victim when she answered her phone.

Probably.

"I said a prayer for them in the Basilica earlier."

Her muse turned his gaze to San Marco's at the top of the piazza. "That was a kindness, *Signora*. May God grant their families peace." Then, with a flinch, her personal Valentino turned, setting out on his customary path. "*Buonasera*, Signora."

Only this time, moments before he slipped from public view, Portia was on the move. He became the flag on the tower, a beacon on the edge of her view, one she kept walking towards but to whom she never seemed to get any closer. The end of the rainbow she'd never reach. The chatter of the crowded square faded, and the walls of the ancient city closed in as they passed from the arches under the Basilica to the court to the left and onward to a maze of cafés and shops hocking their wares. Portia wasn't sure what she expected to happen at the end of this chase, but her interest in the handsome native had evolved. Passive infatuation became active obsession. *Why not follow him?* she thought. It wasn't as though she could ever sit in the square again and observe his daily vigil after actually talking to him. She'd simply die.

Her breath raced, both from the thrill of pursuit and from moving so fast to keep up. Portia's pulse pounded in her ears as they passed into the residential section of town, where the only people on the street were ghosts of the past or locals on their way home from work. His coat billowed out behind him as he hung a right and Portia's feet pounded pavement. She turned…

And found nothing.

Not just a vacant street and a door behind which he'd probably disappeared. Nothing. Only an empty path lay before her, the herringbone brickwork cutting off where one of the many canals veined across the island. Portia stepped to the edge of the water, looking left and right, seeing if her mysterious quarry might be standing on a ledge that jutted out. But he was nowhere to be seen. He'd simply... disappeared.

"Why are you following me?"

"Jesus!" She spun, her arm lashing across her chest to keep her heart from pounding out of it. It was him, of course. She didn't need to turn to know, but she did need to turn to believe it. "How in the hell did you—"

Her tongue stilled as he stepped forward, his eyes intense pinpricks of light in the night as one of his fingers pressed against her lips. Any criticism of "healing hands" she'd had through the years evaporated. When he spoke again, his voice sounded different. Isolated, dominating, as though the sound of the night and the lapping of water on the canal walls had been muted.

"I'm not an easy person to follow—I'm not even sure how you managed—but I'm more concerned with why you're doing it." His head angled and his hand dropped to the side. "Tell me, please?"

A wave of nausea threatened to take her to her knees. She should have eaten dinner before dashing halfway across town after a mysterious stranger. Or better yet, she ought not to have chased a mysterious stranger at all, especially in a foreign city on a solo vacation where it would take days for anyone to realize she was missing. Hadn't he just warned her himself that there was a killer on the loose?

She pressed her fingers into her forehead as his hand dropped away, almost as if she could pin herself to the air to keep from falling. "Because you're so handsome and I... I don't know, really. But when I saw you leave the piazza, I just *had* to follow you."

What was she doing? How could she just blurt the truth like that? And why did she feel like a guest in her own head?

He grinned. "Is that all?" His hand rose to pinch her chin. "No one sent you, then?"

"No one sent me." *Who would?*

"Very well. Then what are you doing in Venice? You're not a student. Too old."

Her forehead creased. No need to throw her age in her face. That was her mirror's job. "It's an anniversary trip, if you must know."

He blinked. In surprise? In doubt? He was so hard to read. "I've never seen you with anyone else in the piazza."

"That's because it's the anniversary of my *divorce*," she spat back. "First anniversary, actually. A year ago, I finally told Richard to go take a flying leap off a… Wait, that's none of your business. Why am I telling you that?" Portia shook her head, trying to make sense of her lack of restraint. Big mistake. The world went from dappled impressionism to Picasso-worthy cubism. "I think… I think I'm sick. I'm dizzy, and you… Wow, why do you smell so good?"

"You can *smell* me? Well, this *is* peculiar. But ultimately, harmless." His hand dropped away again. "Don't worry, *bella*, you're not sick. You're just under my thrall. It can make someone dizzy, especially the first time. It won't last very long."

"Under your what?" *Oh, dear.* She hadn't had an episode of vertigo in years, but suddenly, everything around her began to spin. "I'm going to—"

"*Bella, occhio allo scalino.*"

Arms replete with corded muscle caught her just in time before her legs went out completely from under her. He smelled… divine. Olives and rosemary, like her grandmother's kitchen. Drunk with sensation, she turned up goofy eyes. "I want to lick you."

"Perhaps another time." She could have sworn she heard him laugh under his breath. "You have a very strong mind for a huey."

Portia's hand extended to stroke his cheek. So cold. But again, it was the middle of winter. "What's your name?"

"Massimo, but you won't remember it, or me, after tonight."

"Massimo." She tried the sound out on her lips. It felt good. *He* felt good. She felt divine. Just dizzy. No, not dizzy, euphoric. "Of course, I'll remember you. I have a picture of you," her hand slide down to tap her side bag. "—right here. I've been drawing you for weeks now. Couldn't get the eyes right, though. Or the mouth. Always seems wrong. Never saw you up close." She turned up her gaze not so much at *him,* but to look at his features. "I'm not sure I can, still. There's something about you, something... unique."

"So *I'm* the one you've been sketching. Not an advisable thing, *bella mia*."

"Portia. My name is Portia Kepler."

"Of course, it is. This is Venice, after all." He had such an intriguing smile: both sweet and spicy at the same time. She amused him. That should be insulting. But for some reason, it warmed her to think that she could have that effect on him. "Portia, I'm sorry about this, but I'll need to relieve you of that."

"Hey! That's my..." She grabbed empty air, fully cognizant that he'd taken her bag, but completely unable to coordinate the act of snatching it back. No matter how hard she tried, her hands and her eyes couldn't agree on location. So that's what this was, after all? A mugging? It would figure that the man she'd lust after would be someone who'd take advantage of her. She had a type, didn't she?

His gaze drilled into her, if possible, more intensely than before. "Hush now."

Her tongue cut off mid-word, and no matter how hard Portia tried, it wouldn't loosen. Tendrils of anxiety painted blue fingers across the warm tones of her elation. Had she been drugged? Intoxication by a muse generally remained symbolic, but it would have been simple enough, wouldn't it? She had an established routine: sunset coffee at the same café for almost a month. The waitstaff might slip something into a drink for a small fee. And why else would Massimo have circled back if not for the fact that he knew she'd be ripe for the picking?

Hell, she had practically walked into this willingly.

Only, it had been her own decision to *walk*, hadn't it? How could she explain that part of it?

His smile this time held notes of guilt. "I should take you home now. Tell me where that is."

"Victoria, British Columbia." So her mouth did work. When *he* wanted it to, anyway.

Massimo grimaced. "No, I mean, where are you staying in Venice? What hotel?"

"Not a hotel. A vacation rental. On Via Fanciulla, number six."

Great, so not only had he stolen her bag, but now he knew where she was staying. What kind of an idiot was she?

He nodded. "That's not very far from here. Close your eyes, *bella*." Her world shifted as he literally swept her off her feet. "We're about to move very, very fast. It will be easier on you if you're not watching."

"Why would I…"

But before she could finish, immense pressure made her ears pop. All the air exited Portia's lungs with a burst like she'd fallen violently and landed on her back. She felt both airborne and floundering at the same time. Their surroundings whipped by in a blur, a multicolored patch of everything and nothing. And yet, with Massimo cradling her, she didn't fear. He wouldn't let her fall. Something… Something in his eyes.

It was an apology. Remorse. Remorse was the quality she'd found so hard to capture.

What was it that this beautiful man felt so sorry for?

"I said to close your eyes." Massimo leaned down, his lips tickling her forehead. "Tomorrow, this will all seem like a dream."

"You seem like a dream now."

No sooner had she uttered it than she felt an undeniable need to sleep. The world went black.

TWO

Massimo Bruneli, sixth Vampiric Doge of Venice, used the front door of his palace for the first time in years, sending the guards stationed at the public entrance into a tizzy.

"*SIGNORE PRINCIPE!*"

Four men and two women, all loyal to the Republic over their bloodline, took a knee and folded one arm across their chests, hands fisted, heads bowed.

Massimo grimaced. "You do know that if I had been followed in by an enemy, I could have taken all your heads off by now, don't you?"

Young vampires who hadn't known war. Not unless they'd been human during the huey conflicts of the last century. Most of them, however, had only walked the immortal ground for two centuries or so, a time of unprecedented peace in the Eight Courts. Like the cities that defined them, the vampiric courts tended towards a national identity now. One ruler had not attempted to overthrow another since 1835, when Lazio successfully captured Molise and Campagna. Even in the supernatural world, Rome was a conqueror. His guards, it seemed, had grown lazy laying in the shade of prosperity and peace.

Massimo allowed the Canadian woman's bag to slip from his shoulder. "Giuliano?"

One pale vampire with amber eyes and a scar across his left cheek leapt to his feet, saluting. The captain, and the only vampire in Massimo's court older than he. "Signore."

"I tried to come in through the well outside the palace gates like usual, but it seems the security gate is malfunctioning again." Electronically sealed doors and storm drains didn't mix well, it seemed. "Please ask maintenance to fix it. For good this time, if they can."

"Yes, sire." Giuliano saluted. "But if I can interject, it isn't the draining that's causing the problems. Sometimes when a huey throws a coin in to make a wish, it ricochets off the side and gets lodged in the trapdoor's hinges. Perhaps if you considered capping it like most of the other ones in the city, shutting down Catalina's well..."

Even four hundred years later, he flinched at the mere mention of her name. His beloved, his wife... Her bones were nothing but dust now, as he soon would be too. "I would never deny huey lovers a chance to make a wish for happiness. Never." Massimo shook his head as he handed off the bag and his cane. "Please have one of your men put these in my office and let Pavlos know I am back from my—"

A silhouette on the balcony overlooking the foyer emerged into the light. "*Pavlos* is already aware."

Massimo tapped the captain's shoulder, pulling both items back into his chest. "Never mind. I'll take them up myself."

The captain gave a salute and turned to one of his guards, ordering his troops off to the side, no doubt to dig into them about being caught unawares by their sovereign.

Pavlos descended the stairs with purposeful, jolting steps. As Massimo's second in command, the vicedoge served as part-confidant, part-secretary, and even as his official spokesman when called upon. The former Greek soldier had been turned in the dying embers of the last Great Huey War. Sired into the Dracule bloodline, Pavlos commanded a gravitas far beyond his immortal years. Being a descendant of Vlad Tepeş also helped balance some of the more radical members of Massimo's court. They bought into the name, but nothing the vicedoge had ever done suggested to Massimo he couldn't trust his hopeful heir.

Not that Venice worked that way. Yes, the office of the Doge came with royal powers. His word was law and his command, action. But Venice was a Republic, and only its citizens decided who wore the crown.

His rebuking glare proceeded him, along with a finger wag of epic proportions—Pavlos's weapon *du jour*. "Your Serenity, how many times must we discuss this? It isn't fit for the Doge himself to be patrolling Piazza San Marco nightly. Besides, we do not know if the killer of those poor women was a vampire."

"You read the same police reports I did." Massimo shimmied off his jacket, moving to the coat closet at the side of the lobby to hang it. Yes, the *Palazzo Oscuro* was a formal governmental building for the vampiric community, but it was also Massimo's home, right down to storage. "And I quote, 'as though they had been attacked by an animal and missing a massive amount of blood.' If they hadn't been tourists, if the case hadn't gotten so much international attention, we might have had a chance to examine their bodies for confirmation, but I'm fairly satisfied with my conclusion."

"But every member of your court has provided a solid alibi for that night."

He closed the closet door behind him. "Then it wasn't a Venetian that attacked them. But the question is, was the vampire who did kill them just passing through, or is he or she still in the city? That's why I patrol, Pavlos. I want there to be no confusion on this: I will not tolerate this behavior."

"It's been three weeks without further incidents, Your Serenity. Certainly, if it were a vampire, that means he or she has moved on."

"Yes, well, I still have concerns that..." Massimo saw a flash of auburn hair and brown eyes in his thoughts. "No matter. Is there any other matter we need to attend?"

Pavlos's eyes shifted to the staircase from whence he'd come moments before. "Perhaps in private?"

The Doge's eyebrow arched. "Very well, then. *Guards!*"

The heads of his security detail shot up.

"Please resume being of use to me. Back to your positions. And next time someone comes through that door unannounced, act. Even if it is Death himself."

As soon as they reached the third story landing and maneuvered into Massimo's soundproofed office, Pavlos wasted no time. "Your Serenity, you asked me to reach out to your sister in Florence to see if she could account for Marco's whereabouts on the night of the murders."

Patria's consort was one part snake and two parts slippery eel. "Yes, and?"

Pavlos turned his head. "She cannot."

Massimo's jaw ground. "Will there ever be a day that I don't regret making that match? I thought being consort to the Duchess of Tuscany would sate Marco's thirst for power. What else does the bastard want?"

"I'm certain you did what you thought best at the time. None of us can know for certain what the future holds. But I wanted to ask if you feel there's any connection between Marco's sudden boldness and the rumors coming out of the East?"

"You think Marco is a Dracule sympathizer?" Massimo waved a dismissive hand through the air. He maneuvered the Canadian woman's bag to his lap as he settled into the leather office chair behind his desk. His modern throne sat on four coasters. "Only a fool would think an alliance with Vlad Tepeș is anything but trouble. The Sultan doesn't gather allies; he gathers subjects."

"Marco has never shown himself to be a wise man, sire, and with the sovereignty of the Eight Courts growing weaker with each generation, perhaps he thinks the timing is right."

Younger vampires showed little deference for the treaties and contracts that had kept the Italian vampire population in check for centuries. They moved about hither and thither, disrespecting authority until respect was forced upon them. Did they not understand that the balance between the huey world and the supernatural was tenuous at best? Without the Federation of the Eight Courts, all hell would have broken loose long ago—and that was *before* the most infamous vampire to ever live returned from the dead.

Massimo sighed. "It's at times like these I wish that slayers hadn't gone extinct. Even if a few did tend to overstep their duties…"

"So, you admit, then, that some were killers."

The Doge measured his response carefully. Pavlos had never seen a slayer. The newer generations only knew them as legend, and as with any legend, normality gave way to the legacy of extremes. "There will always be those who kill for sport. The slayers were no more immune from zealotry and misguided passions than we were. Then we *are."* His hands were hardly clean. "When Tepeș reemerged from wherever he'd been hiding after the last Great Huey War, I worried that his radical ways might be reborn, too. Now it seems I was right. The world has changed so fast, and yet, in some ways, not at all."

"Speaking of the world changing…" Pavlos balanced himself on the edge of the desk, leaning over, perhaps trying to get a gander at the sketchbook Massimo was now pawing through. "A man with your looks carrying a cane and dressed to the nines does not walk through the Piazza San Marco unnoticed. I've already had to hire additional staff to scrub the internet for your image and hack them off from the world wide web."

Massimo barely heard what his vicedoge had said. His eyes feasted on the work of an undiscovered talent. Every flip of the page brought a revelation and a memory. There was nothing exotic about the vignettes from all around his city. An old woman and man seated outside their homes, exchanging pleasantries. A mob of pigeons using a woman wearing a hijab and a radiant smile as a perch in Piazza San Marco. A mother handing her child a gelato in a cone, the frozen treat already melting over the edges. What caught his attention wasn't the unique subject; it was that it wasn't unique. Portia Kepler saw people. Saw that the body was the shadow of the soul. She saw his city not for its touristic appeal, but for its living, breathing self.

And then he flipped the page… and saw his own eyes staring back at him.

Amazing. Any artist worth their brushes could capture a likeness. In an age where every huey had the electronic means literally in the palm of their hand, he'd even grown to dismiss the value of a portrait. But this monochromatic sketch of him held more color than every jewel in his treasury. Portia captured him in the true sense of the word. She'd taken the sadness of his eyes prisoner and tortured it, driving stakes through his emotions. How could she see so much of him without ever having met him face to face, and from such a distance?

"Sire?"

"Yes?" Pavlos's question snapped Massimo back into the moment. "Oh, yes, well… The more modern you try to sound, Pavlos, the older you seem to get."

"Bold words from a vampire who's celebrated his four hundredth fanging." The junior vampire made his way to the Doge's liquor cabinet, where he took two glasses from the shelf. "Truth doesn't die from starvation, and its absence makes rumors fat. We survive as a species by remaining in the shadows on the edges of humanity. Your sunset strolls across one of the most frequented places in the world is creating a virtual record of your movements and your presence. You're making it all too easy for your enemies to take notice and strike you down when you are vulnerable: before huey eyes and unable to use your supernatural strengths and powers. This isn't like the old days when the only thing we had to fear was the artists with their charcoal pens and ambiguous memories."

Massimo wondered what his vicedoge would say of the sketches he'd just locked in the top drawer of his desk. "I'll remind you that there is, in fact, a very nice painting of me hanging in the Uffizi at this very moment."

"From when you were still human, four hundred years ago. No huey would think that's you today. In fact, there's a rather popular Reddit thread of modern humans posing next to classical works of art to which they bear a striking resemblance."

Massimo looked up. "Reddit? Is that like Myspace?"

Pavlos's eyes went wide, until a moment later when he sighed, offering out a drink to his sovereign. "Never mind."

Now that Portia had been warned to stay away from the piazza—or perhaps compelled by the embarrassment of their awkward encounter to avoid *him*—the need to patrol it personally no longer seemed necessary. Still, it was an opportunity to allow Pavlos to feel he prevailed that shouldn't be wasted. "Very well, you have my word: I'll henceforth only visit San Marco's when I have specific business in the area."

Besides, if the attacker had indeed been Marco, he wouldn't revisit the scene of the crime for some time. He was evil, not stupid.

"Can we move on with the business of the night, then?"

In ancient times, the Doge's affairs would transpire in the court with supplicants making their cases, pleading for help, or seeking retribution for some grievance in person and in the public eye of the community. Life had changed in the last century, even among their kind. The supernatural citizens of his city expected due process now. Oh, as Doge, Massimo was still the ultimate adjudicator in the Republic, but there were forms to fill out, stamps to be affixed to long, scrolling paper. Consequently, the Doge had gone from being the black shadow of the Venetian night to the black ink of all its paperwork. A half-dozen stacks on his desk reminded him of it each night.

Pavlos presented the first paper and gave Massimo a moment to read.

"A petition for turning?"

The vicedoge nodded. "From Cara di Nali. Seems she has fallen in love. They've already married as hueys would, in the church, but she would like to have her husband turned and granted membership to the court."

"And where does she intend to live?"

"In her home by the lagoon on the Lido."

Massimo shook his head. "No, there are too many vampires in the city as it is. If she wishes to entertain this man as a huey, that is none of my concern, but Venice cannot support any more of us."

"Even as our food supply is vast, with Venice receiving a record number of tourists each year?"

"Frankly, *because* of it." At some point in the last century, they'd gone from being hunters to gatherers. You could practically wait by the port daily for the latest catch. "This city is bursting at the seams. How do creatures that survive in shadows manage when every corner is lit by those—" He shoved a finger in the air. "Little, annoying lights on their cellular phone camera things?"

The vicedoge's eyes narrowed to slits. "Should I mention the hypocrisy of that statement?"

"Absolutely not!" Massimo thought Pavlos's grin was born more of amusement than shame. Cycling a deep breath, he attempted calm.

Pavlos tapped the corner of the paper on Massimo's desk. "Sire, there hasn't been a newly-made member of the court since 1993, and some of our older members can taste the dust of their five-hundred years on their tongues. They will soon be stone for the sunrise."

"Of all people, do you not think I know that?"

The vicedoge absconded his gaze. "I didn't mean to imply that—"

Massimo held up a hand, silencing his second. "I know you didn't. It's just, five-hundred years is an approximation. Some of our kind meet the sun as young as four-fifty, and I'm, well—"

Massimo's voice trailed off. Immortal did not mean eternal. The truth didn't often break bread with what hueys thought they knew of vampires. Case in point: vampires did, in fact, die of old age. Eventually. The English slayers, when they'd been alive, had had a phrase for it: *five-hundred to the day, then pass away*. Death was coming for him, certain as the sun.

If one forgave the pun.

He reached for his pen on the corner of his desk. Pavlos was right. He couldn't keep denying requests just because he couldn't assure that he'd still be around to rule in the way he thought best. That wasn't how legacy worked.

"Fine, but tell Signora di Nali that I must meet her consort and assess his viability as one of our kind first. Also tell her that, if I grant the request, they cannot live in the city until after his first fanging. I can't have a bloodthirsty *bambino* running around. They will need to relocate until he is stable."

Pavlos nodded. His second knew better than to press him on this. "Yes, sire."

"Cara is an Alaric by the blood, isn't she? Has she asked the paterfamilias of her bloodline about turning him?"

"She... haaaas..." Pavlos checked his notes. "Not. She must have assumed that, if you said yes, he would be made here, in your court."

"I'm not a maker, Pavlos—everyone knows that—nor are there any surviving makers in my bloodline and—"

The vampiric elephant stepped into the room and took a seat in the corner, an awkward pachyderm Massimo would immediately exorcise.

"*You're* a Dracule."

A grimace flitted across the vicedoge's face. "And all Dracules are makers. Yes, Your Serenity. But we both know why that is a bad idea."

Damnable facts. Pavlos was precisely the type of vampire a clutch should want as its maker. Problem was, the Dracule bloodline was a dangerous one to belong to these days. No one was certain who headed it, and that confusion had led to infighting, death, and power struggles.

All, of course, amplified by the return of their most infamous members from the pages of history. Where Vlad Tepeș had been for three centuries and how he was still alive approaching six hundred years of age, no one was really sure. The most popular theory was that he and his Generals, collectively known as the Ravens, had found themselves trapped in smoke form, and that had served as an intended vampiric form of cryonics. But what he'd been up to since popping back up in the 1950s was common knowledge: the destruction of werewolves, supernatural rule of Istanbul, and domination on the political stage. Any progeny Pavlos fathered by that blood could fall under Vlad's command, if in fact Dracula ever achieved his ambitions.

And that introduced an even more frightening reality. Vlad Tepeş *wasn't* the paterfamilias of his bloodline. If he were, the infamous vampire humans knew as "Dracula" would have used that position long ago to rally his descendants and create who knew how many more. That meant there was another Dracula out there somewhere even older than six hundred years. How that was possible, even Massimo didn't know.

The Doge bobbed his head before returning to his paperwork. "Consult with members of the court. See what recommendations they can offer."

The other paperwork proved to be nothing more than bills, the payment of which required the Doge's approval. Pavlos would know this, as he was the one who'd readied the stack. So why did he linger?

"There's something you wish to discuss which I don't have in this pile, which leads me to wonder what could be so drastic that you don't want a paper trail."

Pavlos shifted in the chair, his nerves getting the better of him. "We have received a royal request for an official visit."

"Is that all?" Massimo stiffened, his eyes alone moving up from his papers. "It's not from Luciana, I hope." He didn't care if she were on the right side of history this week. He *detested* that woman's presence.

"She goes by Inga these days, and very few of us like spending time with our ex-lovers. Fewer with our former, deposed rulers, particularly if *we* were the ones to depose them." Pavlos shook his head. "No, I've heard she's in Germany these days. The request arrived today, born by a Turkish huey."

The pen fell to the desk as Massimo leaned back in his chair. "Now, *that* is unfortunate."

"Yes, sire." Pavlos bobbed his head. "You don't suppose it's an attempt to get a foothold in Italy, do you?"

"Do I?" Courage straightened his spine and a mask of conjured indifference concealed his thoughts. "In his human life, Vlad considered the Ottoman Sultan his mortal enemy. In his vampiric life, he modeled himself after him. It's a tendency of the oppressed to echo the actions of the oppressor once they've gained power. You've studied huey history, Pavlos. Do you remember who the Sultan considered his enemy?"

"We were." Pavlos's throat bobbed as he swallowed. "As well as Rome, Milan, the Hapsburgs, the Pope, most of Christendom.... Not to mention the Safavids, the Arabs, the—"

"It was Venice," Massimo cut in. But that was centuries ago. While Istanbul was still a major world capital, Venice simply wasn't. Was it archaic appeal, perhaps? The Doge shook his head. "This is a bitter pill, but the only thing that concerns me more than having the Ravens in our city, potentially plotting to overthrow me, is having them *outside* of it after being snubbed. *Keep your friends close and your enemies closer.* We will welcome him and his retinue—Do they still refer to themselves as the Ravens?"

Pavlos shrugged. "I don't know that Vlad and his generals *ever* used that phrase to describe themselves, but it's still used by others."

The moniker was too apropos. Cunning, cawing, pushy vampires that they were. "We'll welcome them as honored guests, up until he makes his intentions known."

His second scribbled a few notes into his folio. "Patria will be furious when she hears."

Massimo wasn't so sure, though he could offer solid odds that her consort Marco di Serpente, would practically climax with joy. "She will see this for what it is: no more than a way to hold together our already fragile alliances and protect us *all*."

The top drawer of his desk held a stack of paper embossed with the official insignia of the Venetian court. Massimo took out a sheet, inked his glass pen, then signed at the bottom with more embellishment than customary. "Draft the invite, add my seal, and send it by personal courier." He handed the paper across the desk. "Key members of the court, as well as the vampire staff within the palazzo, should be alerted that Vlad the Impaler will be joining us soon. Prepare appropriate accommodation and arrange an official court reception, entertainment, gifts, et cetera."

The flatline of Pavlos's features suggested he was not happy with the decree, but Massimo's second was nothing if not obedient. He rolled the paper into a scroll before dipping his head. "If I might suggest, you might consider commissioning a new art piece to mark the occasion. Vlad considers himself the Sultan of Istanbul. He expects appropriate gestures."

"Agreed, but the poets and composers of my court fled the city long ago."

Pavlos shifted. "Something shiny perhaps. He always was a fan of jewels and silver, I've heard."

"The rumor is he uses the Topkapi Museum as his own personal shopping mall. There's enough jewels and gold there to choke a one-ton goose. I think, perhaps, a commissioned piece of art might do." Massimo laid down his pen, crossing his arms over his chest as he leaned back in his chair. "Actually, I may know of someone in Venice who'd be able to accept a last-minute contract."

THREE

The rental apartment had a very comfortable bed. Why, then, was she sleeping on the couch, and in the same clothes she'd been wearing the night before?

Portia gained her feet with trepidation. She wasn't dizzy, and still, something about the world seemed... off-kilter. It reminded her of the time she'd woken up after surgery with traces of sedatives still in her system. Present in the moment, but somehow not a part of it. She went to the window, gathering from the angle of the sun shafting into the narrow street that the day had pushed by without her. It would be dark in a few minutes. *Well, wasn't that great?* She only had two weeks left in Italy, a trip of a lifetime that she'd blown half of her divorce settlement on, and she'd lost a day to...

Sickness maybe? No, that didn't seem quite right either.

Her growling stomach took her thoughts hostage and anchored her to her body. God, she was hungry. She needed breakfast. No, *dinner*. Gnocchi and white wine. Maybe a little biscotti. Gelato was a given.

What time was it, anyhow? Portia looked around for her satchel and the phone that would be inside. Hopefully, the battery hadn't died without being charged overnight, but unlikely. She'd need to replace the old device soon, but she needed to get every moment of use out of it before departing with a single woefully-needed dollar. In the month that she'd been in the residence, she'd made a habit of putting the bag on a hook by the door when she'd come in. Apparently, not last night though. Whatever, she usually didn't sleep on the couch either. She'd probably put it on the dining table.

Or next to the bed?

Maybe she'd left it in the bathroom?

In the coat closet?

If only this flat had a landline, she'd just call her cell and hope it rang.

That was it, it wasn't here. Either she'd lost it or someone had stolen it. But wouldn't she remember something like that? Tendrils of the unexplained began to coalesce in her thoughts; she'd gotten home not knowing how. Her bag was missing. She couldn't remember anything after putting the money down on the table to pay for the coffee at the café in Piazza San Marco after sketching the mysterious man who...

Good gracious, the coffee... She'd been drugged! That explained why she felt so loopy. Suddenly her mind raced with dark possibilities. What else couldn't she remember? Had she... But her clothes were on, no signs of violence, her body didn't feel used.

And yet, that sense of disorientation... *What if?*

Silence shattered as a knock on the door made her gasp.

Portia's hand splayed across her chest, an attempt to keep her heart from bursting out of her chest. She didn't know anyone in town, and the weekly maid service included with the rental had passed through two days before.

"Signora?" Another knock. "Signora, are you in there? You left your bag at the café last night. I've come to—"

Portia threw the door open without a second thought. "Oh, thank god! I didn't know... where it... was and..."

Black hair. Brown eyes. Broad chest, long wool coat, and a fine Italian suit. His cane rested against the doorframe.

Her Venetian muse grinned as he bowed.

Bowed.

"*Buonasera.*"

"*Buonasera.*"

Her response was automatic. Her reaction was anything but. Portia felt like a deer in headlights. Like she was a teenager who'd just opened the door to find the guy whose posters were plastered all over her bedroom wall on her doorstep. Her heart pounded even as her mouth went dry. She tried to blink away the illusion, but he wouldn't dissolve. This was real.

He was here. *Il Reboundo*. It had so much easier to laugh at that name when she was stalking him from across the crowded piazza and not having visions of straddling him as he stood right in front of her.

Speaking of which... "I'm sorry, but why in the hell are you here?"

Now it was his turn to gawk. As soon as Portia realized what she said, she considered slamming the door, shimmying through the bathroom window into the next alley, and leaving for the airport. She'd just buy a new phone and claim her passport was stolen. She'd gladly walk to Milan to apply for a new one at the consulate. That would be easier than having a conversation with the man she'd fantasized about for the last three weeks.

But that all evaporated with his laugh. "*Mi scusi*, I didn't mean to intrude, but..." He lifted his hand—oh, such long fingers—and presented the missing satchel. "I believe this belongs to you. Signora, you... You look pale all the sudden. Is something wrong?"

Was something wrong? Yes, there was certainly something wrong. He had the bag which had the sketchbook which included the rendering she'd been working on little by little for the last three weeks—of *him*. Pale, did he say? That was funny, because suddenly, Portia felt like her whole face burned.

"And now you look like you're on fire." He leaned in slightly, as though to examine her more closely. "Are you certain you quite feel yourself?"

"Yes, I feel myself just fine." Realizing the double meaning, her face burned even hotter. Enough of this. "I mean *like* myself. I mean... I'm sorry, do I know you?"

He grinned, doing a repeat performance of his bow.

And suddenly the term "standing O" wouldn't leave Portia's thoughts.

"I thought you might not remember me," he said, standing erect.

Erect. Standing O. Jesus, apparently her hormones were on vacation, too.

"My name is Massimo. We met last night. I was passing through Piazza San Marco—I walk through it most evenings—and I spotted you from the corner of my eye... *Como si dice? Swooning.*"

"Swooning?"

"You..." He stuck his hand up like a blade, then bent his wrist in the act of a fall.

"Oh, you mean I passed out?"

"Yes, that!" he snapped. "You *passed out*. I rushed over to help, made sure you came home safely."

Another step closer, and something changed inside Portia. Warring factions within battled; she had an almost irrepressible need to tackle him to the ground and to run away screaming as fast as she could. Something about this man... *Massimo,* was off. He was... different.

Duh, handsome as hell and sexy as sin. But there was more. He was more than he seemed to be, and he seemed to be a hell of a lot.

But what was she going to do, call him out for being duplicitous without cause? "That's so funny. I don't think I've ever passed out before."

"It can happen suddenly, for any number of reasons." His brown eyes bore into hers. "Remember me catching you."

And where before there had been nothing... she did. The world had tipped and he'd caught her.

"Oh, yeah..." The memory was so crystal, Portia wondered why it hadn't just popped into her head the second she saw him.

"Massimo…" She said his name slowly, like a confirmation. "Would you like to come in?"

The man blushed. Except for the part where he actually turned red, that was. "No, Signora, it would not be appropriate."

"Oh? Oh." She cleared her throat. "Would you… I don't suppose. That is, I was thinking I would go out and grab something to eat." It was practically night now, anyhow. "Will you let a swooning woman thank you by buying you dinner?"

"I have… uh, already eaten."

Her spirit shriveled. It was a convenient excuse not to spend time with her. After all, this guy was miles out of her league. Just because he'd been kind didn't mean anything more than that.

"Of course. No, I get it."

"But…"

Her head jerked up to see him smiling again. My, that smile.

"If you would not mind the company, I'd be happy to join you. Only one condition: you allow me to choose a place."

"You mean, take me someplace the locals eat?"

He huffed. "Please, Signora. This is Italy. Italians eat everywhere there is food and hospitality. No, just somewhere a little less… touristic."

Ah, so he'd spend time with her, but he didn't want anyone he knew chancing upon them. Maybe Massimo was married and didn't want his wife thinking he was running out behind her back. Only, no wedding band.

Suddenly, Portia heard her grandmother's voice in her ear. *"Don't look a gift horse in the mouth."*

Followed by the voice of her best friend back home, Mae. *"When the hot Italian guy asks you out—and he will—just go with it. You deserve to have a little fun."*

Portia put her bag on the table. "Sounds like a plan. Just let me plug in my phone and give me a few minutes to... um, *freshen up,* and we can go."

FOUR

The waiter's hand shook as he poured the glass of wine.

Portia leaned in over the table. "If I didn't know better, I would say he's scared of you."

Massimo chuckled. "He's simply nervous. It's not every day he's asked to serve the owner."

Portia's bright eyes went wide. "This is your place?"

"*Si.*" The house wine danced momentarily on Massimo's tongue before he swallowed. "Though just on paper. I leave its operation to the house manager and staff. Go ahead, order anything on the menu you want. Andrea is particularly skilled with seafood dishes."

"Seafood?" Her nose crinkled. "Not a big fan, and not something I think when I think Italian cuisine."

"Let me guess: you think pasta and pizza." Massimo leaned over the table as the waiter turned away. "I bet that's all you've eaten while you've been here, isn't it? Spaghetti or Margherita?"

"Gnocchi, actually. But I've eaten other things, too. Soups, bread… Um, lots of biscotti. The first night I was here I actually got Chinese food. Isn't that crazy? I came all the way to Venice and go out for the same egg rolls I can get at about fifty places in Victoria."

"It's not at all crazy. Familiar things bring comfort in unfamiliar places. But if you'll allow me…?" Massimo lifted the menu suggestively.

The redhead—oh, he did like redheads—tipped her chin. "Please. I'd like to taste something a native himself recommends. Particularly if that native owns the restaurant and approves the chef."

Massimo waved the waiter back over before whispering an order in the man's ear.

After a few silent moments, Portia set folded hands atop the table. "You don't look like a restaurateur."

"Meaning?"

Her raised finger gestured in no particular direction. "It's just... the clothes. A little fancy for being around kitchens. And, well, then there's the cane."

Massimo wetted the tip of his finger before tracing it over the rim of his wineglass. He didn't miss how her mouth fell open ever so slightly. "And what is it you think I look like?"

"I don't know."

"If you were forced to guess." He stood, grinning, giving her a slow turn. "A refresher, just in case you've forgotten what I look like."

"Oh, I haven't forgotten." Her eyes narrowed as he sat back down. "Can't put a finger on it, but someone important. Someone other people look up to. Maybe... Maybe even someone other people fear."

He managed to swallow before throwing back a laugh. "I assure you, *you* have nothing to fear from me."

Others? They'd best shake in their boots at his scent on the wind.

"I'm a simple entrepreneur," Massimo continued. "This is my only restaurant. I bought it some time ago. It's never really turned a profit, but it's been run by the same family for four generations and I can't bring myself to part with it. I also have a few trinket shops where tourists mill about. On the other side of town, I also co-own a gelateria."

He may have been a vampire for nigh on four centuries now, but he still had a sweet tooth. Massimo suddenly wondered if Portia might enjoy a visit.

The beautiful woman's fingers wrapped around the stem of her glass. "So, you live off the blood of tourists and all the dollars, then?"

"Signora, I can honestly tell you that I live off it exclusively."

His own glass stilled before lips that failed to hide his amusement. Not only because of the unintended chord of truth, but because he rather enjoyed the way her pupils dilated when the pose forced her to focus on his lips. *Careful*, he lectured himself. *This is hardly the time to be making conquests, with the Ravens circling the city*. Besides, he *did* have an agenda with her, though he was hesitating at getting to it. Yes, Massimo could enthrall Portia, get her to do whatever he wished. If he wanted art, however, then the artist's soul must be free of influence. Otherwise, she'd only produce whatever her human mind thought he wanted to see.

He lowered the glass and cleared his throat, breaking the moment. "But that is no less true for all the *Veneziani*. We have less than sixty thousand citizens, but every year, thirty times that in visitors. It is our double-edged sword, as I believe your English saying goes. They infuse our city with capital because of its history and culture, but that very history and culture are being lost under too many trampling feet."

Her brown eyes flitted away. "I suddenly feel like I should apologize for being part of the problem."

His insides twisted. Insult was rarely a diplomatic means of wooing talent. Massimo put down the glass and reached across the table with both hands, taking Portia's free hand. "Signora, tell me why you are in the city."

She squinted. "I feel like you've asked me that before."

Damn, he must have resurfaced more of her memory than he'd realized. Did he need to manipulate her more? No. After a moment, her countenance eased... even as her pulse increased ever so slightly and her blood warmed.

Stay focused.

"It's been a dream of mine since I first came to Italy as a teenager, to spend a season here drawing and painting."

"You are an artist." He leaned back. Good, now it was out there and he didn't need to admit that he'd already rummaged through her sketchbook for some time in the morning.

She nodded. "I mean, it's not something I do professionally. I don't try to sell my stuff or anything. I just... like capturing the interaction of a place with the people who live in it. The play of the transient and the timeless."

Massimo quirked his head to the side. Were the *people* transient or timeless? Or both? What an intriguing notion either way.

The waiter reappeared with Portia's meal before he could voice the question, reminding him that time was passing and he had places to be. "Most people who come to Italy with artistic intentions visit Florence or even Rome."

Her fork prodded the fish on her plate. She wasn't familiar with the dish. Not surprising, given her temptation towards pasta. "I know, but they don't *feel* like Venice. I get what you're saying; the tourists *have* taken over the city. But Venice is still Venice. It could never be anything else. Maybe it's because it's an island. Um, lots of islands? Rome and Florence had room to grow out, to have life move away from the core and for the core to be repurposed for tourism, but where would Venice grow to? It *can't* change."

"An astute observation." And one not many mortals managed to come to.

Portia shrugged. "It's the truth, and it doesn't take a genius to see. I *am* from an island too, don't forget. And don't get me wrong, I love Rome and Florence, but those are just places you go. Venice is different. It's not just the setting of the play, it's a character. Two characters, maybe. Both the hero and the villain, depending on the scene. Maybe that's what you're talking about when you compare tourists versus natives. Venice is playing you—and us—both."

She finally got bold enough to take a bite of her meal and Massimo watched as Portia renounced her allegiance to gnocchi, embracing a new master. Her eyes fluttered closed and her head tilted back. Even as she chewed, taking a deep breath and letting the play of oxygen in the back of her throat enhance and perfect the palette of flavors, he felt himself tempted. Massimo suddenly became keenly aware of his own hunger, and not just for blood.

"It pleases you?" *Because I suddenly want to please you so very much.*

Her mouth cracked ever so slightly when her eyes met his. Wide, wet, a flush in her cheeks. "Quite."

Suddenly Massimo had an urge to take the fork and feed her himself, if only to be somehow connected to the source of her euphoria. And with the salt from the dish entering her system, her blood pressure would tick up ever so slightly. The endorphins in her blood born of pleasure would sate his own appetite. He'd experience her delight by proxy.

He felt his fangs descend, and with it, Massimo lifted the glass again, letting it hover to block her view. "I will let Andrea know. At the risk of sounding cliché, *mangia*."

Portia grinned as she went in for another bite. "So now you're going to worry about clichés?"

His face screwed up. "Meaning?"

"Meaning... all this." With a swirl of her empty fork, she brought their surroundings forward as evidence. "The handsome Italian man in a fancy suit sweeps the single, plain-looking foreign woman off to some café only the locals eat at, plies her with wine and platitudes and attention until she's putty in his hands and he can assure her seduction, after which he either pretends he doesn't know her or rebukes her for thinking a one night stand was meant to be anything more than meaningless, not-even-very-good sex."

It, in fact, wasn't why he was sitting here with her, but he couldn't help himself.

Massimo leaned forward, a predator teasing prey. "First, you're not plain-looking. Far from it. You are a beautiful woman and I've had problems keeping my eyes off you for weeks in the piazza. Second, if we were to make love, you would not say after that it was 'not-very-good.' I would give you a night of passion and bring you to heights you only hitherto dreamed. I would probably ruin you for all other men. And I would never consider any moment with you meaningless. Just sitting here right now watching you experience *sarde in saor* for the first time is a memory I will carry with me forever."

Massimo wouldn't deny he took some pleasure in the way her mouth had hatched open, or argue that the increase in her breathing, of how her chest rose and fell, fueled his temptation. But more important than any physical effect was an emotional one. He found himself consumed with what her response would be.

Finally, Portia set the fork on the edge of her half-eaten plate and worked the linen napkin against her fingers. "As tempted as I am to call your bluff about the boasts of your sexual prowess, I'm more curious about what it is you're *actually* trying to seduce me into doing."

The Doge feigned confusion. "I'm not certain I understand what—"

Portia's hand flattened in the air, stilling his tongue. "Prove that wasn't complete insincerity and respect me enough to tell me the truth."

Who was this creature, and why didn't she fall for the same tricks other huey women did? It was like Portia had some kind of immunity to his charm. It should annoy him.

Instead, it made him hard.

Tepeş is coming. Stay focused. You cannot engage in liaisons.

"I want to hire you to compose an original artwork in my home."

Portia tilted her head to the side and bit her bottom lip. Well, she hadn't been expecting *that*. "You don't even know what my work looks like."

"I do." He shifted his weight in the chair. "I looked through your sketchbook."

Her cheeks burned almost as deeply red as her hair. "You *looked* through my work? Without my permission?"

"Signora, if you are embarrassed because I saw the sketch you made of me, don't be. It is exquisite work, and I suspected from the second time I saw you at San Marco what you were doing. Your focus could only mean you were drawing me, or—" he leaned back to give her eyes a wide landscape to survey. "—that you wished to seduce me."

Portia's eyes went to her lap. Her voice softened, but a heavy stone, once laid, continued to weigh down. "Still, you had no right. Don't get me wrong; I appreciate that you went back for my things and returned them, but I don't see it as any less an invasion of my privacy than if you had stolen the bag yourself."

Massimo leaned forward. "Signora, aren't you being somewhat hypocritical?"

Her face shot up, her eyes wide and burning. "Excuse me?"

"Not about looking at your work. You're right about that and I apologize. But did you ask *my* permission to look into my soul?"

"Oh, come on, now. It's not like I—"

"The detail of my eyes..." Massimo said, cutting her off. He ran his fingertips over the insides of her wrists, tracing a path over the palms of her hands. "The sadness... Did you have my permission to claim it as your own?"

"I... Well..." Portia snapped one of her hands back, then, after a moment, melted around the edges. "I guess I see your point. I should have asked your permission before I sketched you."

"I give it retroactively." Massimo raised his glass in a toast and grinned when Portia did the same. He waited until she put the glass to her lips to add, "On one condition."

The Canadian woman rolled her eyes. "So you *are* going to proposition me."

"Yes, but not in the way you're thinking. I'd like to commission a work from you. For pay, of course."

Portia guffawed. "Well, I'll give you credit—no one's ever tried to pick me up before by offering to pay me to *draw*."

"Not only draw," Massimo clarified. "I'd hope you'd paint as well."

"You don't even know if I can."

"I've seen your work. I have every confidence."

"Be that as it may, I'm only a tourist. I can't legally work in Italy."

"Don't worry over that. It'll be a one-time payment in cash."

He pursed his lips and considered his options. Another artist was the most obvious choice. Pavlos could call Patria's people tonight and have someone sent from Florence by morning. Of course, that created a debt he'd owe the Duchess of Tuscany, and the last thing Massimo wanted, with the political waters in such turbulence, was an outstanding marker someone could call in. A huey artist with no ties to the vampire world was the perfect solution.

Not to mention, she had a rather shapely and pleasing backside.

Her jaw worked, evidence that she was taking the offer under heavy consideration. Massimo knew the moment he had won. Portia sucked in her bottom lip, then huffed.

"Fine, what the hell. I only have two more weeks in Italy, though, so it better not be a big project."

Massimo shot to his feet. "No, not at all. My assistant, Pavlos, will phone you in the morning with details. Please, enjoy your dinner."

"Wait, you're leaving?"

Massimo took his coat from a peg on the wall. "Don't worry about the bill. It's, how do the Americans say, 'on the house'. In fact, eat here whenever you like, free of charge. The waiter will be given a break in order to walk you back to your flat."

"No, not... I mean, thank you, but..." She stood and took two steps toward him. "You're just leaving?"

"I told you that I am not attempting to seduce you. If I stay, I might change my mind. Besides, I have a meeting to get to."

She looked out the window. "At this time of night?"

"Much of my work is done at night." Well, all of it really.

Massimo stepped forward and took up Portia's hand, kissing it. "*Buonasera,* and thank you."

FIVE

That odd sense of disorientation was back, but this time it couldn't be because she was hungry. Portia stayed at the café after Massimo suddenly split, polishing off every bite of the fish dish because food that good should *not* go to waste.

But, seriously, what the hell? The man she'd been obsessing over for over a month (okay, not over the man, but at least over his face) not only knew about her (not so) covert mission to sketch him, but approved of it to the extent that he wanted to hire her like she was a professional artist or something? Temptation begged her to immediately phone Richard and throw that fact in his face. Her ex had told her repeatedly that her work was amateur. Another part of her refused to believe Massimo's offer was sincere. Remembering the maxim "the simplest solution is usually the correct one," Portia would lay money on the chance that Massimo's ultimate goal was getting into her pants. The thing was, she wasn't sure she'd be opposed to that. Why shouldn't she have a little fun? After the years-long drought that capped off her failed marriage, didn't she deserve a little reminder that she was, in fact, a woman?

But, oh, the embarrassment if she was wrong. So she'd just go along with the probable ruse and wait to see if Massimo made a move. Of course, if she sensed any danger, she'd be out of there in a second flat.

A high soprano let out an amazing run from the kitchen, jolting Portia from her reverie. Looked like the phone battery had juiced up while she'd been out. She crossed to the kitchenette and pulled her device off the charger, catching "Mae Avery" on the screen before she tapped the receive button.

Mae didn't wait for a hello. "Dear Lord, I thought you died."

Portia settled into one of the mass-produced plastic chairs

common in holiday rental units. "Hi, Mae."

"Hi, Mae?" Mae repeated. "All you have to say is 'Hi, Mae'? Didn't you get any of my messages? Especially the last one where I said if you didn't call me back in an hour, I was calling the Venice police?"

"No, when did you leave that one?"

"Two hours ago."

Portia's eyes surveyed the small flat to check for any hitherto unnoticed officers performing a wellness check. "They seem to be running late then."

"Of course, they are; they're both Italian and men." Across the line on the other side of the world, her best friend sighed. "Portia, when you decided to run away to Italy alone—"

"I prefer to think of it as a solo vacation."

"We agreed that—"

"You *instructed* me that—"

"We would check in with each other each day when you were going to bed and I was getting up," Mae concluded, undeterred by interruption or correction. The chastisement disappeared from her tone as she continued. "Babe, I'm just worried is all. Anything wrong? Did something happen?"

Portia saw her choices before her in pale blues. Lie, and risk Mae not having a heads up if, in fact, Massimo turned out to be some kind of creep she needed to worry about, or tell her the truth—that Portia had passed out in public and been escorted home by a sexy stranger who *might* be plotting to seduce her—and risk having her best friend turn on a dime and become fervently Team Massimo in a bid to get her good and fucked.

Literally.

"My battery died and I didn't notice until I woke up." No need to say 'just before sunset because, yeah, maybe there is something wrong with me.' "I left it behind on the charger when I went out for the evening. Sorry for worrying you."

Doubt still lingered. "But everything's okay other than that?"

"Better than okay." Portia made for the much more comfortable Papasan chair in the seating area. "I talked to him."

"Him?" The momentary cluelessness cleared as Mae picked up the context. "Wait, do you mean *Il Reboundo*? The guy who looks like Valentino?"

"I said he *reminds* me of Valentino, because frankly, most halfway good-looking Italian men remind me of Valentino. He and Roberto Benigni are my only reference points. Turns out, his name is Massimo."

Keyboard clicks punctuated the background of the call. "Full name please. I'm searching for him now."

Portia had opened her mouth before she realized the truth. "You know, I actually didn't get his last name."

"What? How could you—Never mind. Just give me the story already. Make it juicy and remember to tell me about how soft his lips were."

"Nothing happened, Mae." Much to her disappointment. *Was* she disappointed? Portia had basically called a spade a spade hoping they could just bypass the theatrics if, indeed, he was trying to seduce her, and instead of jump (on her), he'd retreated into an offer of employment. "It happened in the Piazza."

"The one where all the pigeons crawl all over people?"

"Pigeons don't crawl, but yes. And he… um, *walked* me home last night. And then, tonight, he showed up just as the sun was setting and asked me out to dinner."

"Sounds like the beginning of something romantic," Mae said. "And after dinner?"

"That would be right now. Don't forget about the time difference." Portia couldn't stop herself from blushing, even though nothing had happened. "There was no after-dinner. In fact, there really wasn't dinner, not for him, anyway."

In her mind's eye, Portia could picture Mae's brown eyes

narrow. "Honey, you didn't just set the sketch you made on the other side of the table and pretend it was him, did you?"

"No, of course not. What I mean is, yes, he took me to a café--*His* café, actually. I mean, not like he's a chef or anything. He owns it. And then... He just let me eat but he didn't touch a thing. Then he offered me a job before taking off a minute later."

Mae's words dripped confusion. "What kind of job?"

"He commissioned me to create a piece for him. I told him I can't work legally in Italy but he says he'll pay me under the table."

"Girl, you know if anything's going to go on under the table, it ain't going to be paying you, right?" Mae laughed. "Of all the cheesy ways to pick up a woman..."

"I know, right?" Portia tucked her legs under her as she settled down on the couch. "But the crazy thing is, I think I'm going to do it."

"Sleep with him? Good."

"Well, I'm not sure about that, but yeah, the commission," Portia confirmed. "Hell, even if it does turn out that's all he wants, I could use the money. I don't have a place to live when I get back to Victoria."

"I told you, you could stay with me as long as you want."

"I know, Mae. And I might take you up on that temporarily, but I'm not just talking about a place to live. I mean a *home*. A place where I fit and have purpose. And, you know, maybe even a master bathroom."

"Dare to dream big. And as long as you feel safe, have fun, honey. Just next time, don't make me call the cops while you're off doing it."

SIX

Any notion that Massimo's job offer was part of a well-crafted seduction plan faded when Portia arrived at the address his assistant, Pavlos, had given over the phone the next morning at the crack of dawn.

"If Signora can come as soon as possible, we would very much appreciate it."

She'd grinned and swallowed her morning espresso. "I didn't realize the project was that urgent."

"Indeed. The work for which you've been commissioned is intended to be dedicated to a revered guest who will be arriving later this month," the assistant had returned in Grecian-flavored English. "We would like you to start immediately. Also, I'd like to be the one to personally show you the space where you'll be working, and I'm afraid my schedule only allows an early morning appointment."

"Massimo keeps you pretty busy, huh?"

The attempt at small talk grew tiny in the wake of Pavlos's flat-toned answer. "Signore Bruneli is a very exacting man with great demands upon him, but he has asked me to make—what's the words, *setting you up*?—a priority today."

Bruneli. Portia jotted it down on a slip of paper. She'd scour the internet later to see if anything popped up. "Got it. No problem. I can head over as soon as I finish breakfast and get dressed."

Like so many ancient cities, Venice was what Mae called "a bag of mixed nuts." Small, crumbling homes that still claimed a rustic charm stood next to grand residences which had been given modern makeovers, boasting double-paned windows, refinished walls, and even visible security systems. And of course, there were all those bridges and canals. This early in the day, most of the gondolas, protected by taut leather covers, sat listlessly on the barely-moving streams, an aquatic parking lot that reminded somebody the best way to get around the city wasn't on foot, it was on water. Boat rides were expensive, though, thanks to all the tourist dollars driving up prices. Not only that, but something about being on such a tiny boat didn't sit right with her. She wasn't *afraid* of water per se, but she hadn't been a fan of aquatic activity since the time she'd been electrocuted while swimming as a teenager. So Portia played pedestrian, occasionally finding herself in the length of a few steps going from a perfectly uniform street of old stucco buildings into some small piazza rimmed with fine red brick, marble statues, and mosaic masterpieces dating back centuries. She'd been in the city for a month, exploring its nooks and crannies. The contrast no longer shocked Portia. What did was the building to which she'd arrived after a forty-five-minute walk.

She looked down at her phone, queried the address again, then looked up once more. No, this was the right location. It just couldn't be the right place.

Before her, a large, forest green door with a concrete crest adorned atop it belied visions of a much grander façade rising behind it. She found herself feeling like Dorothy at the unassuming gates of the Emerald City, knowing from what touched the sky behind it that an enchanted world was about to open up to her. Portia craned back her head, counting at least six stories, including a circular tower, and the Middle Eastern-influenced arched windows the residences of the wealthy had. White alabaster walls were broken at intervals by the inset of quartz and granite motifs. Leaded windowpanes made Portia feel more like she'd arrived at a museum than an office building. An inset of tiles along the roof reminded her of the kind on some of the buildings in San Marco's square, though even from here she could see a few broken ones. An outcropping of golden-leafed tree branches over the wall suggested there was a courtyard right inside the door.

To the unfamiliar tourist, the building might look plain despite its height, but this was Venice. The glamorous façade would be facing the grand canal, which it appeared the building faced. She had the sudden urge to pony up enough euros and courage to get a water taxi, just so she could see what it looked like from that direction, because she was willing to bet it would knock her socks off.

Portia leaned on the edge of one of Venice's old public wells and thought to ring Pavlos back and make sure *he* hadn't made a typo when someone said her name.

"Signora Kepler?"

She looked up from her phone. "Sorry?"

A woman in a security uniform had appeared from nowhere, in the shadow of the wall. The blare of morning light hitting Portia's eyes made it difficult for her to pick out any additional features.

"You must be Signora Kepler," the security guard repeated with a smile. "Signore Katsaros asked me to meet you and escort you inside." She bent at the waist, her hand skimming the air to suggest Portia step toward the doors, which had been opened without a sound.

"Oh? Oh, ok." She shoved her phone in her pocket and moved on. "I just wasn't sure I was in the right place. This looks like a palace."

The security guard nodded. "This way please, Signora."

Despite the promising exterior, what Portia saw beyond the gate failed to live up. In fact, it was rather pedestrian. The trees with the mix of blushed and browned leaves did bring some interruption to the plain-Jane concrete path lined by small stones and the occasional rosebush, but it could be the entry to any Canadian office building.

Portia shuffled her feet in a swift walk, but the guard, despite a petite frame, managed to outpace her. "Signore Katsaros? Is that Pavlos? I was told to ask for Pavlos."

"Yes, Signora. He's Signore Bruneli's personal assistant."

"And what exactly is it that he *assists?*" If this was an office building, it lacked the usual signage she'd expect.

Instead of answering, the security guard held open a set of double-doors—glass and metal framed this time—and watched Portia as she passed. The question and the woman who asked it were left alone.

The square lobby smelled its age: musty with a tinge of sea air leaking in from a small, rectangular open window on a nearby wall. Underfoot, polished marble bore signs of use, dipping in the middle where people had walked on it through the centuries. Sconces carved of another type of stone in a refined, baroque design may have once held candles, but looked to be retrofitted with electric lights, giving the enclosed space an artificial glow. When a young man who couldn't be more than twenty and who wore a dark brown suit emerged from the hall leading off to the left, Portia blamed his poor pallor on bad lighting.

He stuck out a hand. "Pavlos Katsaros. Thank you for coming so quickly."

Portia pulled back her head in surprise, even as she held up her hand in kind. "*You're* Pavlos?"

Too young. Maybe he was doing an internship? Or maybe Pavlos had been born with some fortunate genetics that kept him looking much younger than his actual age. Her grandmother had been like that. Nana Alba had been nigh on a hundred when she passed away a few years ago, but you wouldn't have thought her more than sixty if you saw her.

Portia blinked in confusion when, instead of shaking her hand, Pavlos bent over to kiss the back of it. He wasn't trying to charm her, was he? He was way too young for her.

Moments later, the thought cleared as Pavlos straightened. "Welcome to the *Palazzo Oscuro*. If you'll follow me, I'll show you to the space in which Signore Bruneli wished you to work. This way, please."

Massimo's fangs erupted. He rolled onto his side and took to his feet, ready to kill…

The room was empty, just as it was each twilight when he awoke. No one was coming to attack him. No one was coming to drown his beloved and his child again.

No one was praying he would save them, only for him to let them down.

His erratic pulse slowed as his conscious mind abolished the delusions of his predator body. He wiped a hand over his face before looking at the table beside his bed, the screen of his phone lit. The little devices of the modern age were marvels, each generation iterating information flow a little better. When first he'd become Doge in 1687, his chamber had to be protected by guards night and day, huey or vampire, depending upon the hour, and his waking briefing a formal affair in the office of his royal council. Now, a high-tech security system kept his room locked unless he, Pavlos, or the captain of his guard opened the door, and all the matters that had happened whilst he'd been sleeping, were texted to him.

Oh, the paperwork would still be on his desk, awaiting his attention. Perhaps, if he were lucky, the huey developers could rid his remaining fifty or so years of that before too long.

Three notifications awaited him. A message directly from Patria, asking if the rumors about a visitor from Istanbul were true. How she'd found out, he couldn't say. For all Massimo knew, Venice was not the first court Vlad had petitioned to visit, though. He swiped away the message into a box designated for follow-up. The second and third messages had both been sent by Pavlos, one around 9:30 AM, the other just a few minutes ago. Massimo expected the more recent to be more important; if a morning message had required immediate attention, Pavlos would have woken him personally during the daytime.

> ISTANBUL SENDS WORD THAT THEY DELIGHTFULLY ACCEPT YOUR INVITATION TO COURT. SULTAN VLAD LOOKS FORWARD TO RENEWING YOUR GENIAL ACQUAINTANCE. ARRIVAL IS ANTICIPATED IN TEN DAYS.

"Genial acquaintance? Mother Mary!" Massimo dropped his phone and moaned, running a hand down his face. Genial might describe it, if by such one meant that they had sat together last they met in the same room and not attempted to kill each other. That had been, what, sixty years ago? Seventy? Italy had been still piecing itself back together after the last great huey war. Most had thought Vlad dead for centuries, the infamous vampire unseen since the late seventeenth century.

Massimo, of course, had known his return was always a possibility. After all, he knew that Vlad wasn't dead. But even now, Massimo had been unclear on what the purpose of that rendezvous had been. It pointed to one conclusion, however: Vlad didn't know that Massimo had had a heavy hand in having him trapped in silver to begin with.

Hopefully, he never would.

A buzzing noise forced Massimo from his thoughts. He retrieved the phone and activated the screen.

> SIGNORA KEPLER IS ABOUT TO WRAP UP FOR THE DAY. WOULD YOU LIKE TO ADDRESS THE SUBJECT OF PAYMENT FOR HER COMMISSION? I WOULD HAVE SETTLED IT MYSELF BUT I WASN'T AWARE OF THE DETAILS.

Consumed by the verbosity of the message, it took Massimo a moment to come to terms with the meaning. Discuss payment? Surely, he and Portia had already... But as he replayed the discussion they'd had the night before in the café, the Doge realized that in fact, no, he had only promised to pay her with no referral as to how much. The money itself was no issue; the Venice court rarely lacked funds due to the loyal patronage of its vampire citizens and a history of wise investments dating back to the Middle Ages (if one overlooked the whole black tulip fiasco). How much was appropriate though? Too little and he'd insult her. Too much, and Portia might think he was patronizing, and not in the way modern women appreciated. If she walked, he'd be back to square one with a welcoming gesture for the Ravens, and the last thing Massimo wanted, no matter how much he detested them, was to insult Vlad Tepeș. The monster had managed to find a way back from death and rebuild an empire in less than half a century. Secure as he may be in his own throne, Massimo didn't fool himself that he was any kind of challenge for a vampire with that level of gravitas and, frankly, cult status.

Perhaps his sister in Florence could advise on the going rate for commissioned art these days?

In short order, the Doge had arisen, washed, and dressed. He kept it casual tonight: gray slacks and a long-sleeved white tee, tight-fitted to show off his muscular frame. Portia had been attracted to him; most women were. It was an advantage in negotiations he'd be a fool not to employ. Yes, he needed to properly appease her wishes in the matters of compensation, but he didn't need to—what was the huey phrase, be taken to the cleaners?

But when he made his way downstairs and came to the foot of the staircase leading into the grand courtyard, Massimo found another huey phrase at play: the shoe was on the other foot.

He intended to have Portia create a work filling a provided canvas that measured a meter square, then to mount that canvas on the wall at the end of the enclosed courtyard and surround it with stucco, setting it into the wall, making it part of the structure, as it were. In a welcomed coincidence, the wall had long needed refinishing, the stucco having weathered and cracked over the last few decades. Instead, a set of scaffolds had been erected against the wall, creating a platform that raised about a meter off the ground. Portia's charcoal stick worked on the existing wall itself, a space three times the size of what he had intended.

This... was going to cost him more. Massimo forgot momentarily that a huey worked within view and sped across the courtyard, covering the sizable length in a few moments. Luckily, Portia's back was turned.

"Signora Kepler, what are you doing?"

She startled, her instrument dropping from her hands as she spun. The sudden movement threw her off-balance, and before Massimo knew what had happened, he was holding her to keep her from hitting the floor.

With faces inches apart, he was surprised that instead of

attraction, her mannerisms suggested embarrassment.

"Just remember," Portia said, "you hired a glorified sketch artist, not a dancer."

"On the contrary, that was one of the best pirouettes I've seen in some time."

He should put her back on her feet. The fact that he kept her there, leaning into him for support, suggested... something. But he was only a vampire. Portia's accelerated pulse scented the air with the sweet aroma of adrenaline. Massimo closed his watering mouth, lecturing his fangs to obey and stay retracted.

She is not here for this. She is not your prey.

The Doge made an act of clearing his throat as he helped her to regain her balance before taking a step back and lowering his eyes. "Apologies, Signora. I lost myself for a moment."

"Are you... bowing to me?"

When he regained his stance, it was to find a confused glare on the Canadian woman's face. "I am humbling myself in a show of contrition."

"Right, so yeah, bowing." She kneeled to retrieve her charcoal stick. "No worries. And there's no need for the Signora Kepler thing. I'm just plain Portia." The instrument slipped into a pocket as she motioned to the whitewashed wall with dashes of black lines behind her. "I hope you don't mind that I got to work before we had a chance to discuss anything. Pavlos mentioned there was some urgency and... Yeah, since I'm leaving Italy in two weeks, it doesn't give me much time, either."

"I don't mind, of course. Only..." Massimo mounted the scaffold beside her. "I asked Pavlos to provide you with a canvas. I didn't intend for you to work on the wall directly."

"Oh, he did, but then he also told me your plan: stucco the work onto the wall afterward. I figure, though, if you were going to do that, you wouldn't care if I worked directly on the wall itself."

"But the wall is so..." The proper English word teased his

tongue. "...irregular."

"That's what I like about it." She pressed a palm against the wall. "There's history here. These bumps, these cracks... They record that. I did a whitewash on it to give myself a uniform background, but no, I wanted to work with the structure, not paste over it and have it pretend to be something else." Suddenly, Portia pulled back her hand. "I... hope that's okay."

Okay? It was better than okay. "It was not something I considered, to incorporate the wall rather than cover it."

"Yes, well, sometimes it's better to work with imperfection than ruin something with obfuscation." Portia turned all shades of blush and bashful, but she seemed to coach her expression into one of utter sincerity. Embarrassed to be professional, but still dedicated to its pursuit. "I'm also a woman who respects agreements and contracts, even verbal ones. I believe there's the matter of my compensation to discuss still."

"Yes, of course." Massimo swallowed his nerves. "We'll discuss it over breakfast."

The teasing pinks turned to red. "I'm sorry?"

He snapped. "I mean... dinner. Apologies, signora... Portia. English words. I sometimes get confused." His arm swept across the air. How could he make such a beginner mistake before a huey? Something about this woman was undoing four centuries of refined practice. "Please, won't you join me? I was about to take my meal upstairs."

Her eyebrow quirked. "Not going for your evening stroll in Piazza San Marco? This is about the time I see you there each night."

"Now that you're here, it doesn't seem as necessary. But if you'd prefer to go out..."

"No." Her hand landed on his wrist, making his own heart respond. Someone who could force a vampire's heart to beat might be as big a danger to him as he was to her.

"I'd love to join you for dinner, just as long as we remember it's so we can discuss *payment*."

"Yes, Portia. It is my noble intention."

SEVEN

"You seem…" Massimo weighed his words in the shaking of a hand. "…distracted."

Distracted? How did he expect her to focus? At dinner the night before, keeping her eyes fixed on Massimo was easy enough. He was a very eye-fixable subject. But in a room of such opulence, with paintings on every wall she was certain were originals and signed by the likes of Rosa and Caravaggio? Sitting in a gilded chair and eating filet mignon off fine china rimmed in gold? Dining in a room lit by chandeliers demonstrating the height of Murano glassmaking that probably each cost more than she'd make in a month?

And there were three of them!

Portia cleared her throat. "It's the, um… The table."

"The table?" Massimo looked down at the surface before him. "Is it dirty?"

"No, it's clean." Portia lifted her chin, casting her eyes to the head of the table where her host sat, a full twelve place settings on either side away. Each word she spoke was made crisp to compensate. "It's just much bigger than I was expecting. When you said join you for dinner, I didn't realize you'd be sitting in Venice and I'd be halfway to Milan."

Massimo's chin tucked in. "I forgot that your hearing is… In any case."

He stood then, napkin in hand, and set about gathering up both his plate and his place settings. It was the chair to her immediate right that he indicated with a tilt of his head. "May I?"

Was he joking? "It does make talking much easier, assuming that's still on the itinerary."

"Indeed." Massimo settled into a chair. "I enjoy your company. I live the paradox of being constantly surrounded by people and yet, often alone. Most times I eat, it's alone in my office, one floor up."

"It must be a demanding job if you have to eat at the office all the time," she said as a piece of beef slid off his fork and into his mouth.

His chewing slowed. "Portia, this isn't just my office. It's my home."

"Oh?" God, he must be richer than Midas. "It's… very nice."

Despite a marked improvement in logistics, they passed some space in silence, their clacking silverware the only noise. Finally, Portia lowered her knife and fork, tapped her mouth with her own linen, and placed her hands on the table.

"Massimo, about my fee—"

"Ten thousand."

She blinked her confusion. "Dollars or euros?"

"Dollars."

"American or Canadian?"

He narrowed his eyes in her direction. "Does it make a difference?"

She tried not to cackle.

Too much.

"Have you seen the exchange rates lately?"

His head shook. "Foreign currencies are one thing that tends to slip my periphery. But I do know the strength of Euros, so let us just say Euros, and I'll raise it to twelve thousand to compensate for any loss when you bring it home to Canada."

The wine managed to escape her lips and spray the table.

Massimo's hand slashed the air. "Fifteen thousand, but that's my final offer."

"Massimo! Stop outbidding yourself." Portia grabbed the napkin and tried to clean up the worst of the mess. Luckily, none of the wine had gotten on her lap. "Maybe we should agree on the *subject* of the work first, then we'll come back to payment."

His frame eased. "Very well."

With the auctioneer retired, she leaned over and took her sketchbook from her bag. "I tried to think of a way to capture a reflection of the city in a way that isn't often done, but how does somebody do that? Venice is one of the most painted cities in the world. You can't walk into a major museum today without seeing the *Campanile* in at least one work."

He nodded. "As much as I treasure our architectural heritage, you're right. It's iconic of the city, but it isn't its heart."

"Heart: I'm glad you said that." Portia flipped the sketchbook open, giving Massimo a flash of an embarrassed grin when his portrait went by. Finally, she arrived at the page where she'd sketched her outline earlier that day. She turned the book to him and placed it in his hands.

Massimo studied for a moment, his forehead creasing. Nerves took hostage of her hands, forcing them into trembling fists under the table. What would she do if he didn't like it? It was, after all, not a grand work like he'd probably be expecting. No portrait or even a sketch of a cityscape. The outline, while rough, also demonstrated a simple concept with manifold complexity beneath the surface. Her sketch wasn't so much outlining a subject, as revealing its shadow.

"It looks like a map of Venice," Massimo said at last, looking up with a screwed-up expression on his face.

Grinning, Portia shook her head. "It's actually a chart of its canals. You see, I don't want to sketch *Venice*. I want to sketch the world that envelopes it: the sea. If it wasn't for the water that veins these islands, Venice would just be another medieval Italian city."

From the narrowing of his eyes, she guessed that he'd taken offense. Portia tried to remedy her remarks.

"It's a meaningless, hyperbolic statement. It's impossible to picture Venice any other way than in the totality of what it *is,* is what I mean."

"No, it's not that." His eyes returned to the sketch. "I was expecting a portrait, perhaps one on a classical theme. Instead, you've drawn out the circulatory system of my city's body."

She somehow managed to swallow despite a mouth gone suddenly dry. "Do you... like it?"

For a moment, Massimo's features gave no hint of his impressions. Finally, he lowered the book and caught her eye, the intensity striking a note within her to music she'd forgotten. "I think it's brilliant. I have a thing for circulatory systems."

"But...?" Portia pulled back when he said nothing more.

"It's... It's silly. I..." His gaze turned with his head, away from her and to the far edges of the room.

"Massimo." Portia didn't know where the boldness came from, but without thinking, she leaned forward, putting her hand on his. So cold. For a fan of the circulatory system, he certainly had a sucky one. "This is a commissioned work, and having no guidelines and knowing time was limited, I pushed forward with it this morning. But if you don't want this—"

His eyes fixed on her hand before he lifted them. Suddenly, the flesh beneath her fingers fired, and the heat spread up her arm and into her chest. Damn, if that wasn't a lustful gaze, she didn't know what was. Where in the hell had that come from?

He turned over his hand, capturing hers. "Don't doubt my sincerity. I love the concept. It's just, I have certain... painful memories about the lagoon."

"Oh? Oh." Her hand drew back and she sat erect in her chair. "I'll cover over my work in the morning and start on something new."

"No, Portia, I want *your* art, not my vision for it." He nodded. "Fifteen thousand euro, then?"

"No, ten was fine, to begin with." Enthusiasm restored; Portia grinned.

Massimo held out his hand, this time in a formal gesture of a handshake. She slid her hand into his, but the formality did nothing to persuade her body not to react, especially when his long index finger rubbed the inside of her wrist right over the pulse point.

"You might not get a chance to ruin me for other men, but you're definitely going to ruin me for other clients if I ever do decide to become a professional artist. I'm not sure I'm worth that much."

"I'm quite sure you are. And are you so certain I won't ruin you for other men?"

The wine—what was still in the glass and not soaked up in the napkin, swirled on her tongue, the glass held at the rim of her lip. "Am I?"

Squirming in your seat would not be a good look for you. She should pull her hand back. Should, but couldn't. It was like he knew the effect he was having on her, the corners of his mouth twitching.

"Massimo, I—"

A soaring soprano trill rent the air.

"Shit. Sorry, I mean…" Portia leaned over to fish her cellphone from her bag. "Can you excuse me for a minute? It's my friend back in Victoria. She calls every day at this time to check in with me."

Massimo bowed his head. "Of course."

Thank goodness the room was so big; it gave her a chance to get some distance and have some privacy without getting lost in the labyrinthine hallways. Portia hit accept call. "Mae, it's fine. I'm fine. Everything's fine, but I really can't talk right now."

"Where are you? I don't hear any noise like I usually do when you're sitting in San Marco's."

"I'm not in San Marco's." Oh, dear lord, this wasn't going to be easy, was it? "The portrait of *Il Reboundo* is done. But… I'm getting a much better picture of the man who inspired it."

"Really?" Concern turned to glee as self-appointed mother turned to best friend. "Oh, my God, you have to tell me. No, you have to *show* me."

"Sure, I'll take a picture of it after I get back to the flat tonight."

"What? No, not the sketch, you ninny. I mean I want a picture of *him*."

Portia turned honorary red. "Mae! I can't just take a picture of him."

"You did it before."

"From a distance, as he walked across the piazza. Not when he's sitting next to me at a table in his own home."

"Oh, my God. You're at his place?"

"Yes, but not like, alone. It's literally a palace, and there's other people around too." Portia chanced a look over her shoulder and caught Massimo's eye. He grinned; a catlike smirk that made her think he somehow *knew* they were talking about him. When Portia turned back, she cupped her hand over the receiver and lowered her voice in an abundance of caution. "Look, I'm having problems enough keeping myself from crawling over the table and into his lap. I don't need the added pressure of him thinking I'm here for any other reason than a professional one."

"Just tell him your crazy best friend back in British Columbia wants to live vicariously and see hot Italian men. Besides, that one you sent the first time disappeared from my phone."

That was weird, but beside the point. "I'm *not* going to take a picture. Look, he's waiting for me and I don't want to be rude. I'll talk to you tomorrow."

"Just hold up your phone and pretend you're sending a text and—"

Portia closed the connection before Mae could elaborate on her covert plan. When she turned back to the table, it was to find Massimo's smolder could melt ice caps. *Had* he heard what she whispered about crawling onto his lap? But that was impossible;

she'd been thirty feet away when she'd said it. In any case, there could be no doubt what that gaze meant. Perhaps now that they'd reached an agreement on her compensation, he thought he was entitled to get a little more from her than her art.

And suddenly, that thought scared her. Yes, Portia had already pictured them in several variations of passion, but reality didn't die at the altar of daydreams. She hadn't been with a man in three years. The last years of her marriage had been fraught with constant rejection, and though she hated to admit it, Portia wasn't sure she could face that again if she was misreading the situation. Massimo appeared to be attracted to her, but Italian men were famous flirts. *What if that's all he's doing, recreational flirting*? If she made a move and he turned her down, how could she ever come back here and not die of embarrassment?

"Massimo, I... I think I need to get back to my flat. I've been here since early this morning and I'm beat."

Obviously disappointed, he pushed himself away from the table, pulling the napkin from his lap and pushing it to his lips. "Of course, I understand."

Lucky napkin.

"I will have the kitchen package your plate."

"No, I—" She rubbed her stomach. "I'm full, actually. I ducked out for a late lunch this afternoon at a little café a few streets away." A lie, but so what? "But what I *did eat* was delicious and I really appreciate it. I really have to go before it gets too late. There's still a killer out there, isn't there?"

She'd meant it as a lighthearted jest, if in poor taste, but concern suddenly pulled at his brow.

"Yes, there is."

Massimo snapped twice and a man appeared out of nowhere. Well, out of the kitchen, anyway. Was Massimo the kind of guy who just had to snap his fingers and servants appeared? Who in the hell was he? After conversing briefly in his native tongue, Massimo turned back to her.

"Giancarlo will tell Pavlos to cancel my evening appointments. I'll walk you home."

EIGHT

He was doing it for her safety.

Massimo kept telling himself that, as a litany of self-rebuke rained through his thoughts. Pavlos had been right to criticize his carelessness. If Marco was behind the killings, who knew what else he was planning? The Doge of Venice should be cautious. It was no secret amongst the vampires that Massimo's life could be drawing to the end of its natural—or unnatural—time. "Five hundred to the day and then pass away." It was a cute English turn of phrase for an ugly vampiric truth: the creatures were not, in fact, immortal. *Un*mortal was a better term for it. Free from aging and disease, imbued with superhuman and even supernatural abilities, but not eternal. It wasn't an exact timeframe, as the idiom suggested, but that wouldn't change the facts. Vampires endured about half an eon once turned, until one day when they simply became stone. Did it happen in the four hundred and eighty-third year or the five hundred and fifteenth? Depended on the vampire.

Massimo may have a century left. He may just have a few decades. The uncertainty was marvelously and frustratingly human.

Pavlos needed to be ready to assume the Dogado, and he definitely was *not*. The appeal for a new making showed that. His city had one hundred eighty-six undead residents. It sounded like so few, but Venice, despite its dwindling native population, had never burned brighter, attracting tourists like moths. Tourist with cameras who turned their gaze on every street and every canal.

Vampires lived in shadows, but the shadowy places in his city were growing few and far between. Hiding was becoming harder and harder by the night, and that was before some rogue vampire had decided to lure two college students away from the Piazza San Marco and make a meal of them. Coincidence that it was at a critical time in his rule when he'd be most vulnerable to any sign of weakness? Hardly.

"A penny for your thoughts?"

Portia smiled at him as he turned to her, her gait slow, as though she were trying to stretch out the time. Or was that him?

Massimo shook himself from his reverie. "I still think you should have spent your time in Florence. That is the city of artists and poets."

"No, Florence is the city of patronage," she said, turning forward. "It's where all the talent went because that's where all the money was. It's where the Medici were, after all."

And still are, he'd wanted to say. At least, among the supernatural.

"Medici money bought the art *they* wanted to see," she continued, "not what the artists truly wanted to create."

"As your patron, I'm not sure if I shouldn't take insult in the assertion."

A silent laugh lightened her features. "I didn't mean it that way. And there's nothing wrong, of course, with making something somebody wants you to make, especially when the pay is so good." She gave him a wink. "Like I said, there is no substitute for Venice. I came here because I love the balances."

"Scales? Weights and measures? We developed many of those technologies as well."

"Again, no. I mean…" She paused at the high arc of one of the hundreds of bridges, motioning vaguely to the waterway below. "Where else in the world do you have something like this? I mean, I know there are other places with canal culture, but it isn't just the canals. It's the way the city and the sea live in symbiosis. How the citizens and tourists conflict and yet, there's a confluence between them, because both are after the heart of the city. It's the way that the Basilica San Marco and the Doge's Palace occupy the same square, and yet are miles away from each other in form and function."

One Doge's Palace, anyway.

"It's the way that you can't take a step here without breathing the city's history, and in doing so, become part of it. Venice is its own art, and the people who walk its streets are its poetry, all meter and verses overlapping into an epic saga," Massimo concurred. "Also, our food is far better than Florence's."

He was surprised to shift a bit when Portia's shoulder knocked against his. "Admit your bias on that one. I, for one, prefer beef over fish. No offense."

"None taken. You are young, and there's still time for you to learn better."

"Young?" Portia chuckled. "Well, I'm not old, but I don't think anyone would look at a forty-one-year-old divorcee and think she was a spring chicken."

He would. So little time the hueys had, and she had wasted some of it on a failed romance. "You are young at heart, Portia, as all of those pure of heart remain, despite the effects of time on the body."

They both drew to a stop at the flat's door, the air between them charged with possibility. Massimo hadn't drawn Portia into his home and his employ to be here. He hadn't even done it to taste her. Yet suddenly, he found himself wondering if he might not do both. Yes, as she noted, she was not a spring fowl (what an odd saying... hens nursed young all year long), but there was a timelessness to her spirit that had spoken to his own.

"Are you going to try to kiss me?"

Massimo blinked, shocked by her bluntness. "Is that what you wish?"

"I... I don't know." Her eyes darted to her door. She was... frightened. But not by him, no. But something had her off-kilter.

The Doge reached out and took her hand. "Signora... Portia, you are a very attractive woman." His heart ached as she flinched. "You *are*, though someone has managed, either through intent or consequence, to convince you otherwise. And yes, I relish the idea of kissing you. But you have shown part of your soul to me tonight, both with your art and with your words. Exposed, I can sense its fragility. I fear that to make love to you tonight, while pleasurable to us both, would suffer your heart to hide behind the rationales and lies you tell yourself of why you're not worthy of being desired."

She pulled back her hand and stumbled backward. "Wow, you actually just said all that, didn't you?"

Massimo's eyebrow arched. "Is it untrue? You asked me your question plainly, and I thought to answer you in kind."

"It's not untrue." Her eyes returned to his, and the pupils were small. A war raged within her, that much was plain. "I guess we've decided we're just going to be utterly honest with each other then?"

"I have no reason nor desire to deceive you. I will always speak any truth I own to you, you have only to ask."

Her gaze softened as she looked nowhere in particular. "Are you in the mafia?"

Slowly at first, then all of a sudden, laughter seized him. Like a tune, it was a contagious spirit, and soon, Portia was laughing as well.

Massimo took the back of her hands and pressed a kiss to them. "*Cara mia*, I can tell you without amendment that I am not Mafioso."

"It's just... We're in Italy, and you have that big, fancy office and the money and all the staff..." Her cheeks turned to roses. "I'm sorry, I know it probably seems like I'm buying into clichés."

"No, I understand how you could reach that conclusion."

Her muscles relaxed, as did his. Until, that was, her next question.

"Then who in the hell are you?"

This time, it was Massimo who took a step back, wincing.

"I'm not trying to be rude, and I certainly don't want to be nosy," Portia rushed to assure him. "I'm just... I searched the internet for Massimo Bruneli today, and the only thing I could find was the name of a men's clothing line. Same with Pavlos Katsaros. Well, I mean, not a clothing line, but other than a few Facebook profiles, none of which looked anything like your assistant, nothing. In this modern world, what kind of men can both have so much wealth without some kind of online presence?"

Men who are not of this modern world. The words and the admission of everything behind them begged to be told. Something about this woman made him want to invite her into his world, to show her the beauty of the supernatural.

But why? He barely knew her.

How could this beautiful Canadian woman hold so much power over him?

Portia crossed her arms over her chest before adding, "I just want to know I'm safe."

Such hope in her eyes, the temptation to press his lips to hers, to taste of that emotion in her chemistry, almost overpowered him. Still, this was one thing he could not tell her.

Massimo turned his eyes up to the building where her flat was located. "Signora, do you know the history of this street?"

"What?" She huffed through a grin and looked vaguely at the buildings around them. "Not really. I mean, the buildings are old, obviously, but I don't think it has any particular historical importance."

Massimo rested a hand against the outer wall of the building. "These buildings are late eighteenth century. For generations, this street belonged to midlevel city officials and employees of merchants. Middle class, you'd say now. Then came the twentieth century and this part of town... It was, uh... less respectable."

"High-level city officials?"

The Doge laughed despite himself. "A brothel, though sometimes that seems much the same. And then, after the Great Wars, Venice, like much of Italy, had to rebuild itself – both structurally and psychologically. We did a good job. So good, that now the world is destroying us with its interest in partaking of our heritage. And we cannot blame them. Just look around you. My job, Signora... My life's purpose is to preserve the past and embrace the future, without letting one consume the other. *That's* who I am."

Her gaze sharpened. "So, you're, what, some kind of preservationist?"

It was as good a way as any of explaining himself. "I guess you could say that. Only, it is more of a... a provincial position. And sometimes, my job requires the utmost secrecy. For this reason, I cannot tell you much about it. I'm sorry, though."

"That explains why you live in a museum, I guess." Portia pulled her keys from her mustard-colored satchel and pressed one into the lock. "I better get some rest if I'm going back over in the morning to work. Thank you for walking me home, Massimo. And for dinner, even if I didn't eat very much. Oh, and for sharing some of your history with me."

"Of course, I am your servant."

She opened the door before turning back. What she did next, Portia accomplished with a speed even a vampire could admire.

Curling up on her toes, she dotted his cheek with her lips. Stunned, Massimo stood unmoving.

"You might get a chance to ruin me yet. But not tonight." Portia bit her bottom lip, pulling back like an eel that had struck, shocked, and retreated to try again another time. "Good night, Massimo."

And with that, she closed the door.

The Doge waited there for a few moments, listening for the lock to engage. Not that it would matter. Such flimsy restraints wouldn't keep out a vampire—or even a determined huey. He needed to assign a guard to her immediately—vampire at night, huey in the day. When at last he turned to leave, one hand in his pocket and the other cycling the cane in a measure of time and distance, that wasn't what concerned him.

What concerned him was how his heart leaped at the word *yet.*

NINE

The flat only got direct sunlight for two hours each morning, but it turned out two hours was enough for Portia to be reminded of the truth in the bathroom mirror.

She didn't quite have crow's feet at the corner of her eyes, but she might have sparrow's toes. A healthy diet and modest exercise left her in good shape for her age, but it wasn't like she had a cellulite-free body or lacked any curves. Not to mention, a swollen bump on her left butt cheek still hadn't gone away. Damn Italian mosquitos. Those facts didn't mean she was a bad person. She just wasn't the kind of woman who ended up with a guy like Massimo.

After the kind of marriage she'd barely survived, maybe the kind that ended up with *any* guy.

And here it was... the morning after she'd totally embarrassed herself by admitting to an Italian sex god that she'd like him to kiss her. That they *would probably sleep together*, it was only a matter of time. *As if.* Portia wasn't sure how she was going to face him today. Maybe she wouldn't. Maybe she'd just call that Pavlos guy and tell him she'd reconsidered and the deal was off. Massimo had offered to hire her illegally; it wasn't like he could sue her for breach of contract. Yes, the money may have come in handy, but it wasn't essential to her survival.

Her grandmother's voice echoed in her thoughts. "A person's word is their bedrock. What can your character stand on if not its own worth?"

She sagged at the sink, setting down the toothbrush. "Fine, Grandma, but you never had to face off with a man like Massimo Bruneli who now knows you're hot for him. But, yeah, whatever."

Yes, she'd go back. She'd just make sure to leave before dark so she could get home safely, all without *seeing* the man she'd straddled in her dream.

Frankly, the man she would have straddled last night had he been willing and she a little more self-confident.

The sunlight did wonderful things with the courtyard as it danced through the day. Portia wondered why hardly any of the workers came out to enjoy it. Was their boss such a taskmaster that he didn't allow them any breaks during the workday? Surely that was illegal? Or maybe they'd been told to avoid the crazy Canadian woman.

Oh, well. At least the solitude allowed her to work without interruption. At the end of the day, she'd completely finished all the outlines, leaving a diagram for color that was as wide as two men laying head-to-toe and bested her in height by a foot. She hoped her visions had not pulled a fast one on her ability. Or, was her subconscious slowing her down intentionally? As soon as she'd wrap up the project, she might never see Massimo Bruneli again.

"*But you don't want to see him,*" she internally lectured her brain. "*You embarrassed us so badly last night.*"

Her brain just laughed. "*Girl, the part of your body responsible for that is a little further south.*"

The anxiety never dissipated. He could round the corner or come down the stairs at any point. Even as she pushed on in her solitude, she jumped every time a noise echoed into the corridor. When the sun's angle dipped so that no more light came into the courtyard, she breathed a sigh of relief and packed up her things.

She was just about to throw her bag over her shoulder when she turned… and saw a man frozen in place, saluting her.

"Jes—" Adrenaline shot through her body. Portia put a hand to her chest as though she could squeeze her racing heart into submission. "Sorry, I didn't hear you."

The man, a nondescript fellow of maybe twenty-five with ruddy cheeks, bowed his head. "*Mi scusi,* Signora. I am here to walk you home and his grace's request."

Her hand dropped to her side. "His grace?"

Embarrassment brought dimples out from hiding. "Yes, Signora. M... M..." He built up a head of steam. "Massimo. My name is Giuliano Mastroni. I've been asked to make sure you arrive home safely. Assuming you are ready to leave?"

Oh, she was ready.

Of course, he followed.

Giuliano's looks belied his seniority. The vampire who was turned at twenty-six was actually the oldest member of the Venetian court, clocking in just over the five-century mark. He was also one of the most loyal guards, and if Massimo was going to trust anyone besides himself to serve as Portia's escort, a natural selection.

His smoke form trailed the pair's progress through the main promenade, past the piazza in Portia's neighborhood, and through the narrowing streets. For the most part, huey and vampire guard remained silent, with the occasional small talk exchange. It was no slow meander as it had been the night before when Massimo had been in Giuliano's place. In fact, the term 'march' came to mind. Why was Portia so intent on getting home? Did she not trust Giuliano to protect her should something happen?

But to Portia, Giuliano would look like nothing more than a boy.

This had been a terrible idea. He should have asked Claude instead. The Frenchman, once a member of Napoleon's army, had been turned in his late forties. He looked the role of protector, the tallest vampire (or huey, for that matter) Massimo had ever known. Claude's presence would have set Portia at ease, even if, as only a two-hundred-year-old, Claude was considerably weaker than Giuliano.

Pressing in his thoughts, of course, was the obvious question: Why did Massimo care so much about Portia's safety? He told himself it was because he wasn't a cruel man. Feed from hueys as he may, he didn't wish them any harm or discomfort. If only the truth laid down in the shadow of rationalization. He *needed* her to be watched over. He wanted Portia to like him, and that certainly wouldn't be possible if he somehow became linked with an unpleasantness in her mind.

Comic, really, for a vampire to think such things.

The Doge took solid form at the last corner, where the narrow, short distance from there to Portia's flat door wouldn't allow for any covert entry or concealment.

Giuliano stepped away, allowing the beautiful artist to dig in her bag for her keys. "Signora, if I can be of any further assistance?"

Metal jangled moments before Portia said, "No, Giuliano. Thank you. It was very nice of you to see me home."

The scrape of rubber soles on cement told him she'd turned towards her door. Massimo was just about to smoke away to meet Giuliano at the agreed rendezvous point a block away when Portia turned again.

"Actually, do you mind if I ask you a question?"

The guard stood at attention but managed to avoid a salute. "*Si*, signora?"

He couldn't help it. Massimo peeked around the corner just in time to see the flavor of Portia's body language shift from calm to determined. Balled fists pushed into her hips as she took a step forward, her back straight and her chin raised ever so slightly.

"Is Massimo the kind of guy who seduces a lot of women?"

The question roiled him on several fronts. The obvious, of course: matters of the Doge's boudoir were no business of the Captain of the Guard. The other one, not so much. He feared Giuliano would tell her the truth.

As a rule, Massimo didn't engage in romances. But... the immortal life was long, and bloodlust and carnal lust, devilish twins at times. Since becoming Doge, he'd avoided taking vampiric lovers; bloodlines came with politics and he wasn't interested in such schemes. But huey women? They came and went, usually for a few weeks at a time. Once, in the 1920s, he'd even passed a year in the company of a gondolier's daughter, but *never* in the palace. Women had always been recreational, a distraction from royal duty.

The last thing he wanted was to have Portia think she was merely entertainment or stress therapy.

What did he want her to think, though?

He wanted her to think about him, the same way he couldn't stop thinking about her.

Fuck.

Vampires do not fall in love. They explode into it. His maker's sage words had been both a promise and warning: guard his heart or be its slave. Venice had been his only consort since he'd lost his family so many centuries ago. Now, as his life drew toward a close, he had to wonder if the decision to stay alone was the right one, when denying what was happening between him and Portia felt so wrong?

Was he *exploding* into love? With the arrival of the Ravens eminent, could there be a worse time?

"Signora, I understand your concern, but please understand that I do not disclose my employer's personal affairs."

A fleck of pride wormed its way through Massimo's body. No, Giuliano had been the proper choice. Claude, like most Frenchman of his era, loved to gossip.

With pursed lips, Portia nodded. "No, I respect that. Then tell me this: am I in any danger with him?"

"Signora, I—"

"It's important that you don't lie to me, Giuliano. I'll be able to tell." Portia pressed two fingers into Giuliano's chest. Not to injure, but there was an air of threat implied. It should have amused, but the look on his guard's face suggested honest concern.

Why would he be frightened of a huey?

Suddenly, Giuliano's features turned grim. "Signora, enter your home immediately."

"Excuse me?" the huey balked. "Look, I appreciate you walking me home, but you don't get to *command* me to—"

"*Signora, presto! Sta attaccando!*"

The next moments moved too fast, even for him.

Massimo rounded the corner just as Giuliano pushed Portia through her open door. The huey fell back from the force, but she would be okay. His guard's fangs shone in the lamplight, but the attacker took form behind him, a wooden stake at the ready.

"Giuliano, look out!"

But it was too late. The weapon pierced the guard's chest before he could strike back.

"Giuliano!"

The guard's body crumpled. Eyes went wide, arms limp, his body collapsed first to its knees, then keeled over in the street.

He was dead.

Massimo put himself in the frame of the door as the attacking vampire, sprayed over with his victim's blood, took a step toward them. His form fell into the light, but the Doge didn't need it to know who it was.

"Marco, what in the hell are you doing?"

His brother-in-law had no patience for him. Chest heaving, eyes wild with bloodlust, he squared himself. "Let me at her. Give me the huey."

The Doge's backhand was enough to send the Florentine flying into the wall on the other side of the alley. "Leave, Marco, or I swear that I'll—"

"What, kill me?" Marco opened his shirt, his fist pounded on his bare chest. "I dare you! Plunge the entire peninsula into a civil war!"

In his mind's eye, Massimo saw the path. Lean over, pull the wooden stake from Giuliano's body, drive it forward into Marco's chest. But he'd been Doge too long to give into passions. Marco was right; he couldn't kill the Doge of Genoa and his sister's consort without consequence, even if it was justified. But that wasn't what bothered him. The bigger issue was the fact that Marco *wanted* war.

You think Marco is a Dracule sympathizer?

"Massimo!"

Portia's voice stopped his advance. What if he missed? What if, in lunging forward, Marco smoked and went around him, getting to the huey before he could counteract.

Marco grinned. "As I thought."

And then he did smoke, but instead of advance, he retreated.

It didn't matter. He'd accomplished what he came here to do.

Unfortunately, he'd left behind a witness.

TEN

What immediately followed, Portia would never be able to remember clearly.

At some point, she became conscious of other people in her flat. People who spoke too fast, moved too fast, did everything *too fast*. Shock warped her sense of reality, so she sat on the sofa, staring blankly ahead. Surely, someone would want to talk to her eventually, wouldn't they? After all, she'd just witnessed a murder. Why weren't any of the authorities questioning her or even paying attention to her? Why were they all buzzing around Massimo?

And why weren't any of them wearing uniforms?

A panicked mind created its own reality. Homicide investigators wouldn't be in beat uniforms, duh. And they were talking to Massimo because they assumed the tourist wouldn't be able to communicate. That, or they were just chauvinists who thought a woman needed a man to speak on her behalf.

But when they dragged the body into the living room and laid him out on the kitchen table, Giuliano's legs dangling off the end and one of his arms falling listlessly off the side, even rationalization refused to deny the truth.

These weren't cops.

Her body lit up with both fear and anticipation when Massimo took her by the hand and started guiding her to the door. "Portia goes with me."

The words were meant for Pavlos, the assistant trailing in the shadow of his boss, but they triggered her defenses. Jerking back her hand, Portia plastered herself against the closest wall. "I'm not going anywhere with you. If you want to kill me, do it right here so someone will find my body and my mother can at least have closure. You're not going to... to... Make *me* sleep with the fishes."

Pavlos and Massimo exchanged high eyebrows before the former took a soft step in her direction. "Signora, no one is going to harm you. We're trying to protect you."

"I don't want your protection. I know how that works. First, you make me grateful, then you extort me in some way, and then when I refuse to pay anything more, I end up like Giuliano." She jabbed her hand at the corpse in the kitchen.

Pavlos turned to Massimo, speaking in rapid-fire Italian, setting off a dramatic performance easily followed. Pavlos presented an argument, Massimo's brow furrowed. Counterargument. The servant laid out a supplementary aside. The master deliberated, grimaced, conceded.

"Fine," Massimo said, returning to English, presumably for her benefit. He again took her hand and started toward the front door. "But not until I have her safely back in the palace."

Pavlos inclined his head in supplication. "As you wish, *Serenissimo Principe.* I will see to the clean-up here and have Signora Kepler's things moved shortly."

"Have my things—" Everything was happening too fast, and too many conflicts demanded her attention. "Did he just call you a prince? What is he talking about?"

"I'm not a prince. It's just a traditional honorific." Massimo pulled her into the street, nodding at the guard posted outside her door. "No more now until we are in a secure location."

Using every ounce of her strength, she managed to free herself from his hold. Massimo's feet anchored, his eyes turning not to her, but to his empty hand that had just been holding hers. "You are incredibly strong for one of your kind."

What did he mean by that? A woman? A Canadian? A hostage? She didn't really care.

Portia stomped her foot. "Look, I'm not going anywhere with you until I know what the hell is going on. And if you think that I'm—Oh, Massimo!"

The world tipped as her feet went out from under her. Massimo braced her tight, one arm under her back, hand gripped around her forearm; one arm lodged under her knees and the hand on her outer thigh.

The heat pooling in her core as his brown eyes looked down on her made no sense. It certainly was no time for attraction.

"Portia, I vow that I am not going to do anything to hurt you, and that I will tell you everything. But for the moment I need you to give me your trust and close your eyes."

"That's a pretty big ask considering the dead body in my rental flat and the lack of cops."

"And it isn't even the biggest ask I will make of you tonight."

The woman within pulsed with anticipation.

His lips lowered, ghosting over hers. "*Per favore, cara mia.*"

Suddenly, she couldn't help but comply. Everything in her was screaming to trust this man. So she did. She closed her eyes, just as the wind whipped through her hair.

Three minutes later, Portia gripped the edge of a pedestal beneath a marble statue of Mercury. Focusing on how her stomach let loose over the roots of a rosebush allowed her to ignore the fact that Massimo was holding back her hair in a bundle.

After the third heave, she managed, with his help, to walk to a nearby bench and let her clammy forehead fall against the white tips of her fingers. "Oh, my God, I'm going to die."

"No, you're not. You're just motion sick." Massimo released her hair and snapped. A scurry of footfalls told her someone had answered his summons, appearing from who-knew-where and setting about cleaning her sick without so much as a word.

Adrenaline shot through her and she turned, distancing herself from him as much as possible without falling onto her ass. "Massimo, please. I'm... I'm freaking out. Tell me... Something. *Anything*. I need this to make sense, I need to..." She couldn't sit anymore, not with so much energy coursing through her veins. "Did you run us all the way here? I didn't imagine that, right? You... How does a person run so fast? How is that even possible?"

He reached for her hand, and she was so desperate for the comfort, she let him take it.

"The first thing to understand is that no one here will harm you." He rose then, leading her toward the staircase. "Anyone who attempts to even approach you without my permission will meet the sun."

It must be some Italian phrase that he'd translated literally. "Are you saying I'd otherwise be in some kind of danger?"

"Yes. You witnessed Marco kill one of my senior guards."

She stopped on the stairs just as they turned from the second story to take on another flight. Portia crossed the landing and looked down on the courtyard, the one she'd worked in for two days while wondering why it was so empty. It wasn't empty now, not by a long shot. Dozens of men and women filled the space, smartly dressed in a myriad of styles, their silent mouths and hungry eyes turned on her.

"Where did all these people come from? Is this some kind of party?"

He tried to insert himself between her and the guardrail. "Let me explain first to you what is—"

"You mean take me out of sight of so many witnesses?" she bellowed. "Like you said, I just witnessed a murder, one you magically showed up for out of nowhere. How do I know you weren't part of it? That I wasn't the one who was supposed to be killed? That I—"

His hand gripped her forearm, squeezing with just enough pressure to disrupt her thoughts. "I am trying to ease you into this, but you are upsetting my subjects."

"Your... subjects?" Her face drained. "Who are you?"

"I am the only person who can save you from true evil, *cara mia*. Now, since you've demanded attention— Everyone!" Massimo stepped to the side, raising his voice and hooking an arm around her. "May I introduce Signora Portia Kepler. She is now my guest and under my personal protection, both in Venice and elsewhere. I ask of you as you've asked of me, that both her vein and her virtue be secured in our fraternity."

Those beneath said nothing, but what they did do was even weirder. The moment Massimo finished speaking, each and every one of them *bowed*.

Portia's head lashed to the right. "It's worse than the mafia. You're the leader of a cult."

To her surprise, he grinned but said nothing. He started up the stairs again, forcing her to follow. They only got two steps when, out of thin air, a waft of smoke swirled about them, replaced a moment later by a petite slender woman in a pair of grey slacks and a soft pink crop top. "Your Serenity."

"What the fuck?" Thank God there was a landing beneath them. When Portia fell backward from the shock, there wasn't a long way to fall. "How did she...Where did she?"

Massimo's hands tightened into fists. He gave Portia a quick glance, then turned back to the woman on the stairs above him. "Now is not a good time, Signora di Nali."

Signora di Nali must have disagreed, plowing forward. "Pavlos tells me you've denied my appeal."

"On the contrary, I granted your appeal regarding procuring a maker's bite for your consort, assuming that I find he has the proper demeanor to be one of us when I meet him. What I denied was him crèching in Venice."

"Venice is *my home*," Signora di Nali retorted. "I don't see why I have to leave my home and my city for a year or two when the food here is plentiful. My brother was one of your most loyal supporters before he met the sun. My sister served in your guard for half her life. My family is one of the foundations of this city, and I will have my consort under my own roof when he is made."

"We're still trying to contain the aftermath of what happened to those two American girls. I can't risk our community involved in another death in such rapid succession."

"But, Your Serenity..."

Portia scrambled back on her hands when Massimo heaved his chest and let out a hiss like the cross between some angry house cat and a snake. It seemed a childish mannerism, but whatever Signora di Nali had been keen to press for, he succeeded in dissuading her with the maneuver. The woman kept dignity in her expression while simultaneously lowering her eyes in supplication. "Very well, your grace. As you wish."

Massimo turned back and offered Portia a hand. She took it but kept an eye on Signora di Nali as they passed on the stairs. The Italian woman glared at Portia, flashing bared teeth and....

No, that was impossible. Portia had to be seeing things. That, or di Nali had some serious dental issues.

Pavlos stood to attention the moment they walked in the office door. "*Serenissimo Principe,* Signora's flat has been cleaned and the compliance of any neighbors assured. We will contact the property manager in the morning and let them know she's vacated the flat early."

Portia's head whipped back and forth between the door and the assistant before her. She lifted a pointed finger in vague accusation. "How in the hell did you get back here before us?"

"I didn't, Signora. I just arrived."

Portia froze in place even as Massimo strode ahead, circling his desk. *Good gravy, I'd wanted an Italian adventure and I'm certainly having one, aren't I?*

"I've taken the liberty of having your personal effects moved to one of our guest suites," Pavlos continued. "When your business is finished here, I will escort you to—"

"She will stay in my apartment."

Both Portia and Pavlos's attention snapped in Massimo's direction.

Pavlos swallowed hard, his throat bobbing. "As your guest, sire, or your *honored* guest?"

"Sire?" Suddenly, Portia's body was liquid fire. She bolted to Massimo, who'd taken up a position behind a desk opulent enough it would have fit in Versailles, and stuck her finger in his chest.

"You asked for patience and I gave it to you. Now I'm taking it back. I want answers." Portia spun, pacing the room in tempo with her thoughts. "Who in the hell are you people? Did I really just see a man impaled right before my eyes?"

Massimo, busily writing something at his desk, snapped his finger. "*Impaling.* I didn't even pick up on the reference. Pavlos, I believe your theory was right."

"Marco has always had some kind of odd affection for me, sire," Pavlos answered, taking one of the chairs on the opposite side of the desk. "As I've never mirrored back, I suspected that it was due to my being Dracule."

What in the hell were they talking about? Portia slammed her palms down on the edge of Massimo's desk, forcing his attention. "That's it, I've had enough! Now tell me why you aren't calling the cops. Tell me why I shouldn't run screaming right now all the way to the Canadian Consulate in Milan. Tell me how in the hell *you*—" This time, Pavlos was up for the poke in the pecs. "—got back here so quickly. Or do you have an evil twin, because that's about the only thing short of a wedding, mistaken identities, and a hot doctor I'm missing from this soap opera."

The servant deferred to her would-be savior, who waved him off with a gentle flip of his hand. "I'll take it from here, Pavlos. Please personally see to the moving of my *honored guest's* things."

The servant nodded, both to Massimo, then to Portia, and took his exit.

Alone, she turned up her ire to eleven. "Your *honored* guest?"

Massimo busily wrote down some notes on a piece of letterhead. "Yes, as in, not my prisoner."

She didn't know if she should be angry or scared. "You take prisoners, now, do you?"

"Rarely, and only when other means of containment or persuasion fail."

Portia crossed her arms over her chest and cocked a hip. "So then, I'm free to go if I want?"

His mischievous eyes sparkled like he wanted her to try. "Only if you want to *become* my prisoner."

She assumed an ornately carved monstrosity of a chair with sufficient brocade to outfit a military unit and a cushion stiff enough to iron their uniforms on. "Help me make sense of this. I feel like I'm trying to make water hold a shape with nothing but my hands and hope here."

"An apt analogy." Massimo leaned over and a moment later, pulled out from recesses unseen a decanter filled with dark red liquid. Portia had never before been so thankful for the appearance of booze.

He poured a small portion into a crystal glass and handed it across the desk. "I am Massimo Bruneli; that much you know. What you do not know is that I am the sixth Doge of Venice."

The glass stilled at her lips. "I might not know as much as you about Venetian history, but I took the Palace tour the first week I was here. Venice hasn't had a Doge in two hundred years." She tipped a healthy swig and enjoyed the mix of coolness and burn as it washed down her throat.

Massimo put his glass on the table untouched. "The *human* population hasn't."

Her eyes bulged. "The *human* population?"

A single nod, and his eyes found interest in the far wall's art. "I am the *vampiric* Doge. I have ruled Venice since the Argentum Revolution of the late seventeenth century."

"Oh, well then." Portia didn't know why she was laughing,

but her body refused to obey a command to stop. "Okay, then, if you're a vampire, then where are your—"

Crimson stains covered her lap and the glass shattered on the floor.

It was *impossible*. Where the attractive man she'd spent weeks sketching to perfection had sat was an empty chair, and hunched over her, inches from her face, was the same godlike visage bearing one very distinct difference: two gleaming white dagger teeth.

"Is this what you wanted to see?" His voice curled around the fangs, and he squared himself to give her a better view.

Yes, it was. And it wasn't. And she should be scared. And she was. But at the same time, there was something about the presentation, the alignment, the motif. The power…

Portia lifted her hand and pressed one of her soft fingertips against the protruding tooth.

"This was what was missing." Massimo's features softened as her hand slid over his cheek and she examined him like she might a piece of art. "I kept redoing this mouth over and over and I could never get it right because it always felt like something was missing, and this is it. Massimo, it's…" She swallowed. "You're glorious."

The Doge snapped to attention, leaving her hand palming empty air.

She found him across the office, wearing disappointment in his features. "You're supposed to be frightened."

"I am, like I would be if you were a tiger or a big, hairy spider, but my fear doesn't lessen the beauty."

He turned away a tightened jaw. "That doesn't make me any less lethal."

No, it didn't. She had the bloodstains on her shirt to prove it. "That man that attacked Giuliano, then?"

"Also a vampire." Stoicism reclaimed him as he sat on the edge of his desk. "His name is Marco di Serpente, and he's supposed to be in Tuscany."

She gripped the arms of the chair and took to her feet, thankful that the room wasn't spinning anymore. Vampires. Her rational mind wanted to weep from the insanity of it, but something deep within her told her that she shouldn't doubt, nor should she be afraid. Instinct told her to stay, to listen, to move on. She'd known this. Somehow, she'd always known there was more to the world than she knew. "So you're in the middle of a turf war, is that it?"

"No. At least, I don't think so. I'm afraid that there have been some recent... *developments* in our world that might have made Marco think now is a good time to destabilize our region. Whether or not he's doing so with official backing is impossible to say."

Portia nodded. "Is it impossible to learn, though?"

"No, but it's a sensitive subject, and one which must be contained immediately if Marco's acting alone. But Marco is a man with substantial power and allies. I can't just march into Tuscany and scream out *j'accuse!*"

Now the pieces were falling into place. "You want me to testify about what really happened tonight."

Hopeful eyes found hers. "It's a horrible thing for me to request, to draw you further into our world where there is nothing for you but danger, but yes. Please understand, doing so could save hundreds of lives, both in my court and Patria's. You have to convince her."

"And why would what I say convince this Patria if your word won't suffice?"

Massimo avoided her gaze. He was hiding something.

Portia crossed to him, putting a hand on his shoulder. "Look, Massimo, you saved my life tonight. And as scared shitless and overwhelmed as I am, if I can return the favor by testifying, I will. But you've got to be on the level with me. How will this Patria chick know I'm telling the truth?"

"Because she can compel you not to lie. Vampires have the ability to bend human minds."

Portia jerked her hand back. Okay, vampires were one thing, but vampires with psychic mind-control powers? "That's ridiculous."

"Is it?" He pitched himself forward and burrowed into her eyes with his gaze. All at once, Portia felt like she was looking at a consciousness behind glass. Massimo's voice reverberated in her thoughts. "Have you dreamed of me, *cara mia*?"

She licked her lips as the images flashed in her mind of naked flesh and silken sheets. "Yes."

"And what happened in these dreams?"

"We… we made love. Like, a lot."

His grinning mouth hovered over hers as a tightness in her chest went slack, making Portia feel like a puppet whose strings had been suddenly snipped.

Massimo grinned as she collected herself, falling back into the stuffy chair. "Do you think that's something you'd admit to if I didn't make you? And that wasn't even really enthrallment. I only had to clear away your own thoughts, not change any of them."

"Okay, fine, you *can* control minds. But why wouldn't Patria just think that's what you're doing, forcing me to give false testimony?"

"Because a human mind isn't a six-lane highway. Only one vampire can manipulate it at a time. She could clear any work I did in a heartbeat. She's more powerful than me in this ability."

And he was pretty damn good at it. She still felt the impression of his will in her thoughts. Or was that just her own desire to remember how good those dreams had been?

The clock on the wall clucked, a tiny little bird chirping as it darted out from behind a little door.

Massimo rose, suddenly, taking Portia by the hand and leading her to a door at the back of the office and through a completely darkened corridor. "Come. You've been through chaos this evening. You will be safe in my quarters while you rest. Tomorrow at sunset, we depart for Florence so Patria can hear the truth from your own lips."

How could he see to walk straight? Even being led by the hand, she kept bumping into walls. It was so damned narrow. "And what will happen if she believes me?"

"Then Marco will meet the sun, by my hand or her proclamation. Hopefully both."

Whatever that meant. "No, I mean, after that, what happens to me? Will I be allowed to leave?"

They came to a stop so suddenly, Portia faceplanted into Massimo's back. He caught her by the arms even though she was in no danger of falling, just as a wall opened behind him. Massimo's vague silhouette took on definition, even as her eyes tried to equalize the contrast of light and dark.

"Give me your hand."

"What?"

But with no reason not to comply, she did just that. For a moment, she thought he might be making some kind of romantic gesture. Even if he was hotter than Hades, now was hardly the time. But then he reached out to the doorframe where some kind of biometric sensor was mounted on the wall. The device beeped as he punched in a whirlwind of numbers, followed by a high-pitched trill. Massimo pinched her index finger, guiding it to a glass plate embedded in the control panel. Three, two, one… It beeped again and he dropped her hand.

"That will allow you to enter if I'm not here. In the meantime, don't borrow worry. One step at a time. For now, just rest."

"I don't know how you expect me to sleep. I have so much adrenaline running through my veins, I can't stop my hands from shaking."

His head tilted to the side. "Would you allow me to tire you?"

Despite the events of the evening, her body began to buzz thinking of all the ways he could *relax* her. Suddenly, her pulse moved from her ears to a region much further south.

Massimo's hand cupped her cheek as his forehead fell against hers. "No, not that, *farfallina*, though it would be an honor. But if you will allow me..."

His other hand settled on the small of her back, and before Portia could put words together to ask him what his less-sexy plan entailed, her world went silent and dark.

ELEVEN

He moved against the dawn, a hundred things to do before the sun returned. And yet, he couldn't remember doing a single one.

Upstairs, there was a woman in his apartment. When was the last time Massimo had allowed anyone other than his vicedoge and the captain of the guard access to his personal space? With the occasional lover he'd had through the centuries, a separate room had been readied for their... *use*. Rationales bloomed in multitude: Portia was only a huey and not a threat; she was an innocent drawn into court intrigues of which she couldn't possibly conceive; she was a refugee under his protection and easy prey for Marco di Serpente if not protected. All these were true, but none of them led to the strict necessity that she needed to be in *his room*.

By the time the east tinged pink, Pavlos assured the Doge all essential matters had been seen to. Giuliano's body had been moved to the roof of the palace to meet the sun, where it would turn to ash with dawn's first light. Pavlos himself would oversee critical matters at court in Massimo's absence. Preparations for the arrival of the Dracule were proceeding as planned; a chef had been identified and a menu selected featuring the finest in both victuals and vein. Ukrainian would be served, rumored to be Vlad's favorite varietal. Portia's rental flat had been emptied and sanitized, and the property owner notified that she'd left Venice earlier than planned.

Portia...

Something in Massimo's chest tightened at the thought of her name. As a younger man, he'd have called it lust. As an older vampire coming to the dawn's horizon, he knew it for it was. The creature in his room above had what he had not: a choice. He *envied* her. A long life ahead of her. A human life.

He wanted to experience those things again.

He wanted to experience them with *her*.

"Your Serenity?"

Massimo shook himself from his reverie and found Pavlos awaiting his command just inside the door of his office.

The Doge wiped a hand down his face. "Ah, Pavlos. Thank you for coming."

"Of course, sire."

It seemed such a small thing to worry about, but in Massimo's experience, it was often those small things which caused the most problems down the road. "Signora Kepler has a friend back home who phones her every night to check-in."

"Yes, sire. Mae Avery."

He should ask how his vicedoge knew, but one of the reasons he and Pavlos worked so well together was that they both understood when to seek and when to let alone. "I need you to reach out to whomever is Vampire Lord of Victoria, Canada."

"Canada has no lords, sire."

Massimo blinked his confusion. "What?"

"None of the Americas do," Pavlos confirmed. "Though Canada's was among the last to dissolve, only about seventy years ago."

"How, then, is there any order? The slayers are all dead, and now the new world has no aristocracy or administrative heads? How is it not chaos there, blood raining in the streets and huey populations running in fear?"

"I'm not certain, Your Serenity. I've heard rumors that there are *other* supernatural forces at play. Ones, perhaps, not present here."

Curious, though now was not the time to contemplate such things. "In any event, please ask... *someone* to keep an eye on the Mae woman. Containing one huey is hard enough. I don't want an international incident to break out."

Pavlos bowed his head. "I will see what can be arranged, Your Serenity." He straightened. "*Massimo,* can I ask what you intend to do with Signora Kepler?"

"I'll take her with me to Florence tonight so she can give testimony about Marco's actions."

"Yes, of course. But what about after that?"

Massimo turned blank eyes on empty thoughts. "I would hope she'd complete the mural I hired her to do."

"Very good. And then, after that?"

Maybe eventually, once everything had settled down, she could go home. But what if Marco had a faction his intelligence networks hadn't detected? He didn't want Pro-Dracule thugs coming after Portia in retaliation. "She's far too deep in this affair now and too much time has passed for us to simply erase her memories. It would leave too many gaps in her recollections, cause too much emotional trauma. She should stay with us until such time as we can guarantee her safety or make suitable arrangements for her return to Canada."

He tried to ignore the pain of that thought. *Ma che diavolo?* Now more than ever, he mustn't be ruled by emotion.

Pavlos leaned in. "And will she continue to stay in your personal suite?"

Massimo swallowed his nerves. "That will be up to her." He squeezed his secretary's shoulder. "Good morrow, Pavlos. Please check again that our transport is arranged and ready for departure at sunset."

"Of course." The vicedoge turned to leave but paused at the door. "You know, Massimo..."

The Doge looked back over his shoulder. "Yes?"

"The concern you expressed the other night about the saturation of our kind in the city... Not to disrespect the dead, but if there is a maximum limit you'd entertain, Giuliano's death brings us down one from that."

"I don't understand. I already granted Signora di Nali's petition, once she agrees to let me meet her consort."

"I wasn't talking about Signora di Nali's consort." Pavlos turned, pulling the door closed in his wake. "Good morrow, Your Serenity."

The silence he'd grown to welcome after nights playing politics and being accosted by supporters and sycophants alike left him. In its place, a head full of thoughts racing, speaking with his own tongue, and making devils of his intent.

Massimo knew what Pavlos implied. While the Doge wouldn't deny there was an attraction bordering on romantic interest within him, he had no plan to drag an innocent and beautiful woman into a world he prayed to soon leave. That he *would* soon leave. His time was ebbing. Four centuries gone, and how much time remained now was anyone's guess. Sixty years maybe? A hundred? Even if he and Portia were deeply in love, he'd not ask her to change only to condemn her to endless nights without him once he passed. He could think of no greater self-serving request.

A vampire did not need much light to see, and even the gentle glow of a modern nightlight revealed his suite's finest intricacies without effort. It was his nose, however, and not his eyes that assured him of Portia's presence. She was sand and sea breeze with an undercurrent of roses. If he closed his eyes, he might think himself on Sardinia, back when he'd still been a huey learning his family's trade. The aroma hit the moment the security seal decompressed, a wave of feminine essence that made his fangs drop and his manhood twitch. His power had put her to sleep, but the trauma of the events had seemed to keep her down all night. She lay stretched across his bed, shoeless but still wearing her blood-splattered clothes.

Massimo cursed himself. He should have provided her with fresh attire. Only then did he remember that her things were sitting on a bureau inside the closet. Still, if he could get her to take her shirt off, one of his huey servants could take it to the roof. The blood would turn to dust in the morning light, and then a simple trip through the laundry. He wanted her to still have this shirt. She looked so damned... *delicious* in it.

Imagine how delicious she'd look out *of it.*

Portia stirred as he took one of the pillows from the bed and its linen case brushed her cheek. Her eyes glowed when they cracked open. "It wasn't a dream."

Massimo stood on the end of the bed, clutching the pillow. "No, Signora." Curiosity dared him to ask if that was a good or a bad thing but he feared her response. Instead, he threw the pillow on the floor and started to step out of his shoes. "Sorry to have awakened you. Please, go back to sleep. I will take the floor."

"Don't be ridiculous. This is your room and it's a huge bed." She managed to prop herself up on the palms of her hands. "Besides, I'm up now. Once I'm up, I can't get back to sleep until dark."

He reclaimed the pillow and placed it by the headboard before setting about taking off his jacket. "Still, try to nap today. We leave for Florence at sunset. Once we arrive at Patria's, you're unlikely to be accommodated just because you're a huey."

Her face screwed up. "A what?"

"A *huey*," he repeated, sitting on the bed to take off his socks. "That's what supes call humans."

"You mean vampires."

"I mean *supes*," he corrected. The rest of his clothes would stay on because... reasons. Normally he'd strip down to nothing. Portia might welcome a dangerous vampire into the bed, but a naked man was another matter. "There are more than vampires in this world."

"Wizards and witches and hobgoblins?"

Magic was a paradigm hueys created to describe things they couldn't understand or explain. It didn't surprise him that her mind was recalibrating. "There are werewolves, wolf-watchers... Other *creatures* that have gone extinct. As for hobgoblins? I've heard rumors of demons, but I've never met one." Massimo grimaced as he laid down, his back to her. "Do you mind if I ask you a question? Why aren't you... I believe the English term is, freaking out?"

"You're saying you're pulling my leg or something?"

"Why would someone pull your leg? It's far too shapely a thing to rid you of."

"You have an odd grasp on English, you know that? Sometimes you sound like a poet, and other times, like the most cliché movie character ever."

"Blame my age." He rolled over to face her. "I learned your language when I was much shorter in the tooth, and I haven't made much effort to keep up with its evolution."

That smile. He *loved* her smile. Even more so because he caused it. *I have many ways of making you smile, bella. My tongue knows more tricks than humor.*

"It is our way to keep our existence hidden from hueys," Massimo continued. "The discovery tends to lead to hysterics. You, however, seem to accept what I'm telling you at face value."

"Well, the face telling me has a pretty high value." She backed up against the headboard. "That and seeing someone stake another man and turn into a cloud of smoke to escape reset my baseline for what is and isn't possible." Portia threw her legs over the side of the bed. "I guess I'll go find some breakfast and get to work for the day, assuming it's safe?"

His heavy eyes snapped open. "Signora?"

She leaned over him, and despite the power of the unseen sun pulling him toward sleep, his pulse picked up its pace.

"All those people in the courtyard last night," she said through pale lips. "They were all vampires, weren't they?"

"Yes." There may have been one or two huey servants circulating in the courtyard, but this wasn't the time for detail.

She nodded, as if sealing her own assumption. "Any one

of them could do to me what that man— *Marco*, did to Giuliano, couldn't they?"

"That and much worse, easily." He wouldn't lie to her. "Your mortal body, though beautiful—" His eyes quickly spot-checked the statement before shooting back up to meet hers. "—is frail. Don't worry. You're here as my honored guest. Any within these walls would die to protect you."

"Honored guest?" She leaned in even further, her face centimeters from his. "Or prisoner?"

There it was, wasn't it? The weight in that question pushed on his chest. No, wait, that may be her breasts. As she flexed her body so subtly, a huey would have probably not noticed, Massimo was left without doubt. She was trying to manipulate his mind via his dick. Oh, he'd underestimated her. Portia came across as an innocent, straightforward woman, but he'd forgotten she'd had an artist's soul. Such creatures fashioned many masks and changed them according to the company they kept. He'd put this fair creature in a situation where she felt powerless, and she'd found a way to regain some of that power... by attempting to draw blood away from his brain and have it reallocated to less rational parts of his body.

It would be so easy to turn the tables on her, to pull her down to him, claim her mouth and her blood, ride out the morning making love. But what would be the fun in that? No, if she wanted to play a cat and mouse game...

Mouse, meet lion.

One hand petted her shoulder then continued down her back, settling on the soft curve of her hip. Massimo let it rest there a moment before pushing his fingers along the contours of her backside. The tips of his fingers sensed the warmth of her arousal through the material of her jeans.

Portia tried to hide the intake of breath and the quick flinch at the corners of her mouth.

Unsuccessfully.

"If you were my prisoner, I'd have to tie you up. Do you know what I do with sexy women I tie up?"

The tiniest fragment of pressure, and her whole body pulsed. This time, she didn't try to hide his effect on her. Portia's mouth fell open as she licked her bottom lip. Her voice shook when she spoke.

"No, what?"

His other hand anchored on her shoulder, securing her as he teased her below. "Anything they want me to."

She gasped again, a heavenly sound at the back of her throat. Massimo's body began to betray his purpose. His fangs dropped and demanded their place at her table. A banquet of carnal delight was warming before him, and both his hungers demanded satiation.

He would make love to her now if he didn't stop this. If she didn't stop him. If they didn't both stop.

Dio, how was he supposed to stop?

Pulling his hand back was the hardest thing Massimo had done in decades. "*Topolina,* I'd like nothing more than to keep you here all day, to wake to you and make love well into the night... But that's not who I am. You are free to come and go as you wish. I just ask you *not* to leave the palazzo. Until Marco meets the sun, the world is a dangerous place for you."

Confusion marred her features. "Is it as dangerous as this bedroom?"

A good question. "I can say only that I will never hurt you intentionally. This is as good a vow as a vampire can make." Massimo ran a hand over her cheek, hoping to relieve the fret furrowing her brow. "Most of us are rational creatures, and in Italy, there are systems in place for eliminating the dangerous elements of our community. But that does not change the fact that in my world, you are prey."

She pulled back, sitting up at the end of the bed. "*Your* world. That really seals it, doesn't it?"

Yes, and if I brought you into it, you could end up hating me forever, and for a vampire, forever is a very long time. "I promise, after Florence, I'll see you get home safely and compensate you for your trouble and time, if that's what you desire. For the moment, my staff is at your command. Pavlos..." He tried to stifle the yawn, but it would not be tamed. "...has instructed them to grant your every..." *Yawn.* "...request."

"Thank you." Portia sucked on her bottom lip before gathering herself off the bed. "I'll work in the courtyard then, distract myself from the fact that a Florentine vampire wants me dead. You sleep well. You've earned it."

His hand fell back on the mattress, even as his eyes drifted close. "Thank you, *cara mia*. I promise. You are my... top..."

His words tapered off as sleep finally took him. In that fuzzy place between consciousness and oblivion, he wasn't certain if the kiss on his cheek was real.

TWELVE

Portia's first thought, other than how damned good a kitchen staff had to be if they could make biscotti that tasted like *that*, was that she needed fresh clothes. She'd been so tired the night before, it hadn't even occurred to her that she was still wearing a dead man's blood all down her front. Despite overhearing that her things had been brought to the palazzo, Portia didn't know where she'd find them, and as before, the place seemed nearly empty during the day. Luckily, all her artistic supplies were still on the cart where she'd left them the previous night. She got to work, only at some point to look down and see her shirt had magically laundered itself.

"What the hell?" Her charcoal stick dropped to the ground as Portia fisted the bottom of her shirt, pulling it away from her body to give it a closer look. Gone. It was all gone. All the blood, the stains... disappeared. Had Massimo changed her clothes while she'd slept and she just hadn't realized it? Or did vampire blood, like the vampires themselves, turn to dust when kissed by the sun?

She filed that away as one of a thousand questions she could ask Massimo and to which she might not want the answer.

Work focused her mind and eased her spirit. In the lines and twists of her landless mural, echoes of gore and confusion ebbed. All that existed was this wall, these pencils, the paintbrushes.

Ah, the paintbrushes...

Other than a few walls in her house, she hadn't *painted* something in fifteen years. What did she remember of stroke technique and brush pressure? She hoped it was like riding a bike, that it would all come flooding back to her through wishing and muscle memory. No such luck. Turned out painting was another language, and as with any language once learned, *use it or lose it.* At the end of the day, if Massimo thought she didn't deserve full payment, she wouldn't blame him.

Morning became noontime and noontime meandered its way toward evening. By the time the angle of the sun in the sky had the shadow of the roof crawling up the wall of her work, her eyes, mind, and body longed for rest.

"Signora?'

Portia jolted as the servant emerged from a nearby hall.

"*Mi scusi*, Signora." The… maid? Valet?… curtsied. "I didn't mean to frighten you."

Hand over heart, Portia assured her not to worry.

"I can see you are tired," the maid continued, her accent doing summersaults around the English words. "I have prepared a room upstairs for you if you like to rest and refresh before your dinner tonight."

Portia set about cleaning her brushes. "My dinner?"

"Yes, Signora," the servant acknowledged. "With Mr. Bruneli. I understand he will be taking you to the mainland."

Mister, not His Serenity or *Serenissimo Principe*. Was it possible that the human staff were unaware of what their boss really was? If so, it wasn't her place to say. Just like it wasn't Portia's place to correct the servant, if that's the story that had been told.

"Yes actually, I think I would. Is there a chance I could get my things from Massimo… I mean, *Mr. Bruneli's* suite. I'd like to change my clothes."

The maid's eyes turned down. "Oh, no. Sorry, Signora, but staff are not permitted in Signore's suite. I could, however, arrange fresh clothes for you. Something… appropriate for the evening and weather."

Now that she mentioned it, it was a bit nippy tonight. Instinctively, Portia laced her arms. "Yes, please."

Hot water and perfumed bubbles medicated the soul and

body, easing tension from her shoulders and letting her mind wander. By the time she'd gotten out of the bath, Luisa (as she discovered was the maid's name) had turned down the bed, left her a hot pot of tea, and best of all… a warmed cotton robe.

The sheets were silk and as soft as her skin freshly coated with the most luxurious lotion she'd ever used. She thought it would be a sin to put on the cotton nightshirt straight out of a period drama. Portia crawled into the bed al fresco, wanting to bathe in the silk as she had in the bath. A fireplace crackled on the opposite side of the room, and as she relaxed back into the pillows, she noticed an oil painting hung over the mantel.

She didn't recognize the artist or the subject, but the style suggested Late Renaissance, perhaps even Early Classical. The stately young woman was framed by a red gown whose collar was nearly a perfect circle. *She might be a strawberry blonde?* Hard to tell with age, but her hair was an exquisite arrangement of orderly curls so precise in their placement that they resembled a halo. Her full bosom managed to be both prominent and understated, as though the artist wanted you to be certain this creature was fully owning her body but that it wasn't what you should notice. Instead, the thing that really stuck out in Portia's observation, was the transparent lacework forming a high collar. When Portia focused on the details, she could swear that the delicate shapes were birds and snakes.

A necklace around her neck looked like a dozen suns on a string.

Luisa cracked open the door and grinned when she saw her charge in bed and engaged with the art. "Ah, I see you've introduced yourself to Signora Barozzi."

Portia recognized the name from some of her recent tours of historical sites around town. "Barozzi? They were one of the wealthy merchant families back when Venice was a powerful Republic, weren't they?"

"Indeed." Luisa grinned. "But Catalina was a… how do you say, a benefactor? She gave up much for the care of the poor."

"Kind, as well as beautiful. Wait." Portia shifted farther under the blankets as Luisa neared to take the tea tray away. That was, until some footnote of one of her guidebooks resurrected itself in her memories. "Catalina Barozzi... As in, *Catalina's Well*? The one in the street outside the palazzo walls?"

The servant's smile flatlined. "Yes, it's where they found her body after she was murdered."

None of the guidebooks mentioned that part. Portia tensed, overcome with some eerie sympathy with the legend for reasons she couldn't explain. "How did it become a place for couples to make wishes then?"

Luisa took another log from a pile on the side of the hearth and tossed it in the fireplace. "Because she died for love. The legend says that a... how you say, noblewoman? That she wanted Catalina's husband for her own bed. When Catalina wouldn't allow it, the noblewoman threw her down the well. They say the husband killed himself after that, though sometimes the story ends that he just walks into the sea, never to be seen again. Anyhow, now couples ask for help from Catalina to keep their lovers from harm. You throw in a coin, say your prayer, and she watches over you both."

"My experience is that the dead don't make the best advocates."

"That may be true, Signora, but hope grabs even the most slippery surface."

Who was Portia to counter that? Her hope was trying to climb up a wall bathed in blood.

"Thank you for your help. And for the clothes." Never mind the fact that they were still neatly folded in the closet. "I wonder if there's a washer and dryer I might be able to use somewhere in the... uh, building?"

The maid bristled. "Signora, I would die with embarrassment. Leave your laundry in the bathtub for me. You are an honored guest."

Portia nodded. "So, I hear."

She didn't know if it was the scent of his spicy cologne or the weight of his stare that pulled her from slumber, but Portia didn't mind either one.

"Are you going to bite me?" Portia rolled over, opening blurry eyes.

Sitting on the edge of the mattress, a war of emotions played across Massimo's face. A moment of complete longing as his mouth dropped open and chest rose, followed by his eyes shooting to the distant door. "It's not what you think it is."

Stretching her arms over her head, she suddenly remembered that she was, in fact, naked as the day she was born beneath the sheets. Massimo knew, too. His eyes shifted again, and this time the hunger written into his features was one she recognized as oh-so-human.

And damn, if that didn't feel good. After years of rejection by the one man who was supposed to be her rock, it was nice to be appreciated. So nice, that she wanted to be appreciated a little more. A *little*. She gathered the silk sheet to her chest and sat up, the brush of the fabric pebbling her nipples. "Do vampires not drink blood?"

His gaze was locked by a force stronger than gravity. "Yes, but your movies and books make you think that for hueys it's..." His hungry gaze raised back to his eyes, and oh... The desire hit her in a wave, curling her insides. "...pleasurable."

The most delicious tremble shot through her just to hear the word on his tongue. "It's not?"

"I have ways of giving pleasure..." Massimo leaned over, prowling his way up the bed. "...but biting is not one. It's horrifically painful. We cover it up with enthrallment, turning anguish into illusions of euphoria, but do *these*—" His fangs shot into existence just as his hands planted on the mattress on either side of her, his body delightfully heavy atop her. "—look like they tickle?" His mouth lowered, skirting over her exposed neck. "I want your blood, Portia. I am a vampire; I will always want it. But I fear what that might do to our friendship."

She arched her back, pushing herself off and leaning into him. His hot, heavy breaths tickled her chin. "You've heard of friends with benefits, right?"

His flattened palm on the mattress tightened, fisting sheets and threatening to expose her if he just gave a little tug.

A little voice in her head hoped he did.

"I don't want to be that kind of friend with you. Already, these things I feel for you—*Cara mia*, can't you tell how dangerous my control is getting around you? And I'm not a man known to lose control."

"Are you really *losing* it, or giving it to someone else?" One hand lifted to thread through his hair. He leaned into her touch like a kitten. "Trust me. I'm a big girl; I know what I'm doing."

"You are a *woman*." He pulled back before leaning his forehead against hers, his eyes squeezing shut. "And I want you more than I've wanted anyone in a very, very, *very* long time. But this cannot be…"

The mattress rebounded as Massimo shifted, moving from beside her to across the room in a blink. The distance was more than merely physical; it felt psychic. They each came to the edges of their comfort zones, bordering intimacy, until something shifted.

Portia sunk back beneath the blankets, pulling the sheets and the coverlet up to her chin as Massimo assumed the role for which his title branded him.

"We leave in a half-hour. I understand that Luisa has prepared a bag for you but let her evening replacement know if you require anything more. I've also asked the cook to ready a meal. It will be delivered shortly. Eat well, Signora. I vouch for your safety in Florence, but I can make no guarantee regarding hospitality."

And then, like a lamp being turned off, he was simply… gone. Portia waited a minute, making sure it wasn't a game of peek-a-boo. As the seconds ticked by, the reality became plain. Portia didn't even stop to see what Luisa had packed for her. She doubted any piece of clothing could cover her embarrassment.

What was it about Massimo that made Portia into a fool so consistently? She'd thrown herself at him twice, and though he took an initial swing, she had yet to connect with the bat. *Three strikes, girl, you're out.*

Whatever, it wasn't like she could blame him for not taking advantage of her obvious desire. Yeah, she'd had a rocking bod when she was younger, but youth was slipping away. At forty-one and having played the hermit since her divorce, even she was aware of how her curves had begun to soften and her breasts to lose some of their bounce. Thin lines across her face seemed to deepen by the day.

Besides, Massimo was just so... yum. How old he actually was, she didn't know, but his body looked like someone her own age. Except solid muscle and like, no body fat. No wrinkles. A smack of gray hair right in front of his ears, which frankly, she found hot for reasons she couldn't understand.

She paused at the door on her way out, turning to look back up at the portrait over the fireplace. "Hey, Catalina, if you really can grant wishes... Just saying, I wouldn't mind a little time with a guy like that."

To her surprise, it was Pavlos and not Massimo who met her in the courtyard and guided her to the dock behind the palazzo. The wood-paneled motorboat bobbed, not from waves which didn't generally hit the canal except in storms, but from the wake of a passing boat.

"Where's Massimo?" she asked as she allowed the Doge's second to aid her into the cabin.

Pavlos pulled back his hand to accept her bag from the dock worker. "His Serenity is not a fan of boat travel or being on the water in any way." A nod at the pilot saw them push off. "He will rendezvous with us on the mainland."

"He's afraid of water?"

Pavlos grinned but didn't deny it.

Portia turned around, admiring the sparkling wall of the palazzo as it grew smaller in her sights. "Is water dangerous for vampires?"

"Hardly. In fact, most vampires take their day sleep in water. For... anachronistic reasons, I'd guess you'd say."

Massimo didn't. He slept in a bed. She'd slept in *his* bed. What kind of supernatural being capable of ripping through bone and flesh was afraid of a little *agua*? Of course, given her own distaste for waterplay, she couldn't criticize there.

She pulled her sweater at the collar, closing it to the marine winds. "I'm not a big fan of it myself. Ever since I was a kid, I'd had this thing about being wet. Maybe I drowned in a previous life or got swept away by a tsunami or something."

The smaller canal brought them to the famous lagoon, the *Campanile* to her left shooting up above the horizon like a giant pushpin keeping the island in place. Memory flooded as the bells echoed over the water. For a month, she'd sat a stone's throw from the famous landmark, awaiting Massimo's arrival, having no idea that soon she'd step away from her passive existence and into the cusp of centuries-old immortal politics.

She should have just sketched the pigeons.

How quickly the romantic, postcard visions faded once they stepped foot on the mainland. They docked and alighted not at the tourist docks, but alongside a mundane roadway. Pavlos again served as her guardrail, helping her to climb out of the boat without falling in the water. The buzz of the marine motors still echoed in her body as he led her to a small convoy of three glossy, black town cars parked on the breaker's edge.

He opened the backdoor of the middle one. "After you, Signora."

Portia crawled in, scooting to the inner seat when Pavlos followed her.

"I thought you were staying behind in Venice while Massimo

and I are gone?"

Pavlos closed the door, nodding to the driver, already in place and waiting. "I am."

He offered nothing more, and Portia got the feeling from the way the vampire's eyes sharpened, then flashed to the driver and back again, that she shouldn't question it.

Late evening traffic slowed them for a while, but soon, they'd gotten far enough from Venice that Portia could no longer smell the sea in the air flooding in from the opened window beside her. And still, Pavlos remained, though he had spent the last ten minutes busying himself on his phone. Apparently, digital distraction was an equal-opportunity creature corrupter.

"Pavlos?"

He held up his finger, his eyes trained on the screen. "A moment, Signora. We just... Ah, yes." He looked up, but not at her. Rather, he caught the driver's eyes in the rearview mirror (another urban myth dispelled, vampires *did* have reflections) and said something that definitely was *not* Italian.

The breaks slammed. The tires squealed. The car came to a very sudden stop.

"Holy... fu—"

Portia's mouth went still as Pavlos's arm pinned her back. His calm demeanor told her this had been planned. But why? He didn't wait to explain or even ask if she was okay. WHICH SHE WASN'T. Jesus, she'd thought she'd been just about to die.

He opened the door and held his hand for her, even as the trunk of the car popped open and the driver scrambled out to fetch her bag from it. "Quickly, Signora. The illusion must be succinct."

She took his hand and pulled herself out of the back seat. "What illusion?"

No words again. Instead, Portia's feet lifted as Pavlos braced her and lifted her. She had time enough to see that all three cars in the convoy had stopped under an overpass of some sort. No one coming from behind, thank god, but the headlights approaching from the other direction told her they could still be hit if they weren't careful.

Only as the Porsche SUV approached, it too put on its brakes, screeching to a halt right beside where she and Pavlos stood. The hatch popped open, and the driver hastened to place her bag inside.

Pavlos patted her arm, encouraging her to move, even as the passenger side door swung open. "Take care in Florence, Signora. And if you wouldn't mind, send my personal regards to the Duchess."

"Your personal what?"

No time. Vampires could move like the wind and they didn't waste the skill.

Trunk closed, seatbelt on, door closed, engine revving. It all seemed to happen at once, and it took her a moment to realize that the man driving them in the opposite direction they'd just come was none other than the Doge himself.

"Massimo?"

He grinned, shifting the car into a higher gear before taking her hand to place a kiss on it. "*Buonasera, cara mia.*"

Total tease.

"Thank God. For a minute I thought I was being kidnapped." A sign they passed labeled the road north-bound. "I thought we were going to Florence?"

He squinted at her before turning back to the road. "We are, but I don't know if Marco has allies on the lookout for us. It is easy enough to stage a car crash, and I wouldn't put it past him to try, if he has learned of our impending arrival. My convoy will serve as a diversion while you and I slip into the city by more—" He tapped the steering wheel. "—common means. If you'd prefer the town car on the return, we can leave this one behind. Assuming Patria grants my request to have Marco meet the sun."

"And if she doesn't?"

His smile soured. "Then my sister is not the person I've always supposed she is."

"But there's a chance I'll end up dead instead, isn't there?" *You don't just plop yourself in the middle of a supernatural conspiracy and come out unscathed.*

His body tensed. "I will do everything in my power to protect you."

"That wasn't a no."

Massimo shook his head. "There are bigger issues at play. Patria doesn't want war, nor do I. She will end Marco rather than take our two cities into battle, even if it means killing her own consort."

"Marco is Patria's *consort*? You mean, like, her husband?" Every inch of her body seized. "How could you *not* tell me that?"

"I didn't?" He didn't even bother to look at her while daring to sound all innocent.

"No, you didn't." Portia's teeth ground audibly. "Seriously, you think your sister is going to believe me, a nobody huey, over her own husband?"

"You're not a nobody. You're my friend." This time, he did look at her, with eyes begging and mouth hanging open. "That is… It's okay if I call you my friend, isn't it?"

"With where your hand was this morning? We better be *at least* that much." She tried to make out the contours of the landscape in the darkness, but couldn't see much more than vague outlines, blurred by speed. "Put yourself in her position. Would you believe me?"

He looked to mull that over a moment before clicking his tongue. "It doesn't matter. When she enthralls you, she'll hear the truth. Then she'll have no other choice than to give in to my demands where Marco is concerned."

"Suddenly I'm feeling very played. You do remember that I

have a life, right? It might be short and simple compared to yours, but it's still all I got. I didn't just stumble into Venice for your convenience."

"Believe me, Portia, nothing about you showing up in Venice has been convenient." The blinkers clicked as he changed lanes, going around a late model Renault with more rust than paint. "Besides, you're assuming that Patria cares anything for Marco. She doesn't. They have a political marriage and spend most of their time apart. She wouldn't hesitate to—"

"Don't." Portia's hand shot up. "Don't sit there and dare to tell me you know what their relationship actually is. A marriage—*any* marriage—is a hall of mirrors, and anyone who walks through never gets a real view of the structure that lies beneath."

"Vampire hearts don't work that way." His eyes darted between her and the road. "Patria and I are born of the same maker. Bloodlines pull tighter than heartstrings in my world."

"You can't seriously believe that." Her jaw clenched as she wove her hands over her chest and huffed. "And even if you do, it just means you've never been in love."

Massimo's voice sounded more like a growl as he punched the gas pedal. "You'd be surprised."

The rest of the trip passed in silence other than when Massimo asked Portia if she needed to stop to use the bathroom. She bit her tongue, crossed her legs, and dug in her heels. This car trip needed to be over. Her eyes stayed trained on what she imagined might be beautiful countryside but, under a new moon, it kept its secrets from her. Two hours in, she brought her thoughts out from the cocoon of her anxiety enough to realize that the smooth highway had begun to undulate. They must be approaching Florence, as the rolling hills meant they'd definitely made it to Tuscany. A *click-click-click* proceeded their turn off the highway and onto a smooth, single-lane road.

"This isn't Florence."

"No, it's Fiesole. Florence is another half-hour drive."

Her nerves ticked up. The outlines of buildings were masked against ambient light, but it was the opposite of Venice. The car's headlights highlighted green hedges and yellow stucco walls. The roads were comfortably wide and tree-lined. Rather than mobs of tourists, only the occasional couple or solo local walked with purpose-filled gaits. After passing through a roundabout, Massimo turned onto a lane that crawled its way up a steep drive. Above, landscape lights revealed a house peeking out from lush gardens.

"It would be a great place to bury a body."

Massimo tried to hide a laugh. "If you want to kill me, you won't need to dispose of a body. Just leave me to the sun and I'll turn to dust."

She couldn't tell if he was joking or not. "I didn't mean that. I... I don't know why I said it. I mean, it's not like I could kill you anyway. How would I even try?"

"Wood to the brain or the heart. Distracting me first would help. A cut large enough to force your blood would probably do it. Alternatively, you could just cut off my head. Few creatures survive without a brain."

"Obviously, you've never met my ex-father-in-law."

He must have seen her attempt at humor for what it was. Massimo moved the car into park alongside a few others at the end of the drive before turning in his seat to her. "Portia, I know I'm asking a lot of you to trust me that I can keep you safe. But you don't think you're the only one extending trust, do you? I know I seem very strong, but I have weaknesses, too. I just told you plainly how to kill me. I did that trusting that you never would."

"What reason would I have for killing you?"

"What reason would I have for wanting *you* to die?"

He took her hand. Her trembling hand. Her shaking hand. Because even though she was still mad at him, he was still... just wow. The kiss he placed was the simplest form of affection, and still had her burning in effigy.

"I should have told you about Marco and Patria. But as I've

trusted you, trust me. I know my sister. I know what she will do, and I know what I must do to convince her, even if she hesitates."

"I don't want to die, Massimo." She tried to bite back tears, but the truth abhorred light and clawed at the soul begging shelter. "I just wanted to spend a winter in Venice, make a few sketches, eat gelato and gnocchi, maybe have some tawdry love affair if I got really bold. Or drunk. I didn't want all—" Her free hand splayed out. "—this."

"*Cara mia*, get through tonight with me, and I promise, you'll have all the rest. I'll see to it personally."

Could he see her blush even in the dark cabin of the car? "All of it?" Her voice rasped. "Personally?"

"Do you mean a tawdry love affair? No." His jaw hung down and his head rolled to the side. "But I'm open to other interpretations of—"

Knock, knock.

Portia recoiled as a woman who hadn't existed a moment before solidified from a bank of fog and tapped on her window.

Massimo grimaced in frustration, but he didn't signal anything to suggest they were in danger. The Doge pivoted in his seat, pushing the button to roll down the window. A woman with dark brown hair and wearing a burgundy pantsuit leaned in, speaking the native tongue with some sort of jesting threat. Massimo wagged a finger, issuing his rebuke, and the woman grinned in amusement.

"I'm serious!" the Doge said. "I *just* got this one. Get a scratch on it, and I will drive the wooden spike into your heart myself."

The woman feigned fear, following him into English. "Look, Massimo, how I quiver."

Tension took root in the following silence, until a moment later when the two vampires broke into smiles and Massimo opened his door. He embraced the woman, even picking her up off her feet. The spike of contempt that shot up Portia's spine was undeniable, even if it was irrational.

Massimo turned back to the car almost as an afterthought. "Portia, *vieni qui.*"

Oh, she'd come, all right. She wanted to face down this trollop making moves on her...

He'd said *friend*. They'd almost kissed once. She'd practically dry humped him in his bed. But, while Massimo could win the FIFA cup of flirting, he'd made it clear that he didn't intend to do anything more with her through passive denial of her advances. Besides, a man who looked like that only stayed single by choice. Of course, he had a gorgeous Italian hottie girlfriend. Probably had one in every city.

Rebuking herself, Portia crawled out of the passenger seat and rounded the hood. As if to add insult to injury, Massimo's hand settled on her shoulder, drawing her near, but not in anything even resembling a romantic gesture.

"May I introduce my honored guest, Signora Portia Kepler. Portia—"

His hand moved down to the small of her back, both bracing and giving a rub. *Well, now.*

"Please allow me to present you to Her Grace, Grand Duchess of Florence and my blooded sister, Patria de' Medici."

THIRTEEN

Patria's receiving room didn't scream out seventeenth-century royalty the way his did. No, the expansive lounge looked like something out of a movie where a rich executive steals away some peasant love interest to wine and dine her into seduction. Low couches, acrylic tables twisted in unnatural shapes, a preference for the large and squarish over the detailed and intricate. In the center of the room, two one-armed chaise lounges, one on which Patria was spread out at length, the other where he sat on the edge, folded in on himself. And Portia...

She attempted to disappear into a wingback stool at the far end of the space, where a well-stocked wet bar stood ready for raiding.

He'd done this to her; plucked her from her serene if lonely existence and subjected her to the company of two infamous vampires. Made her feel like a toy being dragged about the country by a selfish child. Being sidelined as inconsequential as he and his sister caught up. It would be worth it in the end, he told himself. If things went as planned and Marco met the sun come morning, he would take Portia away from all this to make up for it. Maybe they could stop in at one of his vacation homes in Paris or Prague.

Or maybe he'd just whisk her away to his house in Cagliari, where their only agenda would be relaxation. She could paint. He could read and forget about the world. What was the huey term for it? Oh, yes... *checking out.* Massimo tried to picture it in his head. Dinners overlooking the ocean. Walking the beaches under the moon.

Making love until evening.

Even as the Doge tried to keep focused on Patria's pleasantries, he felt the pull in his loins. There was no doubt in his mind now; he was going to make love to her. The only questions unanswered was where, when, and for how long.

For the moment, though, he had to protect her. Not so much from himself, though if Portia knew what he was thinking, she might think otherwise. But from the purview of his sister, whose involvement with Marco's schemes he had yet to ferret out.

"Massimo?"

"Hmm?"

Patria grinned when his eyes turned up at him.

Caught.

She scooted to the edge of her chair. "I'm uncertain if you've heard anything I've said for the last few minutes, so I'm going to skip the rest of the small talk. Tell me why you—" Patria lifted her chin in Portia's direction. "—and the woman you can't stop staring at are here. It wouldn't have anything to do with the guests you'll soon be welcoming in Venice, would it? Here to scout Florence for signs of weakness pending an upcoming bid?"

Massimo shook his head. Thank God that Portia couldn't speak Italian. If she truly understood the deep end of the ocean she'd fallen into, she might take off at first light. "Unlike you, Patria, I've never coveted power."

"Now that's a lie so deeply planted, I fear you've allowed it roots." The Duchess returned the poker to the stand next to the fireplace and crossed to a bureau where she poured herself a glass of wine from a clear decanter. "There may be few still alive who know the truth of how you came to rule Venice, but I do."

"I only overthrew Luciana… *Inga,* to rescue my city and keep it from falling under Vlad's control."

"An admirable goal. A worthy endeavor, indeed. Only now, you have a vicedoge of the Dracule bloodline. If your goal was to keep Vlad's influence out of your city, what is the rationale in that?"

Massimo stood, shaking his head. True, Pavlos was a Dracule, but that didn't mean he was a usurper-in-waiting. "Signore Katsaros is many makers removed from Vlad. I trust him enough with my city to be here now. I would trust him enough with my life anywhere. And do I not remember properly that you and he seemed to get along quite well when you visited Venice last?"

Patria's smile evaporated as she averted her gaze. "I don't know what you're talking about."

Massimo crossed his arms over his chest and leaned back in his chair. Fine, if his sister wasn't about to pin her heart on her sleeve, he wouldn't blame her. Romantic ties weakened a ruler, particularly if those ties were to the vicedoge of another court.

"Regardless," Massimo continued, "you must have heard the same rumors coming from the east as I have. I need to know that we're on the same side of this, Patria. You and I united sends a message to the others: the Dracule and their way of thinking is not welcome here."

"Are you not the one welcoming them to your city?"

"I am the one allowing them to *pass through,*" Massimo clarified. "We both know there are those among our citizens who would embrace the Dracule's rule, to be freed to feed on all hueys at will without regard to discovery. Not to mention, their ability to outlive the term of their unnatural lives has drawn... curiosity."

"Not yours, though?"

"As long as I'd be leaving Venice in good hands, what have I to remain living for?" His eyes flashed to Portia of their own volition.

Yes, romantic ties weakened a ruler...

His sister turned slowly, methodically, following his gaze to the huey. "And so, we come to the Canadian elephant in the room." Patria fanned her fingers as she pivoted back. "She has something to do with your sudden need to see me, and *alone,* and *outside of the city*?"

Massimo broke his gaze with Portia only with supernatural effort. He took to his feet to draw away Patria's attention, leaning on the mantel over the fireplace. "I needed to meet with you to inform you that your consort killed one of my guards openly and without provocation."

"Marco?" Patria cackled. "Ridiculous. What reason would he have for killing a vampire without cause?"

"Let me clarify. Your consort killed a member of my guard *right in front of my eyes* and challenged me to take vengeance on the spot, knowing fair well what kind of instability that would cause." Massimo planted himself behind Patria, giving her shoulders a squeeze. "Like you said, there are those who would welcome Dracule rule. I don't know if Vlad is coming here with intentions, but the Pro-Dracule factions would be eager to provide whatever aid they could."

"You speak of conspiracies, but the only ruler of one of the Eight Courts to win his throne by violence lives in Venice." Patria mused a moment before continuing, "If I were to accept your charges and make them public—and I do mean, *if*, Massimo—what compensation would you seek?"

"Justice. Only justice."

"One man's justice is another's tyranny." Patria leaned forward in her chair. "Tell me this: if Marco was ready to die at your hand, to become a martyr, what makes you think that will be any different if you kill him here? If he is attempting to trigger a war between Venice and Florence, he will have planted seeds of conspiracy in the richest fields already."

Patria was right. She usually was; he'd been highly educated in the rules of conflict but she was born and raised a Medici. "Now that I think about it, I'm not sure he really intended for me to kill him in Venice. In fact, I'm certain he didn't. He knew I was nearby, watching, when he killed Giuliano. If he'd simply had wanted to trigger a war, he would have assassinated me and made it well known he'd done the deed. Pavlos wouldn't have hesitated to avenge me."

Something he'd need to make sure to discuss with his vicedoge.

"If I were to take you at your word about what happened, do you want to know what I think, brother? That my consort did what was needed to draw you here. Think of how much more glorious he'll be to *his* followers when he kills you in front of them in a challenge you called for. Of course, your vicedoge will not see it that way. Pavlos is too young. Too... *passionate.*"

Massimo tried to ignore the mischievous smile that kept sneaking across his sister's face. "Patria?"

She cleared her throat and straightened her expression. "Anyway... I said *if* I were to believe you, but we both know it's not just about me. Members of my court would question the validity of such accusations. Is there any other witness to this killing?"

Massimo looked to Portia.

"The huey?" The Duchess turned to English, spitting out the term like a four-lettered insult on the way. "You want my court to act on the testimony of a huey?"

Massimo scowled. "What reason would Portia have to lie?"

Patria notched her head to the side. "You mean besides the fact that she's in love with you?"

"I am *not* in love with Massimo." Suddenly, the woman in question sprang to her own defense. "How dare you insinuate—"

"Watch your words, human." Patria held up one hand at arm's length. "Men can be so obtuse about these things, but we women know. I can see it in the way you two—what is the English term? *Eye fuck* each other?"

"Patria!"

Portia squared herself, motioning for Massimo to keep his distance. "I can definitely tell you two are related, you know. You speak English just fine, but every time you want to imply you might have a vulgar side, you act like you're just learning it."

"She does know you well, doesn't she, brother?" Patria studied Portia through squinted eyes. "Allow me to enthrall her?"

Massimo huffed. "She's not my property, Patria. Seek her permission."

The ancient vampiress nodded. "Signora Kepler?"

"Of course, it's the only reason I'm here." Though in the wake of her boldness, Portia's nerves staged a rally. "Will it... Will it hurt?"

"Being enthralled? Not at all. The memories it brings to the surface? Only on an emotional level."

Portia cast her gaze to him, throwing Massimo for a loop. She didn't seek permission; he knew her too well to think Portia would willingly defer to him on anything. Then it could mean only one other thing: she sought his reassurance. She *trusted* him. Or at least, she was making an effort to.

"Patria speaks the truth," he said. "And I will be right beside you, making sure she only seeks what you've given her permission to obtain."

Portia's fear fell away, taking with it some of the walls between them. "Very well, Duchess, you have my permission."

FOURTEEN

They sat her in a chair and tied her wrists to the arms, though both vampires were quick to reassure her it was only because the enthralled could sometimes flail or fall unexpectedly.

"Like anything I could do could hurt you at all."

Portia had meant it only as a joke, but Massimo looked as though she had intentionally impugned his honor. "You have no idea the pain you could inflict on me."

Portia wanted to call him out on taking a moment of jest and imbuing it with global implications. She was still reeling at being accused of being in love. She *couldn't* be in love with a man she'd only known for a week. That kind of thing only happened in movies. She'd dated Richard for two years before she even experimented with the thought. Sure, she liked Massimo. Maybe even she *lusted* him. But love? No way, no how.

Patria leaned over her, her face inches from Portia's. "Do not worry, Signora, my brother is given to dramatics in all things romance. A carryover from his mortal days, I'm afraid, but of course, you know all about that."

"No, I don't. What do you—"

Her words died on her tongue and her will followed suit as Patria's eyes became her world. A warm wave of serenity crashed through her, separating Portia from her anxiety, her curiosity, her thoughts. Like being on a boat just offshore but completely able to see land. She could swim to any point on this beach, she just needed to know which direction to go and when to dive in.

The Duchess's voice echoed in the sky of her imagination. "Turn your thoughts back. Tell me everything you remember about—what was the guard's name?"

Massimo cleared his throat and stepped closer. "Giuliano."

"The night *Giuliano* died," Patria pressed on. "Where are you, Signora?"

Suddenly, serenity fled. The world became streaks of black and gray and red. She stood, her back pressed into the doorway of the flat. "We're in the street outside my vacation rental. Giuliano walked me home after I finished my work at Massimo's office for the day."

"You're working for my brother?" Suspicion stained Patria's words.

Massimo clicked his tongue. "Portia is an artist. I commissioned her to create a piece to mark the Ravens' arrival."

"You didn't just ask for one from my stable?" Patria spit back. "Is she *that* good?"

Portia sensed the question wasn't for her but answered anyway. "I'm not. I don't have any professional credits and the only salon I ever had was in college before..." She swallowed. "Before I met my ex."

Even behind the shield of her will, Portia could see with her eyes perfectly well. That didn't mean, however, that she understood the sight. Massimo's face contorted, a combination of surprise and... if she didn't know better, determination. Or was that possession?

"I'm not interested in your huey love life," Patria said. "All I want to know is how Giuliano died. Tell me what you saw."

And so Portia did, reliving every quaking moment in tandem with recollection. Marco's arrival. Giuliano's attempt to defend her. Marco impaling the poor guard with a wooden stake. The light going out from Giuliano's eyes. Massimo's embrace as he protected her, comforted her, dragged her inside.

Massimo's embrace... It felt so real, even in memories. His scent filled her nostrils and she felt a desire... no, a *need* to be near him. For a moment, Portia reconnected with her physical being and felt her cheeks burn, heard her heart pound. Her mouth fell open.

His voice was right beside her when he spoke. "Enough, Patria. Don't force her to linger in that horror."

"I don't think it's the memory of Giuliano's murder that's making her grin that way."

"So, you believe it then? Good, release her."

Patria's finger shot up. "Not yet. Portia, tell me what you *felt* when Marco killed Giuliano."

"*Patria...*"

"Hush, Massimo!" the Duchess snapped. "I want *her* to tell us."

She licked her lips. The vessel of her thoughts rolled on a wave summoned against her will. "Scared."

"Obviously, but I'm not talking about your lizard brain reaction. Your mind was racing. Too many thoughts. Violence, danger, yes, but you'd just seen my brother appear out of nowhere and Marco with wild eyes and long teeth. Then, after, you saw him turn into a pillar of smoke and float away. Your rational mind was grasping at straws, but it was still grasping. So tell me, tell *us,* beyond that moment, what did you *feel.*"

"I felt..." Suddenly, the silk cords binding her felt too tight, too restrictive. "I felt..." All she wanted to do was turn over her wrist, to open her hand. To... strike. "I felt like I had to attack."

Like that would achieve anything. The vampires could break her neck before her hand landed.

"Self-defense, or..." Patria pulled back, turning to Massimo. "Something more, perhaps?"

Wide-eyed, Massimo shook his head. "It's nothing. A nervous tick."

Curiosity nibbled at Portia's gut. "What is it? What are you talking about?"

One perfectly shaped eyebrow arched above Patria's eye. "She is asking that while enthralled. Really, Massimo... I'm surprised you didn't see it before."

"And I'm surprised you see it at all. You're trying to find a way that Portia could be enthralled and still lie to you instead of accept the truth for what it is."

"I am more concerned with how you're lying to yourself. Nonetheless..."

With a wave of the Duchess's hand, Portia fell forward, a tremendous conflict of feeling both free and burdened. Massimo was at her side in a moment, bracing her shoulders before she collapsed forward, but his words were for his sister.

"You heard what she said. Now, will you allow me to do what I must? Or will you let Marco pull the strings and bring our cities into open conflict?"

"No one pulls my strings, brother. You of all people should know that." Patria balanced her chin on the tip of her finger, sucking in her bottom lip. "I believe your witness, but you forget that my union with Marco brought together the courts of Florence and Genoa. You say you make this request to keep us from turmoil, but did you ever consider the consequences for Tuscany if I kill their Doge and Genoa cedes?"

"Of course, I have. The smaller of two evils if his infatuation with the Ravens' world vision gives them a path to wile their way into either of our cities."

He stood, leaning in, turning his tongue back to Italian. How interesting, Portia thought. Did Massimo think that hid anything? Maybe Patria was right and for all his experience and intelligence, Massimo couldn't see the truth right in front of him.

She could understand almost every word.

"Perhaps the solution is to give Marco exactly what he wants," Massimo said.

"I don't see how my head on a spike will help, even if Vlad would appreciate the homage."

"What? No, not..." Grunting, Massimo shook his fist. "If your court would think my avenging the killing of a guard overly wrought, then maybe I just need to add more weight to my side."

"Meaning?"

"Meaning, what if he also threatened the life of my betrothed?"

"Except you haven't got a—" Realization struck a bell in Patria's thoughts, her eyes going wide. "You honestly think anyone's going to believe Europe's longest-reigning bachelor has pledged his fang to defend that... thing?"

A flushed Massimo gathered his impressive height for a man of his era and stiffened his spine. He looked down at his sister, chest heaving, fangs long and threatening. "Her name is Portia, and any man—vampire or otherwise—would be lucky to have her."

"All right, all right." Patria threw up her hands in defeat. Rather than be intimidated, she appeared amused. "Fine, I'll convene my court an hour before dawn. I'll give Portia an honorary place beside me and do my best to keep any of Marco's sycophants from her. A few words, and they'd have the truth out in no time flat. And of course, don't forget the most important thing of all."

"What's that?" Massimo asked.

"If Portia's going to be your fiancée tonight, she should also know there's a risk that she'll be a widow come morning."

He'd long ago lost faith that the Almighty heard his prayers, but who else could Massimo beseech? *Please let this work*, the Doge begged in the medium of his thoughts. *I don't know how else to protect Portia and Venice at the same time.*

Because that's what he was doing now, saving Portia. Florence wasn't Venice. While Patria too had banned the killing of hueys for anything other than self-defense, Marco wasn't just another member of her court. Here, as royal consort, he was free to take whatever random huey he wanted. Portia was in even more danger than if they'd just stayed home.

The Doge of Venice walked the Duchess of Florence to the lowest terrace of the hillside garden, leaving Portia on the balcony high above with a glass of water and a cold compress. Enthrallment often had lingering effects on hueys, but Portia's reaction seemed to endure longer than others.

Though, perhaps, it was simply a shadow of the things she'd been forced to relive while under.

"Shall I send a car to collect you before dawn?"

Massimo shook his head. He wanted to arrive on foot. It was more intimidating. "But perhaps one for Portia?"

"Of course. I'll go to the city now and make the necessary arrangements. Portia will sit beside me in the balcony. If things don't go your way... Well, I'll be certain she stays safe."

"Thank you, Patria."

"Don't thank me." She tapped him on the shoulder. "Win."

"Win what?"

Both vampires turned, looking across the foyer and the kitchen beyond to where Portia had just come in. Massimo couldn't help but feel a little pride in the fact that she'd moved so gracefully that she'd managed to take two immortals by surprise.

"Don't worry, Massimo will explain everything." With that, Patria bowed, turned to Massimo, gave him a look that said *I hope to high hell you know what you're doing*, and dissolved into a pillar of smoke that zipped its way down the hillside.

"Jesus... criminy!"

"*Cara mia!*" Again, he was at her side before she lost her balance. "Are you okay?"

He'd meant to catch her, to *comfort her*, but as Portia found her feet, she also found her tongue. "No, Massimo, I'm not okay, okay? I'm definitely *not* okay."

His hand flattened against her forehead, feeling for a fever as he gave her a top-to-bottom survey. "I don't see anything wrong but stay here and I'll bring you more water and perhaps some ginger candies if I can find any."

"I don't need water and I sure as hell don't need candy. What I *need* is an explanation." She pressed blanched fingertips into her forehead as she sank into a nearby chair. "We're engaged?"

Suddenly, Massimo knew what it must feel like at the end of a vampire's life when they turned to stone. "You speak Italian."

It was a statement, not a question. Or perhaps better stated, it was a realization.

Portia crossed her arms over her chest. "I mean, I can't compose poetry or hold discussions on existentialism, but yeah, I have basic functionality. My grandmother was from Cortona and she never really warmed up to English. But engagement? That came through fine."

"No, you misunderstood." He kneeled beside her. "I didn't say we're engaged. I said we'd *pretend to be engaged.* It gives me enough grounds to challenge Marco to open combat and kill the cur like I've wanted to for two hundred years."

"Oh, well, if it's only to satisfy your bloodlust, then…"

"It's not about bloodlust," Massimo insisted. "Marco threatens to destabilize Italy with his actions, and as the Italian courts go, so will the rest of the continent. Even though he killed Giuliano, his supporters here in Tuscany won't see it as reciprocity if I kill him. It will trigger a bloody vendetta with vampires picking each other off, and humans will fall in the crossfire. But if he threatened my *bride-to-be*," he took her shaking hand, pulling her gaze along with it, "then I have grounds to end it all here tonight before things get out of hand. All I'm asking is that, for one night, you *pretend* that I'm the kind of man with whom you'd consider spending the rest of your life."

FIFTEEN

Yeah, pretend. Didn't he know how hard she was pretending right now? She'd done her best to quell it. After what she'd just come out of, the last thing she wanted was to fall into the middle of another doomed relationship, but that didn't stop her imagination hijacking her thoughts and attempting to seduce it with fantasy.

But, perhaps, if it was for the greater good…

"You promise me it's only for tonight?"

Massimo nodded. "Of course. The rumors will run rampant the moment you sit beside Patria at court. But once we are back in Venice, I'll announce our dissolution."

Portia tried to ignore how the sentiment saddened her.

"Besides," Massimo continued, "no one will believe that I would ever really marry someone like you."

The insult sizzled all the way up Portia's back as her mouth gaped and electrified her hand. She almost managed to slap him. Almost.

Wasn't he supposed to be able to move so much faster than her?

Massimo's hands shot up in surrender. "That's not what I meant."

"Then what *did* you mean, Massimo? Like me, *what*? A middle-aged nobody? A foreigner? A high school art teacher? A divorcee not possessing virgin's blood?"

"No, none of those things matter to me. What I meant is a human, of course. A vampire of my power and influence, married to someone so easily corruptible? I'd not only be inviting trouble, but I'd also be signing over my life to it. Not to mention, it would put you in constant danger. You've only been part of this world for less than a week, and already you're in the middle of a clusterfuck of politics."

Portia blinked. "You cursed."

"I do, when occasion recommends."

Massimo seated himself on a stone bench on the side of the garden, turning his study to the ground beneath his feet as his toe dragged a line across the moist dirt path. Humility or embarrassment? In either case, she knew whatever he was about to say put him in awkward position vampire royalty often did not entertain.

"I just want to protect you, Portia. This conflict with Marco didn't start today, or last week, or even this century, but that won't make you any less dead tomorrow if I don't do this tonight. For years, Marco's kept his antics here is Tuscany. I didn't condone them then, but it was outside of my power to act. Now he's committed multiple crimes in *my city,* and he'll do so again if *we* don't stop it. So, I'm asking you..." Puppy dog eyes set in the face of an attack dog, like a petulant Pitbull. "...please, be the one to help me end this."

The fire within her died, leaving her awash in some kind of delirium. Portia pulled in a deep breath, enjoying a lick of jasmine in the air, as well as a hint of something... ancient. She took measured steps toward the bench before turning and settling herself beside him, her arms crossed over her chest. "What do you need me to do exactly?"

Keeping his eyes down, she still caught the uptick in the corners of his mouth. "Just be there and don't say anything to contradict me. Look like you're in love with me and pretend to be devastated if he kills me."

"Why do you think I'd be pretending?"

Their eyes met, and nothing Portia had ever experienced before equaled the pull at that moment. She felt like a wave had crashed into her and pushed her towards him. Only, she didn't move. She couldn't. She refused to do this to herself: fall for a man who wanted her as a convenience, not as a partner. Hadn't Massimo just said it himself? She would topple his security, not to mention put herself in mortal danger if she were with him. Borrowing the gravity of the earth for a moment, she somehow managed to look away.

"So tell me what I should expect down there."

Massimo appeared as dazed as she was but pushed on as well. "It's called *Il Anello di Fuoco*: *the Ring of Fire,* but that's more of a metaphor. With the sanction of the Duchess, two vampires meet in the courtyard of the Palazzo shortly before sunrise. They fight until one is dead, or until the sun rises overhead and kills them both."

"Wait, are you telling me that your way of protecting me is to go get yourself killed?"

"You're so certain I'd lose?" Massimo pulled one of her hands to his mouth and ghosted a kiss across her knuckles. "Have you so little faith in your lord, wife?"

"I'm not your wife, and yes, I do. I saw what that guy can do. He went fully medieval on Giuliano. How can you possibly fight someone that dirty?"

He took her hand, tracing over the creases that time had started to etch into her wrists. "Don't worry. Marco fights for his misguided ideology. I fight for a greater power. Not to mention—" he grimaced. "I am much older than him, which makes me far stronger."

Despite the swirl of emotion within, Portia let the humor bubble its way up, making her laugh silently. "So vampires are like wine, then? Getting better with age?"

His features transformed, and now in place of comfort, his gaze inspired heat. "In every way possible."

Sweet baby lord. Portia wasn't sure she would ever love Massimo, but lust wouldn't be an issue.

"I don't know how I'm going to stomach seeing two men trying to destroy each other."

She left unsaid that she thought seeing him die was her sole concern. As to Marco, that bastard deserved anything he got. Would Patria mourn him? As a younger woman, she wouldn't have questioned that. After surviving a failed marriage and bitter divorce that had left her heart wounded and her pride beyond repair, not to mention the things Massimo had said about the nature of his sister's relationship with her husband, she was second-guessing that.

Which also made her wonder...

"Massimo, have you ever been married?"

He blinked, his whole body pulsing once. Obviously, he hadn't been expecting that.

"I... had a wife once, when I was still mortal. Of course, I wasn't Doge then. Merely a merchant."

"Did you love her?" An odd question for a modern westerner, but she knew that romantic marriages as the norm were a fairly modern phenomenon.

"More than life itself." The answer was evident even before he spoke. Massimo winced, a pain still tangible after so many years. Then his face broke into a wide, placid smile as sweet memory washed away the anguish. "Truth be told, I love her still."

"And why didn't she..." Portia realized suddenly the nosy path she pursued. "You know what? Never mind."

"You want to know why she's not beside me as a vampire, too."

"I don't want to pry or cause you pain." Because if she did want a relationship with him...

Whoa, girl. Her brain pulled on the reigns of her heart. *This isn't about you. Tell him to stop. It's none of your damned business.*

"No, it's a fair question."

He continued before she could intervene, and he did so with so much echoed joy, Portia couldn't bring herself to cut him off.

"Do you remember how I told you that there are other supernatural creatures besides vampires?"

Portia nodded. "I distinctly remember werewolves being mentioned."

"Yes, and the wolf-watchers. Hueys, I believe, call them riding hoods after the story from Grimm, though how the fairy tales portray them is considerably lacking. They're sort of a binary pair, werewolves and hoods. A balance, matching strengths with weaknesses. Well, for vampires, there's something similar."

"A balance?" Portia didn't lack imagination. Still, she was having a hard time figuring out what kind of creature could counter a vampire.

"In Italy, we call them *soldati del sole*. In English, they're simply called slayers."

"You mean like Van Helsing and Buffy?" Her eyes skimmed the patio, like she expected one suddenly to be standing right there. Crouching, she readied a defensive stance. "So, on top of assassin vampires, I have to worry about celestial soldiers killing you?"

The amusement chased from his face. "*Cara mia*, no. The slayers only killed *bad* vampires. Or have you not yet figured out—" The tip of his index finger traced a line up her arm, twirling suggestively in the crook of her elbow. "—that I'm not evil?"

Her breath hitched despite her best efforts. "I'm still deciding."

He grinned before pulling back his hand. "In any case, it does not matter. They're extinct now. The last slayer died in 1953. And no, not like Buffy or the Helsings, who are real, by the way. Well, not Buffy, but the latter. They had their own abilities to match ours. We're fast, they could sometimes be faster. And because it was our biggest threat, nature gave them the ability to create sunlight. With a single powerful hit, they were able to turn us to ash."

"And your wife was one of those, a slayer?"

Massimo nodded.

"Then how did you end up a vampire? Wouldn't that make

you, like enemies?"

His expression drooped. "I didn't become this until after she died. She was attempting to contain a dangerous element inside the Venetian Vampire Court when she was killed. Drowned, actually. A slayer is made powerless by water."

The pieces started coming together in Portia's mind. A fallen love, a powerful merchant family, a well with a legend of a drowned wife and her grief-stricken husband who attempted to reclaim her soul from hell.

"Catalina was *your* wife."

Massimo's eyes went wide. "How do you know this?"

She hated causing him pain, and the name seemed to do that. She put a hand on his shoulder, squeezing. "One of your staff told me about her when she caught me looking at the portrait hanging in my room. I'm sorry for your loss, Massimo."

He labored to smile. "You say that like it's a fresh injury, not a scar on my soul."

"What is a scar but the part of us that can never heal?"

He gave her a curious look before taking her hand, rubbing circles over her knuckles. "Can I tell you something only a man as old as I can? There is a saying, *time heals all wounds*. It's a lie. Retribution quells the pain for a while, but vengeance is a shallow pool easily crossed."

Portia moved her hand to his cheek. "You became a vampire to avenge her."

"Catalina never hid what she was from me after we were wed, and so I had already come to know many powerful vampires before she passed. Patria sponsored me, took me to the paterfamilias of her bloodline. No wise man said no to a Medici back then, especially an immortal one. I became vampire, wormed my way into the Venetian court, and then waited for the moment I could tear it all down. I have been Doge ever since."

"But you must've been so lonely, especially after knowing

such happiness."

An awkward smile overtook his face. "I am not a priest, *topolina*. I've had many lovers, even if I've never found love. I never could find a way to let go of the pain to give anyone my heart. How do you reach for love again after fate struck you so hard the first time?"

Portia nodded. "I know. I mean, my situation wasn't as nice as yours but believe it or not, Richard and I were madly in love once. Or maybe only I was and I was too happy to see he didn't feel the same? But the last two years of my marriage… I felt like a dog whose owner spoiled him as a puppy but then locked him up outside once the novelty wore off. And then, worst of all, beat him when he dared bay for attention."

Massimo's eyes turned fierce. His fangs erupted into view.

Portia realized her mistake immediately. "No, I don't mean he beat me. It's a metaphor. The point is, though, it warped my whole outlook on life. I don't think I can ever fall in love again without already knowing it ends badly. And if that's what's going to happen, what's the point? I can't imagine how you've gotten through centuries feeling that kind of hopelessness."

"I think pain pilots its own vessel, and we're just passengers until we reach the shore. For some, the journey is longer." Massimo reached for her hand, pulling it from his shoulder to his lips, placing a kiss on the back of her hand. "I hope you reach your shore soon, Signora. You have little time in this world to waste on agony."

She curled her fingers around his. "So do you. You're an old man, remember?"

His laugh dissolved the tension growing in their stare, and Portia knew she had to turn a corner on this conversation soon or her *vessel* would crash on his rocks.

"So… Ring of Fire in the courtyard of the vampiric palazzo," she said, reclaiming her hand and exhaling. "Okay, well, at least I'll get to see a little bit of Florence."

The Italian vampire pushed a palm into his forehead as he shot to his feet. "Ah, *mannaggia a me!*" His hand settled low on her back as he guided her towards stone steps leading up and away from the garden along the hedgerow. "Come. I should have shown you when we arrived."

"Shown me wh—"

Two more steps, and the view answered the question.

All of Tuscany was a crown, and Florence, its shining jewel.

The Duomo crowned the skyline, and from it fell stringed pearls across winding streets. Amber lights glowed in the clear night, illuminating the city and making Portia feel like they'd punched a hole through time. The medieval tower above Palazzo Vecchio winked as her wide eyes scanned the horizon, indexing dome after dome, ancient wall after archaic arch, a sublime intersection of art and function.

She didn't realize she'd taken a step forward until Massimo's hands gripped her hips, pulling her back. "Careful, Signora. Contrary to popular belief, vampires cannot fly. I might not catch you if you fall."

Her head wiped to the left, their smiling eyes locking as she looked back over her shoulder. "You would. I know you would."

Gravity pulled between them, and she didn't miss how his mouth dropped open, like he was either going to kiss her or bite her. She didn't know which she feared or desired more. But a second before the space between them closed, Portia rescued herself. Worming out of Massimo's embrace, she put some distance between them.

"But you're right. I have to be more careful. *We should both be more careful.*"

"But Portia, please—"

She didn't wait around to see what he had to say. As fast as her feet could walk, she made her way for the house.

SIXTEEN

It was like a scene out of every poorly staged production of *Romeo and Juliet* or *The Merchant of Venice* that Portia had ever seen, only with more participants looking at smartphones.

Below, a prototypical Renaissance Italian courtyard: wide-open space horseshoed by the house it belonged to, interrupted at intervals by stone benches, carefully-curated topiary, and in the center, a trickling fountain laying down a belying serene soundtrack. Porticos lined the ground level, hosting a plethora of vampire spectators. A second-tier of porticos anchored the balcony to which Patria had guided her, flanked by guards behind, and to their left and right, a dozen or so immortals Portia took for supernatural nobility. Looking over the railing from the plush chair she'd been given, the lone huey spotted shadowy recesses on either end of the courtyard. If she remembered her theatrics correctly, this would be where the opposing foes emerged. Despite the circumstances, she congratulated herself on her predictions when a pillar of smoke darted in from the passage on the west end and formed into the shape of a familiar friend.

After which, a bomb could have gone off and Portia wouldn't have noticed. Her eyes had robbed her mind of concern.

Wearing no more than tight blue pants secured by a golden strip of cloth, his bare chest and arms revealed their beauty. Vines of olive flesh replete with muscle caught the glint of a torch's flicker as Massimo marched toward the middle of the courtyard. For a moment, Portia wondered if that silly yet enthralling book she'd read once upon a time that suggested vampires' skin was like diamonds held some truth. A moment later, however, a simpler explanation presented itself. Massimo had been oiled up. As had Marco, it seemed, who entered the space a moment later attired much the same, only the strip of cloth around his waist, red.

A muffled sound hit her ears, and Portia spun her head, trying to identify the source. It turned out that all the attendees were... snapping.

This had gone from an ancient Greek fighting ring to a 1960s Berkeley coffee house in two seconds.

The human leaned toward the Duchess. "Is this... cheering?"

Patria's face cracked into a smile. "It's louder in our ear. We can't risk too much noise. It will wake the hueys in the surrounding neighborhood. Remember, everyone here but you is vampire."

Portia hadn't felt scared until that moment. "Everyone?"

Patria tapped the Canadian woman's hand. "No worries, *cara mia*. You are my honored guest. No one here will hurt you."

"As long as I'm your honored guest, and not just your guest." She tried to swallow down her sudden nerves, but her throat was scratchy. "Are humans... *hueys* forbidden in your world?"

"No, but we choose whom we share our secrets with carefully." Patria turned, splaying her hand out to indicate the hundred or so ringing the space in general. "They are kept at the edges, for their own safety. In fact, as auspicious an event as this is, you customarily would be barred from attending. I've allowed an exception for the future *Dogaressa*." The Duchess capped the statement with a wink.

"Thank you." Was she really thankful, though? It might have been nice to have an excuse not to have to witness death. Speaking of which... "I'm sorry to ask this, Duchess—"

"You must call me Patria. After all, we'll be sisters soon, won't we?"

"Okay, *Patria*." Portia left unspoken 'di Medici', but she still felt the impact of the unspoken. "Why are hueys banned?"

"Because they would bleed themselves, of course."

The statement was presented so matter-of-factly, Portia didn't know where to grab to reposition it.

Only then, Patria continued. "We are not sharks. We do not swarm when there's blood in the water. Or the air, as the case may be. But when two vampires are engaged in a fight to the death like this—" She motioned at the pair below, circling with the fountain between them, acting like "manly men" and all the peacocking that entailed. "Sometimes that proves the exception. At the very least, blood is a distraction."

Portia nodded, eyeballing the pair, who stopped right at that moment, turning their eyes to the balcony. Massimo stepped forward. Because he was the challenger, she guessed.

"Your Grace, most benevolent Duchess of Florence, beloved sister..." Massimo paced his words, over-accentuating. "I come seeking retribution against Marco di Serpente for the slaying of my friend and a loyal guard of my court, Giuliano Mastroni, and for the further offense of threatening the life of my betrothed, Portia Kepler."

Suddenly, the warmth was gone from Patria's tone as she sunk into her royal role. "You are granted permission to challenge, Your Serenity," the Duchess proclaimed. "How does my consort respond to these accusations and the challenge made?"

Marco pounded his chest. "I deny nothing. The *Veneziane* are allying with the Ravens, openly welcoming them to their city. I attempted to lure the Doge into an exchange which would allow us an opportunity to block the arrival of the Sultan of Istanbul. As is the head affected by the disease, so are its limbs. If Venice wishes to be decapitated in our great city and not on its own decrepit streets, so be it."

Portia wanted to roll her eyes, even as she recognized the political tactic. Claim your own goals as your enemy's, that way when you succeed, you need not take the blame for it.

The court procedures didn't distract her from remembering the truth, however. Most things were rarely one thing, as her mother used to tell her. Yes, there may be drama because of the Ravens (why they were so horrendous, she'd need to remember to ask later), but the trigger of the conflict on Massimo's side was his desire to protect her. He was fighting, to the death, to save *her*.

Richard wouldn't even wash a dinner plate for her, and they'd been together for years. Since college even. Massimo had known her—really known her—for less than a week, and he was risking his life and the fate of his city to protect her from both its politics and its terror.

Was she worth all that? What was she to him but some silly human on vacation who liked to sketch pictures?

"So be it. Fight with honor, but fight with haste. Dawn approaches."

Portia glanced up through the open-air courtyard, catching sight of the pink hue creeping into the sky to her left. Below, both men bowed to the balcony, and for a moment, Massimo caught her eye. She expected softness, some kind of reassuring *don't worry about it, kid* look that told her to just sit tight and this would soon be over. What she got, however, was a bone-stripping, soul-shaking intensity that she felt physically. That look was a pledge. It was a promise. It was his ardent intention.

But what were those intentions? Not just to kill Marco di Serpente; that much was clear. This battle may have been brewing for centuries, but there was something bigger going on. She wished she knew what. Some irrational pull inside her looked at Massimo and whispered out a crazy thought.

I should be down there fighting.

Portia laughed at the voice in her head. She never took herself for the sacrificial type. But then again, maybe it had been a while since anyone had valued her enough to suffer for her, and the step from that to reciprocity was easily crossed.

She leaned forward on the bench, her breath bated, and mouthed the only thing she could think to say. "Win."

He nodded.

Patria's arm jutted out to the left as one of her nobles placed a long, wooden pike into her hand. "Even the defeated deserve mercy. As has been our custom for centuries, you are honor-bound to render death when your opponent can no longer rise. One strike to the heart by this spear is a death of honor. A spike through the head... shame. Your fight commences when the tip lodges in the ground. Are you prepared?"

Both challenger and challenged voiced their readiness.

"Then—" Patria angled the spear overhead, aimed for the ground between Massimo and Marco. "—begin."

SEVENTEEN

Win.

Did she think he'd do anything less? After that moment in Patria's garden, the second he looked in her eyes and he just… knew. No, some wounds never healed, but sometimes you were lucky enough to find someone who would accept the scars you carried. She was the one. Even to a vampire who'd lived long enough to believe almost anything was possible, it didn't make sense. He barely knew Portia, and yet, Massimo felt like he'd known her all his life. There was something… instinctive driving him towards her. He'd tried to quell it, to deny it, to keep his distance, but every time he got close to her, Massimo's urgency to protect her and claim her and—*Dio*, let *her* claim *hi*… The need for it overpowered logic.

This challenge wasn't just about Marco anymore. His future with Portia lay on the other side of victory. He was tired of fighting it. It didn't matter that she was human. He'd protect her from harm, keep her safe in his world. In Venice, no one would oppose him and only a fool would dare hurt the Doge's consort. Making an example here by assuring that Marco met the sun, however, would do more than protect her than any declaration he could make in words.

The spear hit the dirt between them. Marco spit on the ground as he turned back, fangs bared, eyes wild. "You'll regret that I didn't end you in Venice."

Massimo broke the gaze, focusing on the threat before him. He squared his shoulders, crouched, and readied himself for battle. "Just fight me, you Raven-loving bastard, so you can finally get what you deserve."

They came together then like bulls. Marco surged forward, strong hands finding purchase on oiled skin. Tar and sand. It was the only explanation. He'd cheated. Of course, Marco had cheated. But as Massimo dropped to his knees and thrust up, Marco flew backward, landing with a grunt on the hard earth behind.

His opponent had already regained his feet by the time Massimo turned, but he'd lost his composure.

"What bothers you more about me, Massimo? That a vampire born a huey peasant will soon command your precious Venice, or that as Patria's consort I get to fuck a Medici bitch whenever I wish?"

Fight with determination, not deliriousness. "No one *fucks* my sister," Massimo said. "If she allows you into her bed, that's her showing pity."

"Yeah? I wonder if your bitch human will have pity on me after I rip your head off?"

It was the animal that raged, not the man. Massimo's hand wrapped around the hem of Marco's pants, using the leverage to jerk him forward, bringing him face to face. "You'll die n—"

His vision went to black as Marco's forehead smashed into his.

Sky became ground and earth, the heavens. Massimo lost his grip as his hands went to his head. Beneath his fingertips, he pushed at his spiderwebbed skull. Luckily, not a fatal injury. It would mean he'd be working without his eyes for a few minutes, however.

His ears became his lifelines as he listened for the light shuffle of loose pebbles over compacted grit. Only silence met his search. Then, wind brushed his cheek. The air swirled moments before Marco landed atop him, sending a piledriver of a hit down over Massimo's collarbone.

"Time to abdicate, *Your Serenity.*"

The pain... so much pain. His collarbone broke, possibly into his heart. Good, he deserved it. The humans' only mistake about karma was that you needed to die to experience it. Suddenly, his attacker's weight lifted as Marco moved with immortal speed, making his way toward the center pike. Given Massimo's shattered cranium, it would be the more likely target once Marco had the weapon.

He had to get up. If he couldn't manage his feet, not even Patria would call the killing unfair. Massimo tried to roll to his right; his shoulder collapsed beneath him. In his periphery, broken bone peeked through bloodied flesh. His vision began to return, but what use was it to him now? Overhead, the shadows took the form of a man.

Marco prepared his strike. At least it would be quick, and the sunlight creeping into the courtyard would dispose of his body soon.

Portia screamed from above. "Massimo, roll left!"

The Doge didn't hesitate. He obeyed his heart's master. Still, not even love could force him to move fast enough. The spear missed his vital organs, grazing a path down his back and piercing the ground. Curses ancient and vulgar sprayed from lips dripping blood, but he managed his feet through sheer force of determination. Hunching over in pain put him into prime position. Marco's foot connected with his jaw, sending him spinning.

"Lay down now, old man, and I'll make it quick."

The Doge's fuzzy brain and battered body shouted at each other, but one thing became clear above all the chaos: he'd underestimated his opponent. Little good that did him now. Hindsight was not a strategy.

Only then came the sound of hurried footsteps and a scented breeze dusted with lilac.

And iron.

Massimo's head shot up just in time for his vision to clear. White as a sheet and trembling like a vine, Portia stood at the edge of the courtyard, her shirt sleeve rolled up to the elbow, a red rivulet running down from a fresh slice across her forearm.

Above, the crowd split, some cheering the move, others calling on Patria to intervene.

The Duchess shouted something about "state nothing about the act itself," but Massimo didn't listen. He couldn't. The animal within shoved away temporal concerns like self-preservation and pain. The blood, however, courted Marco's control as well. Two vampires eyed her succulent vein feeding the earth and wanted to taste the offering.

Damn you, Portia. Don't you know what you've done?

Only then, Massimo realized *exactly* what she'd done. She'd given him a chance.

Supernatural speed paired with a reservoir of emotion dammed for centuries. He would *not* let a vampire kill the woman he loved. Not again. Not ever.

The spear filled his hand and gave up its anchor without a fight. The Doge's aim was true, sending the weapon sailing before he'd even realized what he'd done. Forward, forward, forward… final.

Marco turned, the bloody, wooden tip sticking from his chest. Confusion marred his features, and he looked to Massimo with a questioning gaze. The man who'd murdered Giuliano buckled, falling first to his knees and then, forward onto his hands, until, with a shuttering breath, his entire body surrendered to the earth.

Silence. Utter silence. The crowd above. The woman below. Even Massimo's heart refused to beat.

"Portia—"

The words cut off as pain seized his frame, making him a slave of his body. Massimo's knees hit the dirt. Moments before he fell, she was there, holding him up.

Portia's eyes shot to the sky. "Massimo, the sunlight is almost here. Move."

He raised a weary, shaking hand to brush over her cheek. "You saved me."

A momentary smile flitted across her face before anxiety reclaimed her features. "Not if you don't get going, I haven't."

God, this woman... He'd have let himself die in that moment content that he'd done what he'd set out to do, if someone in the gallery above didn't suddenly shout "*Lui vive!*"

He lives.

The Doge's eyes went wide as Marco stood erect, the tip of the spear sticking out from his chest. One step, then another, even as the rays of the sun raced to catch them both. Massimo tried to move, tried to pull Portia into his arms and run. His body, however, refused. Too broken. Too abused. His victory, shattered. He must have just missed Marco's heart. If the vampire reached his beloved, it would just take a twist of her neck to kill her.

"Portia, run!" His words split the air, but she didn't heed them.

Instead, to his amazement, Portia turned, saw Marco, and jutted her hand up as if to tell him to stop.

And somehow, Marco did. Just as the sunlight emanating from her palm bit at his ankles.

Some vampires took hours to burn. Some, minutes. The mathematics of it involved calculations of age, distance from the equator, and time passed since last taking a vein. The dark blue ooze dripping down the tip of the shaft told Massimo Marco hadn't fed recently.

He turned to ash before Massimo could blink.

Portia's looked at her hand for the briefest second before it dropped to her side. She spun, hooking Massimo under the arms and dragging him as fast as her huey body could manage, the sunlight biting at her heels.

"Portia, I love—"

"Shut up!"

Her heavy breaths were hot against his cheek, and the air filled with the scent of her own blood still seeping from her self-inflicted wound. It smelled... heavenly, like Ambrosia, like something he'd known once upon a time, many centuries ago.

"Just... shut up," she said again, though he hadn't said anything else. "Just survive!"

EIGHTEEN

In the master suite of Patria's Fiesole estate, Portia begged for a taxonomy lesson.

"I don't understand, I thought vampires were immortal."

The Duchess's face curdled. "Did you not come here because a vampire was murdered before your eyes by my consort? Did you not see that very same consort dissolve into ash before your very eyes not an hour ago when sunlight hit his body?"

"Sunlight?" Portia's eyes went to her hands. She had to be mistaken. It must have been a figment of her imagination. Something impossible.

She closed her eyes, trying to relive the last moments in the courtyard. Portia had gotten Massimo into the portico as quickly as she could, where Patria's guards took over. It was all so rushed from there that Portia still wasn't sure she followed. Two men dragged Massimo through a passageway as she struggled to keep up with them. A car stood in the street, but an awning had been lowered to block the light. Massimo was placed in the backseat; Patria sat in the front. Portia leaped in without invitation, trying to cover Massimo with her body as the day took hold. No need, Patria said. The glass of the car, it seemed, had been treated in such a way as to protect vampires from combustion.

Then, somehow, they all ended up here.

"Right. Marco must have been too distracted to see the danger." Portia's voice tapered off as she waited to see if Patria was going to challenge her. When she didn't, the huey continued. "Okay, but what now? Massimo isn't dead, but he's not healing. Why isn't he getting better?"

Standing at the foot of the bed, Patria crossed her arms and stared at her brother. "Because he needs to feed. Normally not a problem, but I have no feeders here. Even if I did, I would dismiss them. I can't assure your safety. Even now, my court is in chaos and every moment I stay away, it worsens. I need to return immediately and learn who's loyal to me, and who will stand ready to accuse me of being in league with Massimo to murder my own husband. If I have any hope of coming out of this with my throne intact, I'll need to start a public display of mourning. Besides, Marco was true to his people. He deserves a widow's honor."

Patria sucked in her bottom lip as her glistening eyes dashed away. Massimo had been so certain his sister cared nothing for Marco, but Portia knew from experience that even a desired separation wasn't free of all regret.

She placed her hand over the Duchess's cold knuckles. "I'm sorry for your loss."

The vampire's gaze swung back, a tempered smile on her face. "I didn't love him. I hated most everything about him. But Marco was never cruel to *me*. He tried to love me, I just could never..."

In a blink, Patria seemed to recall the time and place. She bit her tongue and cleared her throat, resuming without the slightest bit of emotion in her voice.

How very Medici of her, Portia thought.

"I have done everything I can to help, Portia. Got you out, took you to a safe place, but now, I have my own affairs to attend to. You'll need to find someone to feed to Massimo yourself. Shouldn't be too hard. You're not exactly bad-looking. I'm sure you can lure some dizzy slob of a tourist here."

Portia turned toward the bed, squaring herself, realizing that the simplest solution was probably the best. "He can drink from me."

Patria's hand gripped Portia's shoulder, spinning the huey around. "Are you insane? He's so delirious and lacking blood that he could kill you before he even realized who you were."

"So, what, I should just trick some innocent tourist into that risk instead?" Was she serious? "Look, I might not be a Medici or a Bruneli, but I get that there's a ticking clock situation here. I don't know the intricacies of court politics, but I *am* Canadian and I understand hockey."

The Duchess blinked thrice. "I'm sorry, what?"

Portia continued. "If your court is really divided, then Massimo and I can't stay here. You've put us in the penalty box, but the second the sun is down and the ice is beneath their feet, they're going to slam us into the boards and hard."

Patria held her tongue, though that might have been because she didn't understand the metaphor. Did Italians even have hockey? What was life without a good hat trick and *Hockey Night in Canada*?

"I have to get us out of Florence and him to Venice and safety before the sun goes down. If what you say is true and he could attack me and kill me without realizing it as soon as he's conscious, I'd much rather have that happen while you're here instead of when I'm behind the wheel of your fancy sun-proofed car. Oh, by the way, I'll be taking that car of yours. Pretty sure if Massimo's had that special glass that keeps the sun from burning you, he wouldn't have made us wait until dark to drive here."

"Of course, his car doesn't have it. *Ha il braccino corto*. My brother is many good things, but he is cheap as hell. He leaves Venice so rarely and drives even less, so of course why would he spend a single euro on something for his own comfort? And now you want to deny me mine? Ah, I should've known that when Massimo finally found a woman, she would be as pig-headed as he is." Her head lifted, and with it, her hands in surrender. "Fine. I'll take the passage beneath the city and pray you won't be here when the sun sets. I wish you luck, Portia Bruneli."

"Kepler."

Patria paused at the door, her hand on the knob. "What?"

"My name. It's Portia *Kepler*... Or, well, it was when I was married, but I did file an order asking to have it changed back to my maiden name."

"I don't care what your huey name is. After that stunt you pulled tonight, you are Portia Bruneli, Vampire Dogaressa of Venice, even if you're not actually a vampire. Wear the title with pride. You are the first in four hundred years to carry it." Patria made another attempt at leaving but paused just outside the door. "Besides, Kepler is such an ugly name."

"You didn't take Marco's name, sounds like." Portia pulled a lock of hair behind her ear. "Besides, what makes one name better than another?"

"You're asking a Medici?" Patria leaned forward, reaching for the doorknob. "If he does lose control while feeding from you, don't do to him what I think you did to Marco. I can make peace with my consort dying, but I will destroy anyone who hurts my family."

The door closed before Portia could ask exactly what Patria meant by that.

Vampires were such enigmas, but frankly, humans weren't much better. Portia had just seen a man—a murderer, yes, but still a man—die before her and she was... peaceful with that fact. More than that, looking at Massimo, knowing the alternative would have been his death, she was damned near relieved. She couldn't imagine what would have happened if he hadn't come out of the challenge alive, but she knew it would have left her world forever altered.

This made no sense. Her initial infatuation had been born of Massimo's dashing good looks, but she'd obviously grown beyond that. Her heart throbbed looking at his broken and scarred physique. Sunlight had hit as high as his knees, blistering and blackening his legs. She could still smell the stench of burning human flesh in the air. One of Patria's guards did his best to put Humpty Dumpty back together again, literally shoving Massimo's right humerus back into the meaty flesh from which it had erupted. The torn flesh and ripped muscles wept navy-colored blood onto a bandage wrapped to hold his arm in place, refusing to knit together. The limb sat at an unnatural angle.

"I don't know if you can hear me, Massimo, but I really need you to wake up." Portia settled on the edge of the bed, her hands folded over her lap. "We can't stay here, and I can't carry you. Please."

Tentatively, she reached for him, but her hand lingered over his head. Was it safe to touch him?

"Massimo?" She pulled up the hair covering his face, his locks just long enough to achieve the effort. To her surprise, his sapphire eyes were open and focused on her. Was he awake, or did vampires sleep with their eyes open? They were kind of dead, weren't they? And dead people tended to have their eyes open. And...

She should have asked these things when there had been a better time.

Only, then, she noticed his lips move.

"What?" Portia scooted closer, craning her neck to get a better angle.

His voice was hardly more than a whisper. "Marco?"

"Oh, Marco. Yeah, he turned to dust."

"*Bene*." His blinked, wet his cracked lips with a flick of his tongue, then grinned. "You saved me."

"What did you think I was going to do? Just let the sun get you? Let some wacko vampire take you down?"

"I'm not talking about that."

Portia crossed his arms. "Then what *are* you talking about?"

"I'm talking about..."

Massimo's voice cut off, replaced by a groan as his good arm slid up his side and the vampire attempted to roll himself over. Portia swooped in without thinking, moving his limp arm for him, pulling on his shoulder to aid in his leverage. When he settled back into the pillows, it was to find his face only inches from hers.

His working hand lifted, rough fingertips bitten by gravel stroking down her cheek. "You should go. It's so hard to have you this close and not—" His hands lowered, encircling her throat, giving it just enough of a squeeze to send a shot of panic (and something more enticing) through her. "—take you."

Courage and faith are the companions on the way to love. Portia hadn't thought about her grandmother's sage words in years, whispered to her on the day she'd married Richard, no less. Only now, in memory, had she recalled the sadness mixed with hope in her nana's eyes when she'd said them. Sadness, because her whole family thought Richard didn't appreciate her. Hope, because they held faith she'd become aware of that, too. It took years of denial, even more of resolve to come to the place where she truly felt ready to embrace the truth.

"But you need blood." Portia brought her hand up between them, brushing his aside, then turned her wrist out toward him. "Please, let me feed you."

Twin dagger teeth sprang into being as Massimo's mouth stretched wide, but it wasn't only her blood he wanted. His eyes quickly reached beyond her pulsing vein, his gaze going to her mouth. Portia's own lips parted as she sucked in a breath. Oh, the bite would hurt; she had no doubt. But something within her still longed for it, longed for that connection.

"If I take too much... Portia, I could kill you."

"You'd rather wait until sunset and risk killing some innocent person?" she asked. "You didn't hesitate to step into that courtyard even though there was a chance you wouldn't survive. You did it for many reasons, but I was one of them. I owe you my life, and this is *my* courtyard. Take my vein."

He licked his lips. "Very well."

Portia closed her eyes, waiting for the strike. The courage came in not pulling back; there was no shame in feeling anxious about the pain. Only, no pain came. The mattress shifted, and when she opened her eyes again, it was to find Massimo forcing his body to obey. He managed a seated position with agony made plain, muscles in his face tensing and his breaths heaving. She joined in on that when the sight of his bare chest and its fine definition played havoc with her hormones.

His good hand reached out to her. "At least let me enthrall you so you won't feel the pain."

Portia's eyes narrowed. "As weak as you are, won't that cost you more of your energy, make you even more likely to hurt me?"

"Yes, but—"

"We're not discussing it, then." She moved like a cat, sleek and quick and noiseless. Portia pulled herself up, settled herself atop his lap, her legs hanging off to the side, and pushed her wrist to his mouth. "Take. My. Vein."

His mouth came down rough, but not over her wrist. Injured though he was, Massimo was still stronger. He hooked his good arm around her back, pulled her hard into his chest, and sank his fangs into the meaty flesh just below her neck.

It was a pain beyond screams, a sudden invasion of her nervous system that made her instinctively try to run. Massimo, however, dominated. He held her in place like a child holding a teddy bear. Her blood blazed, searing heat shooting from the puncture point out through her limbs, scorching her cells. Her body called on her to make use of it, to draw that heat into a collective and light it. It was insanity. It was a solution.

Portia lectured her instincts, became master of her impulses. Massimo needed this. *She* needed him. She swallowed her torment, gulping down air and spit, and... And something shifted. His heart beat, and it did so in perfect unison with hers.

Portia lifted her hands and laid them flat over Massimo's shoulder blades, finding a smooth plane of flesh, free of the cuts and scrapes he'd gotten in the courtyard. Dusty perhaps, but whole all the same. The anguish eased to ache, and the ache, to something very *not* painful. Her body relaxed, sensing the worst of it was over.

His fangs retracted, but his mouth sucked at her wound with gentle draws. The pain disappeared, and in the vacuum, a different kind of heat flooded her senses. Portia looked down at Massimo, his eyes wide in wonder as he pulled back, a drop of her blood at the corner of his mouth.

"*Ti scorre luce del sole.*"

"Sunlight flows through me?" Portia's forehead furrowed. She ran one hand down the side of her neck, feeling for a wound that seemed not to be there. How had it healed so quickly? "Is that some Venetian idiom I'm not familiar with?"

A moment of confusion, then laughter as Massimo wrapped his arms around her and leaned his head into her chest. His hands framed her face. "No, *speme mia*, it's quite literal. It's weak... perhaps a grandparent or great-grandparent, but I can taste it in your veins. You're descended from slayers. Your blood heals me just as your eyes soothe me and your heart woos me. And I... *cara mia, ti amo.*"

Every nerve in her body iced over, so much so that Massimo's brow furrowed with worry.

"Portia? Maybe you didn't understand. I said that—"

"You said you love me. And that I'm part-slayer." She sucked on her tongue before spasming into a smile. "My Italian isn't *that* bad. I just... It's impossible."

"Which one?"

"Both, of course!"

Fresh off the scarred battleground of her divorce and having crawled from the smoking ruins of her marriage, to dive into another castle, praying it wouldn't burn so soon, was lunacy. But this castle was made of sturdier stuff than any she'd ever seen. She barely knew Massimo, and yet, she felt like she'd known him her whole life.

Massimo dropped one hand to the mattress, giving him leverage to push himself closer to her. "I'm not asking anything in return." His free hand smoothed down her face, pinched her chin, and angled her mouth in line with his. "I'm just offering you everything I am and everything I have. Take what you need and ignore the rest. I will never—"

She swallowed his words and claimed his lips.

Portia's breath fled as her breasts crushed against his hard chest and Massimo's hand slid down, shifting her from a side mount to a full straddle. Even the skirt of her dress and the thin blanket between them couldn't conceal his condition. The man was hard, ready, thick. Her arms curled around his neck, using the hold as leverage as she rolled her hips—teasing him? Teasing herself? It didn't matter. They were in this together.

"Portia." Massimo's hand settled on her hips, his strong grip kneading the flesh like dough. He groaned as she slid over his length again, another wave lapping the shore. "*Bella,* please, let me..."

One more undulation and something in his eyes went feral. Without warning, Massimo thrust up his hips. She would have bucked off the bed if he didn't have a good grip on her. The vampire's strong hands and stronger will, however, repositioned her with ease. Suddenly, Portia found herself staring at the ceiling as his hands gripped the v of her bodice, pulling the sundress left and right, sending buttons flying. Massimo sat back on the balls of his feet to take in the view: Portia laid out before him, only her bra and panties barriers between his eyes and her truth.

"You are... such a beautiful woman."

The blankets that had been covering him fell away as he tipped forward on to the palms of his hands, crawling up the bed, toward her. She couldn't help but look down, catching a flash of all his features, even if at an odd angle. Massimo was flawless, a tapestry of sinew and hard lines and male perfection. He was a Michelangelo statue, a Grecian relief. An actual vampire prince. And she was...

Laying there in underwear she'd bought at Walmart on the clearance rack. A middle-aged divorcee from Victoria, B.C., soft in places that should be firm, dappled cellulite on her belly and thighs, and with breasts departing for all stations south. Suddenly, she felt very underqualified to be the lover of a man who literally looked like he'd been carved from granite (and whose cock felt like it might actually be).

Portia covered her chest with her arms. "Massimo, I haven't done this with someone new in a really long time. Well, not with *anyone,* really."

His eyebrows angled. "How long?"

Well, apparently, they'd leaped from friends to no-question-too-personal-to-ask in the past ten minutes. "Three, four years, maybe."

His eyebrows arched. "But you've only been separated from your husband for a year."

He didn't mean to blow on the embers of pain, but it still hurt. "Yeah, well... After I hit thirty-five and gravity started doing things, Richard wouldn't... What I mean is, with *me* he didn't want to..."

He stuck out his chin. "Your ex is an asswipe."

Portia blinked her confusion as she propped herself up on her elbows. "Sorry?"

"I used that term correctly, didn't I? A man who only values his own pleasure and sees his woman as an object to be used and discarded. Asswipe? Though I've picked up other terms from the young people visiting San Marco's. A dickhead? A fucker? A c—"

"Oh, my God, stop." She planted a hand on his chest. "You had it right. Asswipe. And a dick. But the point is that you're so..." Her hand quickly gestured down to nether regions sadly hidden from view due to the angle of his hover. "And this?" This time she indicated her own body. "This is as good as this gets and it only goes down from here. I just want to make sure you understand that a mortal body decays."

His reaction wasn't the one she expected. Massimo grabbed both her cheeks between his hands and planted a kiss on her lips.

"You seem really happy about the fact that I'm turning into an old lady," she said when he pulled back.

"I'm happy because you're warning me about the future, and that means you see us being together long enough for that to matter."

Wait, had she? But she didn't... Portia shook her head. "I'm not saying anything about the long term. I just... Look, when you buy a house, they tell you if you're sitting near a flood zone or a fault line. It doesn't mean you're going to live there forever."

Her words cut off when Massimo's finger pressed to her lips. The look in his eye... The sincerity. The utter commitment.

"Portia, I love *you*. The body is only a vehicle that carries me to your soul when we are joined. Unless..." He pulled back slightly, pushing himself off the mattress to gage her. "Perhaps you find me unappealing?"

And maybe chickens did crosswords.

"Oh, no. Not at all. I—" Her eyes traced down his chest, to where her view cut off, right where the shoreline of his hard stomach disappeared and the plane of flesh met her own. "Wow, just wow."

Forget the age-old vampire and any talk about souls—Massimo clearly delighted in her approval. He eased himself down, his forearms anchoring on the mattress on either side of her head. "I am not this body. *This* is a monster's body. It lives on blood and hunger. But my soul drives it to places it can find grace. This is what you are for me. You are my grace. And if you will have me, I will give you tenfold in return everything you give. *Bella mia*, let me make love to you and wash away the pain that... *asswipe...* made you feel. Let me fill you with my gratitude and allow you to overcome this mortal coil."

What else could she say to that?

Portia's hand went up to his cheek, followed by her mouth. The kiss was slow, languid, peaceful. She delighted in its simplicity. The next kiss, however, *wasn't* simple. A movement of lips over lips that felt more like an encounter of souls. A taste of iron on his tongue and the smell of copper in his breath. Massimo put a hand behind her neck, supporting her, as he pulled her mouth hard to his. Below, his body began to stir, and hers answered in kind, each kiss adding to a flame growing into a fire.

Massimo gave Portia a chance to breathe as his mouth went to her neck. Portia thought for a moment he was going to bite her again, that even though he'd healed, he still needed more blood. Her body instinctively tensed. He must have sensed it, because a moment later, she felt his lips grin.

"No more biting today. At least, not the kind that hurts."

"Not the kind that hurts?" Portia's head jerked up just in time to see Massimo pulling down the cup of her bra. "What other kind is—Oh? Oh. *Oohhhhh!*"

The man was a maestro. His tongue darted out, tracing a lazy circle around her left breast, making the pink peak salute before his teeth nipped, a balance of pressure and pleasure. Portia threw her head back, her moan catching in her throat, just as his left hand went to working on the right. He looked up from his work long enough for their eyes to meet and for Portia to signal her approval through a heavy-lidded gaze. After a few moments, she gasped as she felt a pinch sharped into a puncture.

Massimo pulled back, a drop of fresh blood on his lip, blood which he licked languidly.

Portia asked with heavy breaths, "I thought you said no more hurtful biting?"

He leaned over, sampling the pebbling bead on the top of her breast like a cat at a saucer of milk.

Meow.

"It didn't hurt, now, *bella*, did it?"

No, it hadn't. In fact, she found it deliriously erotic. Who'd have thought, sweet little Portia, a masochist? "Not really."

As Massimo visited the well once more and his mouth drew away, Portia watched in amazement as the moistened skin healed over. She would have asked how, but she was suddenly distracted by Massimo's attention heading south. He worked his way down her with his mouth before sitting up on his heels to examine her cotton briefs with some trepidation.

The anxiety crept back in, and Portia hitched up on her elbow, her other arm strapping across her breasts. "Massimo?"

He looked up at her like a kid caught staring. "*These* are what you wear?"

Self-conscious to the point of an ache forming in her stomach. "Um, yeah. I … I don't have much money, so I—"

"You do now. What's mine is yours." He shook his head slowly, clicking his tongue and returning his eyes to the subject of his consternation. "When we get back to Venice, I'm going to buy you a whole lingerie shop. Until then, however…"

His hand grasped the hem of her underwear with vicious speed. Cloth surrendered to the pull, the garment ripping down the center, exposing her sex. Part of her wanted to yell at him. They may be cheap and mass-produced, but they were still hers. The other part of her, however, purred in delight.

"Better." Massimo leaned forward, hovering over her. "Do you know that I've wanted you since the moment I first saw you on the palazzo? But to have you *and* love you, it's more than I can—"

"Too much talk."

She couldn't say what came over her, or how she managed to pull off the maneuver, but somehow, Portia pushed Massimo over, reversing their positions. Throwing one leg over his hips and weaving her fingers in his, his hands next to his head on the mattress, she used the hold to lower herself on to him in one tantalizing move.

Portia's eyes fluttered closed, trying to process so much sensation all at once. The feel of him inside her, the warmth and grip of his hands as he clasped hers, the duality of instincts warring within: one voice yelling at her to dominate, another warning her of imminent danger.

She let her hips command all.

Push, pull. Forward, backward. She lingered in the adagio, savoring his movement. Massimo stared up at her in amazement, letting her lead unchallenged except to lean up, begging her kiss. She gave it gladly until her own body started making demands. *Harder. Deeper. Faster.*

"*Ah, dio!*" Portia's head fell back, changing the angle of attack ever so slightly. He held her hands as she used the tension to gain traction. "*Mozzafiato!*"

"You speaking Italian," Massimo gasped. "I need more of this. I need more of *you*."

He reversed their position without asking, his renewed sinewy body rising over hers. Portia gave him a wicked grin when she found herself on her back again. So this is how it was going to be between them?

Instead of fight back, however, she did something which took more courage. She let him take control. Not just physically, though that seemed a small sacrifice given the way Massimo moved. Portia let go of her care, all her concerns. She let herself deserve to be worshipped, then let Massimo worship her. His body commanded her, sequestered her, played her. Hours might have passed. Day and night may have risen and fallen and taken emperors along on the ride. When she reached her zenith, Portia closed her eyes and saw stars. When he followed, she'd never heard a man cry out her name with such conviction. By the time he collapsed on the bed next to her, his breath racing, her body limp and awash in waves of release, and his hand laced through hers, the sun was in the sky.

And she couldn't say how she understood that, but somehow, she did. Either the world had just changed, or she had.

And in the same way, Portia Kepler knew she was in deep, deep trouble.

NINETEEN

Massimo hadn't been this happy—or this angry—in centuries.

He was in love. He *loved* Portia. And he was going to lose her. Not today, not tomorrow, but someday. When he'd felt himself tipping over the edge, any thought of taking her to a paterfamilias of some bloodline and having her made vampire disgusted him. So they could have what? Eighty, ninety years before he met the sun, leaving Portia to live on in her loneliness for four more centuries? Now he'd trade his crown, his fortune, and his good name for every moment he could win. And it didn't matter. She was slayer enough that it wasn't even a choice.

Truth be told, the stray thought that she might be something other than huey had darted through his head during the last few weeks. First, there was that instant attraction he'd felt when he'd first seen her at the piazza, the instinct to track and conquer. Lust might explain a passing impulse, but the third night in a row he'd strolled through San Marco's, Massimo had recognized his hunting for what it was. Even then, through the centuries, there had been the odd woman—generally, a redhead—who caught his fancy. Normally he'd move in as soon as he acknowledged interest, but there was something about Portia that made him keep his distance. *Instinct that was just as dangerous for me as I was for her,* he now realized.

Questions cropped up again when at his home, she'd moved faster than a huey should, when her strength, given her genteel, soft frame, took him by surprise. When enthralled, Portia had retained a rare ability to think beyond the frame of their interactions. Still, Massimo let doubt be the master of possibility. How could he or Patria enthrall her at all if she were slayer?

Doubt died the moment her blood touched his tongue. The

sun in her veins was weak, suggesting her closest link was at least two generations back. It didn't matter; it took away a choice they may have had. A pure slayer, like any variety of supe, wasn't susceptible to vampirification. A huey with weak slayer traits might be, but given that Portia could create a contact solarium, it was unlikely the attempt would take.

But that brought another question to mind. Even given her heritage, how could she conjure sunlight at all? Like hoods, the supernatural balance to werewolves, slayers needed to go through an awakening ceremony for their gifts to come to fruition. Clearly, Portia had no knowledge of her abilities, and wouldn't she remember standing in a pool of water, being hit by the magic of one of her own kind? She would have felt like a witch being burned at the stake.

Portia turned over, curling into his chest, tearing the vampire from his contemplations. "So, daytime doesn't automatically turn you into a corpse or something?"

Massimo grinned, twirling a piece of her auburn hair around one of his fingers. "And you're diurnal, but you can force yourself to stay up all night if you try, can't you? I will admit, though, it's been decades since I've been this tired."

"Really, decades?" Her index finger poked him across the pecs. "And here you were thinking three years for me was a Greek tragedy."

"It was. Someone with your beautiful spirit should never go home to an empty bed."

And if he had his way, she wouldn't from that point forward. Of course, that would be up to Portia. Just because he loved her didn't mean she felt the same. Hueys were paradoxes: more sensitive to life-changing decisions while having far less time to make them. Portia, spurned by a bastard Massimo pictured tormenting with ease, had drunk in caution like wine. It was obvious to him that she wasn't the type of woman to give little parts of her heart. She would have put the entirety of her soul in Richard's hands when they were together, and that ass squeezed until Portia's heart broke.

Massimo wanted to make her whole, but Portia would have to trust him with the damaged pieces for that to happen. That took time, patience, and most of all, communication. But for now, he just wanted to lay here, holding the woman he loved, basking in the afterglow of their union.

It was at this precise moment that Portia rolled away and scooted to the edge of the mattress. "Come on, we have to go."

He forced himself past his weariness just as she stood, framing himself behind her, pulling her body flush back against his.

Massimo trailed kisses down her neck, her breasts pebbling under his touch. "When we have such a beautiful estate to ourselves?"

"You have to… *Ungh*." A slight bend in Portia's knees let her fall back, and his cock responded to even the smallest lick of her skin, waking to opportunity. "Massimo, no. We *have* to go."

"There's a grotto beneath the house." His right hand trailed down the curve of her stomach until his middle finger settled on the pearl of her sex. Still wet from their previous encounter or readying for their next? Did it matter? "Artificial, of course, but it can be an exciting place to—"

"*MASSIMO*." Portia broke free, spinning out of his hold, but quickly leaning against the wall, panting. "You killed Marco. When the sun sets, his followers could head out, looking for your blood."

He quirked an eyebrow. "Of course, they would. They're vampires."

Portia huffed her frustration. "I meant that figuratively. Well, maybe literally. I don't know much about how vampires fight. And while I have no doubt that the *grotto* would be awesome, can you please let me finish saving your life before you put it in danger again?"

Only if you let me save yours… He swallowed his thoughts and nodded.

"Good. I told Patria that we're taking her car, since that one is safe for you to travel by during the day." She looked around for her clothes, sorting through pillows and blankets that had fallen off the bed during their rendezvous. "And by the way, how does that work?"

The vampire headed for the bathroom, all while wondering if he could canoodle Portia into joining him in the shower. *Another time.* Many times, if he got his way. "There's a company based in Chicago that manufacturers a special kind of glass. It blocks out the wavelengths that harm us. Expensive as rubies, though, so I only have it in the windows of a few key rooms in my palace. Please, don't tell anyone about it. I employ some of Venice's most renowned traditional glassmakers, and I would like not to insult them with the knowledge that I bought glass from, of all places, America." Massimo reached into the marble-paneled shower to test the water, amused that the pattern painted on some inset tiles was that of the... "Sun."

"Did you say something?" She came in wearing something hideous and black that looked more like a shroud than a dress. Probably something from the 80s Patria had stuck at the back of the closet and Portia in desperation had discovered. "What's taking so long? Get in, get out, get on with it. We need to get as far from Florence as we can before nightfall."

"*Tesoro*, I am Italian. Driving a car at high speeds is second nature."

"Yeah, but if you're really as tired as you say you are, *you* probably shouldn't be driving."

Massimo took a fluffy towel from a basket on the floor and threw it over a hook next to the shower. "I was just thinking, how did Marco die so quickly?"

Portia's hands dropped to her side. "Um... The sun came up. You were right there. You saw it."

"Yes, I was right there, but *I* don't have burns. Broken bones, cuts, a concussion, but no burns. How is it that the sun got to him, strong enough to turn him to dust in a few seconds, and I didn't even get a tan just a meter away?"

"Don't you remember? I dragged you away."

"No, I remember. I just..."

Was it really such a leap to make? He knew for certain now that his beloved was part-slayer. Would it be so ridiculous if she, like the full-blooded of that kind, had the ability to conjure the sun? To destroy a vampire outright? A talent he was glad she had, if she was going to live in his world, but one that could equally bring him to harm. Especially if she wasn't aware she could perform such a feat, or if she hadn't any control over it.

Only, if that were true, that would mean that Portia had killed Marco. And if Marco's followers somehow came to the same conclusion...

He had to get her back to Venice and keep her there. Only then could he assure her safety.

"Massimo!" Portia clapped twice right in his face, bringing him out of his reverie. "Maybe you are as tired as you say."

Massimo blinked, coming back to the moment. Every relationship had challenges. Theirs would be no different.

"Right, well..." He dropped the towel and stepped into the shower. "I'll be quick. Unless you want to join me, then I'll try to be slow and steady."

It had been many years since he'd had a lover. Luckily, they still reacted the same when sex became a priority over safety. Portia rolled her eyes, shook her head, and left the bathroom.

Portia rubbed the flesh just above her collarbone.

"Does it hurt still?"

She ripped her hand away like a child being caught touching some precious object. "What? No, don't be silly. I'm fine."

"Portia, you and I are going to have some challenges as we try to figure out this thing between us. Lying will only complicate that, even if it's only to protect each other's feelings."

An attempt at confession blew away. Portia grimaced. "Yes, it still hurts. But not much," she was quick to clarify. "More like a dull ache, like when you stretch a muscle. I... don't suppose you know what that's like though."

"Of course, I do. I was huey once. "Massimo's eyes fluttered closed as he shifted in the front seat. "I'm sorry for your discomfort, but I am thankful for what you did. Your blood allowed me to heal very quickly."

"Yeah, well, I'm thankful for what you did, too."

A broad, dreamy grin stretched across his face. "I can happily do that again tonight. Or tomorrow. Or every night."

"I don't mean the sex."

But he didn't miss the way her pulse ticked up. No, she wouldn't be opposed to further exploration of *that* side of their blossoming relationship.

"I mean being so restrained, taking so little blood," Portia continued. "The way you looked at me when I suggested it, I thought I was going to look like some mummified corpse or dried out flower afterward. You didn't really take all that much, and I didn't even feel dizzy afterward. I usually do when I donate."

Massimo's eyes snapped open. "Portia, you must never donate your blood again. Not ever."

She looked surprised when she passed him a glance. "Is that some kind of alpha vampire thing? I don't know if that's how you guys do things, but in the huey world, blood donations are desperately needed. I'm a universal donor, so..."

"I am an elected prince, not a tyrant," Massimo insisted, sitting up. "It has nothing to do with me exercising the bounds of my dominion. It's because there are hueys—few, but still—who would recognize elements of your blood as having some slayer quality to it. Don't you remember me telling you that the slayers were extinct?"

"Yeah, but that's obviously not true, because here I am."

Massimo shook his head. "You only have ancestry. Yes, you're a little stronger and faster than if you didn't, but the fact that Patria and I could enthrall you means the slayer genetics aren't—"

"Wait a minute." Portia lifted a hand from the steering wheel, her index finger sticking up. "When did *you* enthrall me? Oh, wait. You mean when you first told me you were a vampire and got me to admit I'd been having sex dreams about you?"

"Yes, then." Guilt punched him in the gut. It had been decades since his tongue had slipped so phenomenally, but didn't he just tell her they had to be honest with each other? "And the other time, too."

The temperature in the car lowered by ten degrees. "What *other* time?"

"There was no malice involved."

"That's an answer to a question I didn't ask. Let me try again, slower to make sure the language boundary isn't an issue. When. Did. You. Enthrall me?"

Massimo got ready to eat crow, a dish he'd never grown a taste for. "Do you remember the night you don't remember?"

"What kind of ridiculous question is that? How could I remember a night I don't—" Portia gaped, letting out an accusatory gasp. "You mean the night before you showed up at my—Wait, why am I even asking you? Of course, it was that night. How could you not tell me, Massimo? How could you lie to me like that?"

"Nothing happened." Was this what shame felt like? Now he remembered why he tried not to feel it. "It's no big deal. I enthrall hueys all the time."

"So, you're saying, what, that I'm no one special? That I'm just your latest conquest? Is this a game you play with a new huey every month? Enthrall her, find out some dirt to get into her underwear, tell her she's somehow partially supernatural to make her think that there's some kind of destiny going on and that's it's okay if she's falling in love even though her heart is still broken from the last guy she trusted?"

"What? No. I enthrall hueys before I drink them to keep

them from feeling pain. Remember, vampire? And I—" His words stopped on a dime once he'd digested everything she'd said. "Did you just say you are falling for me?"

"Did I? No. I didn't mean that, and I—*Ooof.*"

Before Massimo knew what was happening, Portia had moved the car to the edge of the road and slammed the brakes, making everything squeal. He bolted up, surveying the street behind them, making sure another car wasn't going to smack into them... which gave just enough time for Portia to open her door.

Massimo lunged, trying to catch her, but the angle of light pouring in worked against him. His hand drifted into the midday sun, sending pain shooting up his arm.

"*Porca puttana!*"

He smoked into the backseat, where he could roll down the window while still avoiding a direct hit. "Portia, please! I'm sorry, but don't go. It's dangerous for you now if another vampire finds out you have sun-laced blood."

"I was in Venice for a whole six weeks before you decided to tap this." She surprised him by making a rude gesture. "If no vampire discovered me then, what makes you think they'll come after me now?"

"You sat next to the Duchess of Tuscany as the fiancée of the Doge of Venice while he killed the Doge of Genoa. There won't be a vampire for a thousand kilometers who doesn't know your name by tonight. And if they know you're missing, they'll come in droves to find you. I am not without enemies."

Portia spun, eating up the road she'd already gained. "Well, that's just great, isn't it? So, now what? I have to watch my back everywhere I go?"

"Of course not. Once we're back in Venice, you'll be safe."

"But I'm not planning to stay in Venice, am I? Or did you think a good fuck was enough to make me give up my life for you? Or maybe you were just planning to enthrall me and force me to do whatever you wanted for *your* convenience?" She turned again, waving her hand dismissively. "You know what, no. It doesn't matter if *I am* falling in love with you. I'm not going back into a relationship where I'm only an accessory. Goodbye, Massimo."

Damn it, he was going to have to do it, even if it hurt like hell.

One deep breath, and Massimo's hand pulled the lever. No cars nearby let him speed to her unfettered, but he couldn't outrun the sun. Hot irons pressed to his skin, sizzling, baking the pain in. For a brief moment, he schooled his features. The next, his teeth ground and his hands fisted so hard, he felt bone snap.

Portia's eyes went wide. "What the hell are you doing? Get back in the car."

Gruff words powered past a tight jaw. "I'm old and I'm freshly fed on supernaturally-laced blood. It will be an hour at least before I turn to dust." He refused acknowledge the pain. That was his own cross to bear. "Portia, please. Don't leave. Not for me. Dangerous vampires are coming to Venice soon, men who might try to find you and use you as a pawn against me. I won't be able to protect you from them if I don't know where you are."

"Simple solution to that: I'll leave Italy."

"How? Your passport is back in Venice."

Her hands tightened into fists. "I have a friend who lives in Marseilles. I'll go to her place."

"How, on foot?"

Portia held her arms out wide. "I'm wearing Morticia Adams' disco dress and pretty much nothing else. I'm sure with a few suggestive moves I can hitch my way."

The thought of her in some strange Italian man's car alone while dressed like *that*... Massimo *was* an Italian man, and knowing the possibilities, he'd invite hell to freeze over first before he allowed that to happen. His need to protect overrode all else. He closed the space between them, grabbing Portia by the arm.

"I promise, if you want to leave after I've made it safe, fine. But I won't allow you to—"

"I said *no!*"

All ability to master his own body fled as Portia pushed her flat palm against his back. Searing heat blazed across his shoulder blades, creeping into his ribs, up his spine, singing his brain.

A solarium. *Dio*, Portia could make a solarium. Maybe not throw it, but it was enough to make her hands lethal. If Massimo hadn't vaccinated himself against its full effects by drinking her blood earlier, he might be dead now.

Ancient instincts returned to him, ones not born of a vampire body but of a mortal mind frame: fight or flight. Even as the pain drove him to the edges of sanity, love anchored him. Massimo would never raise a hand to Portia. He'd sooner die. But if he didn't give into *flight*, that's exactly what was going to happen.

The vampire dove into the car and into the passenger side, where the slice of sunshine from the open door couldn't reach him. Portia silhouetted against the daylit sky, leaning over.

"Massimo!" Panic filled her voice. "Massimo, are you okay?"

Was he? Massimo held up his hands, pulling back his sleeves to examine his forearms. Darkened, but not blackened. No blisters or toughened flesh. He'd toasted, not burned.

But he knew his back where Portia had touched him would be cracked and oozing.

"You..." He turned his palms over, checking both sides. "You burned me."

"I didn't... I don't know how..." Guilt etched deep lines into her features.

He knew. Because she was a descendant of slayers. Because a slayer's power against a vampire was the ability to call sunlight into being, to project it. Genetics was a game of chance as much as it was a science, and apparently his beloved's had favored slayer traits. Portia might not be able to cast the sunlight she could summon away from her body as could the fully-blooded slayers, and perhaps she couldn't even control it, but some of that power still resided in her.

"You didn't mean to." Massimo shook his head. If his injuries bought him a chance to explain, it was a fair price to pay. "I should have told you about enthralling you as soon as you became aware of this world, but I was afraid you'd leave, and I wanted you to stay more than anything I've wanted in centuries. But, please, understand that this isn't about me. There's so much more to this world that you need to know, and no matter how it came to pass, you're a part of it now. To let you go away ignorant would be to condemn you."

Her eyes softened. Not forgiveness, resolve. Without another word, she got into the driver's seat and closed the door, her gaze trained on the road. "This all happened so quickly, Massimo."

With effort, he sat up, trying not to wince as the baked flesh on his back shifted. "It did."

When she spoke again, Portia's voice cracked at the edges. "You know, my friends used to ask me why I stayed in such a bad marriage for so many years, even as it became more and more obvious that I wasn't just unhappy, I was being damaged by it. And maybe it's taken me being done with it to understand, but I get it now. I stayed because it was predictable, and that made me feel safe. Yes, I was miserable, but I knew the rules of the game. There was a lot of comfort in that. Sure, Richard broke my spirit, but I built walls to protect myself. Locking him out was the only power I had. And then, one day, Richard walked into the kitchen while I was washing dishes and just said, 'Just wanted to let you know that I filed for divorce this morning.' Just like that, like he was telling me he'd be home late from work or that he'd pick up a liter of milk. And those walls I built? They were a fantasy. It wasn't until that moment that I really got it: my safe but sad world wasn't a fortress to protect me. It was a prison, and keeping quiet about my feelings, a key I made for him to keep me locked up."

Massimo chanced taking her hand, relieved when she didn't resist. "Portia, I'm not that kind of man."

"No, you're like me. Or at least, like I was. You think walling off parts of yourself protects me, but what you're doing is eliminating my options, leaving me with one choice: take it or leave it." She turned, and the tear running down her cheek became his world. "You say you love me?"

Massimo fought his pain and turned fully in his seat, putting both his hands over hers. "I do."

"I don't know if that's true," Portia said, "but even if you think it is, honor this thing between us enough to risk losing me. Because if you're not ready to lose it all, you can't have anything."

Massimo slunk back, recessing into his own truth. She was right. If he wanted a chance to be with her, he couldn't do it partway. It had to be all or nothing. "The group coming to Venice is called the Ravens. You probably heard Patria and I talk about them. They have a cult following among our kind, partly because they have a very elitist morality, a belief that vampires should be permitted to take as many huey victims as they want without regard to consequence, and that we are the natural rulers of the supernatural world. Also, some see them as deities because they've found a way to cheat death."

"Cheat death?" Portia's face curdled. "What do you mean? Aren't vampires immortal?"

"We're immune from disease, from aging, able to heal from most injuries, but eternal? No. After we are turned, we live for about five hundred years. But the Ravens? The eldest among them was taken into the crèche in 1450. Even allowing for a slight variance among terminus, he should have turned to stone decades ago."

"You guys turn to stone when you die?"

Massimo nodded. "If we die from age, yes. And then, when the sun hits the stone, we turn to dust."

She took a moment to digest that. "Okay, so what does that have to do with me?"

"Maybe nothing. But I want to be open and honest with you. The work I commissioned from you? It was meant to mark the occasion of their visit. Just as I'm the Doge of Venice and Patria, the Duchess of Tuscany, Vlad is the Sultan of Istanbul. Once upon a time, however, he had plans to rule over the Trinity World. That's what we call Asia, Europe, and Africa. No one knows why the Ravens have suddenly decided to visit Italy now, but it could be because he's dusting off old ambitions."

"I see. And a vampire bent on world domination…"

She let the thought go unfinished, but he wouldn't. "A slayer, fully in command of their power and well-trained, could end all that."

"Yeah, but…" Portia let out a nervous laugh. "Unless a paintbrush is a deadly weapon, I haven't had any training, and I certainly don't have any powers."

"Except you do. That's why Marco dusted so fast. It wasn't the sun; it was you. You felt threatened and your power… just emerged on its own. Self-defense without consciousness. You might not have even been aware you were doing anything."

"Self-defense?" Portia held up her hands, examining her palms. Ah, so she had noticed. Either she didn't recognize her ability for what it was, or the thought was too bizarre for her to accept at face value. "A moment ago, when you grabbed me…"

"I deserved it." But even as the pain of his burns began to ebb and the blood still in his veins began to heal his wounds, the hour and the avalanche of his world collapsing in on him was getting the best of the Doge. "*Cara mia*, I promise I will answer all your questions. I will hold nothing back. But now—"

"You need to rest." She gave one final nod before straightening in her seat and moving the car into first. "I understand. But Massimo, before you fall asleep?"

His eyes cracked back open. "Yes?"

"That part where I said I was falling in love with you?" Portia asked. "Can we pretend I didn't say that?"

He let his eyes fall shut. "*That* is a very good question."

TWENTY

They arrived at the docklands near Venice a few hours before sunset. At Massimo's direction, Portia pulled Patria's car into an unmarked commercial building after he punched in a remote unlock command through his phone. Once the bay doors were shut, she found that the building was fully equipped for huey comforts. A bathroom allowed her to ease her most pressing need, and a locker room with a shower gave her the opportunity to feel human again. She wished she had other clothes, but for the moment, the garment she'd dubbed "Gothic Saturday Night Dead" would have to do.

Massimo was sound asleep when Portia made her way back to the car, allowing her the opportunity to make a closer examination. His skin tone had crept back toward olive, and more of the cocktail than kalamata variety. Should she give him more blood when he awoke? Would he need it? It looked like he was already healing, after all, and honestly, she wasn't sure if she was ready to have that kind of intimate experience again.

Portia eased back the driver's seat and quickly joined him in resting. When the last rays of sunlight had fled the sky, they rose, she used the restroom once again, and they decided to head for the train into the city.

"You must be thirsty after such a long drive." Massimo took her by the hand, leading her toward a nearby hole-in-the-wall a few blocks from the station. Definitely not a place that catered to tourists, or at least, not the affluent ones. "Coffee? Tea? Limonata?"

Her dry throat wouldn't allow her modesty. "Actually, I'd love an *aranciata*."

Massimo purchased two of the orange-flavored sodas, asked the clerk to pop the lids off for them, then handed her one while taking a drink of his own.

"So I guess you still eat and drink regular food?"

"I don't *need* to," Massimo admitted as they made their way casually through streets still flocked by the huey dinner crowds. "It's more recreational than anything. I do enjoy a good cut of beef, though. And this—" He held up the soda. "Fruit tastes like the sun to me. Even if it's carbonated, which—"

Massimo lowered the bottle and made a fist, bumping himself in the chest. And then, to Portia's amazement, he burped.

"*Mi scusi, amore,*" he said, his cheeks glowing as he grinned. "It's not a pleasant thing to do before a beautiful woman and I drink these things so infrequently that I forget it—"

Before he could finish his sentence, Portia pressed a balled fist to her mouth. It wasn't quick enough to muffle the truth.

Well, if he was going to love a huey, he had to love all of her. That meant the ugly parts, too. "Don't mention it."

Massimo grinned, pulling Portia's hand up to his lips, pressing a kiss into her knuckles. "Humanity is so beautiful on you."

"I think that's the first time a guy ever thought my having gas was cute."

"Not saying I would want you making a habit of it in bed necessarily." Massimo shrugged, weaving their fingers together as he walked them up a road less occupied. "I drink blood. If you can accept me knowing that, how could I hold an occasional bodily function against you?"

"Good to hear, because we haven't had a chance to discuss it, but I'm planning on remaining human."

He snickered.

Portia pulled back her hand, drawing to a stop. "What, you wouldn't want me to be a v—"

"*Shhh!*" Massimo pressed a finger to her lips, his eyes darting in the direction of an old woman who had just emerged from a house. "*Buonasera, Signora. Como sta?*"

The old woman looked up at them like she just realized they were there, swatting the air in their direction. She'd probably thought Massimo and Portia were two lovers sneaking away from the busy streets to share a moment of intimacy. Which, it seemed, they were, but not in the romantic way.

When the woman shuffled on, Massimo dropped his hand. "Careful of your words in public, *cara*. Remember that most hueys do not know about our world."

Our world. If he thought giving her ownership of his secrets was going to woo her... Yeah, it was working. Her weak knees told her as much, but her brain wrestled back control.

"It isn't about what I want. It isn't even about what you want," Massimo continued as they began to stroll in the opposite direction. "Only a huey can become one of us. You're *mostly* huey, but you're also partly not. There's a chance the process could rip you apart on a genetic level."

"Yeah, not a big fan of being dead." *Though you certainly make it look sweet in a pair of nice pants,* her brain completed. No, wait... Not her brain. Definitely a different part of her body. "And what about you? Are you stuck like this forever? Is there a way to reverse vampirism?"

"No."

The word was so quick, Portia didn't think to pursue the question further. Then, Massimo's shoulders lifted and his hand shook in the air.

"Probably not."

Hope bloomed in a corner of her mind. Until, that was, Portia realized how selfish it would be for her to ask Massimo to give up his supernatural existence just to grow old and die with her instead. What did she think, that the Vampire Doge of Venice would want to move with her back to Victoria, B.C., get a little apartment, and raise babies?

Raise babies.

Portia froze in place. Where in the hell had that come from? She'd never wanted kids. NEVER. But suddenly, her mind took off without permission, drafting novels about their life together. Massimo's gray eyes and her red hair bundled in a bouncy little cherub. Teaching their daughter how to ride a bicycle or telling their son to straighten his tie and stay still in the pew until the end of service. Sitting at the table after painting the fence and sharing a bowl of gnocchi. It was nothing she had ever wanted, and suddenly, the only thing she wanted in the world.

"Portia?" Massimo's brow furrowed as he took her hand, bringing her back to the moment. "*Amore*, are you okay?"

"Um, yeah." Portia shook her head, clearing her mind. "Just curious, you said maybe. What's the maybe?"

A grin spread across his face. "Just a fairy tale I heard once when I was young, and then never again. And if there's one thing I've learned in my many years, it's that fairy tales aren't true."

No, they are not.

Even if she was going to believe in vampires. Rather than dwell, Portia changed the subject. "So, these Ravens, what's the plan when they show up?"

"By the time they arrive in a few more days, the rumors about you and me will have gotten around the community. They'll hear of it, of course, so I'll introduce you and set them straight, tell them we're only affianced."

Her eyes heated.

Massimo put up a hand. "Just to remain consistent with the story we used in Florence. There's no reason for anyone to suspect what you really are, and they'll likely dismiss you as a passing huey fancy of mine." He turned, leading them onward. "They should only stay a day or two. Politics require that I grant audience, and of course, it will allow me to find out what Vlad's really after. After they leave, we'll do whatever you want. If you want to go home to Canada, I'll take you. And if you want to stay in Venice for a while…"

His words tapered off as they took one turn more, coming to a pair of elaborate iron gates mounted at an ancient wall. It was an entry to Massimo's palace she didn't recognize, definitely not the canal-side one that she'd used during her previous visits, and not the public-facing entrance outside of which Catalina's Well sat. In fact, it was only by looking up and recognizing the arched windows above that Portia understood they'd reached the palace at all.

So we've hit a wall, both figuratively and literally. "Let's just get through this ominous visit, then we'll deal with… whatever this is between us."

Massimo's grin was downright devilish. Oh, they would deal, but she had a feeling Massimo was one hell of salesman.

TWENTY-ONE

"Your Serenity, Dogaressa." Pavlos beamed as he came into Massimo's office, a clipboard under his arm. "The whole staff wishes to offer its congratulations on your engagement."

Portia put on her flattest of expressions. "We're not engaged, Pavlos."

Massimo cringed, even though he told Portia in private she could trust the vicedoge with confidentiality in any matter. Outside of being a slayer descendant, of course, because *no one* should know that.

"No?" Pavlos turned to his sovereign for clarification. "But Patria's lady's maid said..."

Before Portia could attempt anything in the way of clarification, Massimo sent her through the door behind his desk, telling her to freshen up, take a nap, and that he would come fetch her in a little while to take her to dinner.

Once they were alone, the Doge invited his second to sit. "Situations in Florence required us to present as betrothed, but no, we are not, in fact, affianced."

The voice in his head added a silent *yet*.

"Oh." Pavlos's jaw went slack. "Is any of the other news I heard coming out of Florence untrue?"

Ah, so that's why the Greek vampire had been so swift in greeting them within minutes of arriving home. "Marco is dead; to that, I can personally attest. But to say any more, I'd need to know what else you've heard."

His loyal vicedoge did his best to hide the grin, but Massimo knew the man well enough to recognize hope shining in his eyes. "Other than your seemingly-faux engagement? Just that the Duchess mourns her fallen consort, the Doge of Genoa, and has let her court know that, while deeply saddened, she recognized your challenge as legitimate. There have been grumbles about countering, but so far, a nexus of intention and action has failed to form."

"Good." Massimo began to sift through the papers on his desk, thankful he'd have a chance to breathe before dealing with any fallout, if in fact fallout ever materialized. "Pavlos, I feel it prudent to state that custom and common sense require Patria to observe a certain period of mourning before she entertains other suitors."

Pavlos lifted an eyebrow. "Why that should be of interest to me, I wouldn't know."

Massimo coughed a laugh under his breath. *Of course, you wouldn't.* "In any event, Portia agreed to bolster the grounds of my challenge against Marco by claiming to be my fiancée."

"A keen piece of maneuvering, indeed. Of course, the consequence is that half of the vampire world now thinks you *are* betrothed. When the time comes, how is it precisely you intend to *end* your engagement?"

The Doge stared blankly at the wall. "One of the traditional ways, I suppose. Find out she squeezes the toothpaste tube the wrong way... Sleep with her best friend... Appeal to the Pope on grounds of consanguinity."

Pavlos's eyes went wide.

"Perhaps that was funnier three centuries ago." Massimo grimaced. "Truth be told, my goal is that the engagement should *not* end."

"You'll take her as your thrall, then?"

Massimo's face curdled. "What? No, of course not."

The Greek vampire cocked his head to the side. "Put her in your dungeon?"

"It's at times like these that I'm reminded you're a Dracule, Pavlos."

"One doesn't often get to pick the family they're born to, sire." The vicedoge hid a smile as quickly as it emerged. "Perhaps you can illuminate my understanding where Signora Kepler is concerned?"

Massimo fell back into his seat. "I'm in love with her. I want to marry her. I just need to convince Portia that she's in love with me, too."

"How convenient then, that you're already engaged." Pavlos scooted the edge of his seat. "As your second-in-command and the chief administrator of your court, it's my duty to state the obvious. If you hope to wed her, she'll need to be made with haste. Until then, she's open to attack from any number of political—"

"No." Massimo's hand slashed the air. "Out of the question."

"I understand since you're only pretend-engaged and she thinks she's just playing a role, that it might be a taboo topic to bring up. I could arrange to have her kidnapped by friendly forces and taken to a paterfamilias to receive the maker's bite. I know that forced conversion isn't always smiled upon, but I managed to adapt to the supe life in short order."

"You might not have been given a choice about becoming a vampire, but you were also a soldier with a mortal wound when you were made," Massimo said. "There won't be any forced conversions. There won't be any conversions at all. Even if I do manage to convince Portia to marry me—*of her own free will,*" he emphasized, "she will remain huey."

"It sounds like this is something you've discussed already then?"

Massimo nodded.

"I hope you forgive me for pressing the issue, then, but I feel it's my responsibility to ask where the future Dogaressa is concerned: is she aware of the danger that puts her in?"

"I'm not holding back anything from her, not anymore." And

though Massimo wouldn't say it aloud, the fact that Pavlos would even ask just proved again what a good choice he'd made for his protégé. "Portia is aware of the dangers and believe me," he instinctively rubbed a hand over the still-healing scorch mark she'd given him on the side of the road, "she has her own way of dealing with threats."

"Then I'll say no more."

But as the vicedoge rose to exit, Massimo understood what Pavlos really meant was that he'd say no more *for now.*

Except when he did. "Oh, sire, I almost forgot... Our contact in the *Carabinieri* informed us that Portia's friend, Mae Avery, filed a missing person report. We've been able to have it deleted from the system as we did last time and our contact reached out to Signora Avery to let her know Portia was located and in good health, but you might wish to discuss the issue. It seems Signora Avery is no longer deceived by the pirated text messages we've been sending. Last night, she presented an ultimatum: a real phone call or she'd call the police again. Unfortunately, she carried through on her threat, and I don't know how many times we can circumnavigate such acts until she takes them to a higher authority."

Massimo nodded. "Thank you. I'll make sure Portia gives her a call."

TWENTY-TWO

Her body rolled instinctively when the mattress beside her dipped. "Is it time to get up already?"

Massimo's arm hooked over her, pulling Portia in close. His scent permeated her senses. *Ocean mist and leather*. She could live under a blanket of that aroma.

His laugh was barely audible. "That is entirely up to you. But I do have the kitchen staff making a light meal, so if you're hungry..."

His voice trailed off as she nuzzled into his shoulder. "Probably a good idea. I feel like being around you will require me to keep my strength up."

"I'm planning on drinking extra blood as well. I've asked Massimo to increase our supply of house thralls. It will help keep me from temptation to take you by the fang again."

Portia's eyes shot open, until she realized the obvious. *What did you expect, sweetheart? He's a vampire.* But after making love to him, the thought of Massimo drinking from another woman made her... God damn it, she was jealous, wasn't she? Maybe she was overthinking this. She wouldn't be envious if he'd been human and drank a protein shake. Or was there an underlying sexual charge to each encounter? Massimo himself had said he tricked his victims into feeling pleasure in the place of pain. Was that only for their benefit, or did he get off on the experience too? How could she ever be with him if she was always wondering whose neck he was dipping his fangs in?

"Questions are burning in your eyes." He pulled back ever so slightly to take in her expression. "You know you can ask me anything, right?"

"Anything?"

"Of course." Massimo pressed a kiss against her forehead. "I told you: honesty, and you weren't raised in this world. I'd be surprised if you didn't have a single query when the man you love turns out to be a four-hundred-year-old vampire."

"I haven't said I love you." She pushed herself up on the heels of her hands.

"No, you haven't." He grinned, raising a hand to stroke her cheek. "What is it you want to know?"

"I don't know. A lot. I guess to start, the drinking blood thing. How often does that happen?"

"Depends on the strength of the blood."

Portia's head cocked to the side. "Beg the question much?"

But Massimo beamed. Oh, he was planning to tease her often, wasn't he? She *should* be upset about that, but she couldn't seem to force herself.

"Not all blood is equal, and it depends on how much I actually need," Massimo said. "Very similar to caloric intake. If I'm just going about my nights being diplomatic, a salad is fine. If I'm going to be hunting down and killing a rogue member of my court: steak and pasta. Your blood has more calories than a huey's. It might have lasted me two weeks under normal conditions, but I burned up a lot of energy healing from my injuries. Otherwise, I'd take a huey vein every four or five days."

"And how do you decide who to tap?"

"You make it sound like I'm opening a keg in a pub."

She shot him a dirty look.

"Okay, straight answers." His hands went up by his head on the mattress "Venice has a steady stream of tourists. Finding a fresh meal is never difficult. The easiest prey are those attracted to us sexually. It allows us to get close enough to enthrall without rousing suspicions."

"And you always enthrall your victims?"

He reached up to play with her auburn hair. "I don't consider them *victims*. And yes, always. You've experienced what it feels like to be fed from by force. I would never subject someone to that unless they were guilty of a great wrong."

Her hand went up to rub the skin on her neck. The wound was completely healed because.... *Vampire magic?* she guessed. But the memory remained. "Lucky me then."

Massimo nodded. "I'm not a cruel man, Portia. I feed to live, but only sadists and tyrants forgo enthralling their prey."

"And if I stay in Venice?" Portia's head slowly bobbed as she traced a finger down his chest while sucking on her bottom lip. "Could you make do only feeding from me?"

It was like somebody flipped a switch inside Massimo, turning the vampire parts of him on. His lazy smile disappeared as his mouth cracked open, fangs dropping into being, his mouth actually watering. His eyes said it all: *yes, he would.* But that wasn't all he'd want to do with her where his mouth was concerned.

Damn, it felt good to be looked at that way, and *she* had done that to him. To see she could have that effect on a man, to draw animal instincts from him with just a few words, a fingertip across the flat of his stomach...

"Is... that a condition... of your staying?" Massimo managed to say past deep, slow breaths.

"What? Feeding from me?" She swung a leg over his hips and pinned his hands on the mattress, her head inches above his. "Or *not* feeding from others?"

He uttered something under his breath in Italian that Portia was pretty sure translated to, *oh, fuck.* "Which do you want? I'll promise either."

"I'm not sure." She rolled her hips, dragging herself over the erection straining inside his slacks. "I'd have to know what it feels like to have your fangs in me while I'm enthralled to make an educated demand. After all, you must be hungry after being in the sun yesterday."

"Portia, you.... *Ah, dio*." His eyes rolled back in his head as she moved against him. "You don't act like most hueys when you're enthralled. I'm not sure I could convince your mind to disconnect from your body and...*fuhhhh*...."

Her hand reached down between them, working at the buttons of his pants. "We should try, so we know for sure." Her hand found its way down the plane of his stomach, wrapping around his member. Portia squeezed his length, loving how he filled her grip. "What is it you make your prey feel instead of pain, again?"

He was doing everything he could to restrain himself, to let her be in command, and Portia had to admit... it was a high she hadn't felt before. It was one thing to drive a guy wild with want. It was another thing to seek—and be granted—complete control.

"Glee," Massimo said, his eyes closed. "Serenity. Calm."

Her thumb swirled around the tip of his cock. "Pleasure?"

"*Si*! Pleasure." Massimo's eyes flew open, the hunter's glare falling on her. Until now, he'd been at her mercy, but in a click, Portia felt the dynamic change. The Doge was taking command, and God, she loved it. "Ask me nicely, Portia, and I will demonstrate."

Her hand went still as she leaned down and kissed him. Not too deep. More of a promissory note than a payment. "*Per favore*."

She was on her back before she could blink.

Massimo's eyes bore into hers. He didn't say a word. Not. A. Word. But something... something was happening, because everything in her body was swimming in the most glorious ocean.

"Massimo?"

"*Shhhh*...." He pressed a finger to her lips as a devilish grin spread across his face. "Don't talk. Just... listen."

There was nothing at first, because he wasn't saying anything. Not with his mouth, anyhow. But then, without warning, his voice was inside her head.

And the rest of him was everywhere else.

She was going to explode. Portia's mind *understood* that they were both fully clothed, that they weren't even moving, and yet, it *perceived* the feel of him sheathing himself inside her while simultaneously kissing her dizzy. Her nipples grew hard as his mind told hers his mouth was on them. It had to be, hadn't it? It felt *so good.* But her eyes saw the truth, and the truth was Massimo hovered over her, remaining completely still, without touching her beyond where his erection pressed into her stomach.

"Massimo, I'm going to…"

"I said don't talk." His mouth actually did come down on hers then, drawing her breath from her chest before he pulled back. "Naughty little slayer."

Portia's will warred with invasion. She didn't want to say a thing, but she did want to scream. That wasn't really talking, was it? She hoped not, because suddenly she realized she was moaning.

Massimo's mouth moved to her neck, and she felt everything in her tense in the most delirious way. *It's going to hurt.*

No, it feels good.

No, it's going to hurt like hell.

"I'm going to bite you now, *amore*." His voice was barely a whisper. "And when I do, you're going to come harder than you ever have before."

The filaments of anxiety drifted away, leaving only the pleasure.

"Ready? In three… Two… Now."

"Massim….*ooooo*." Portia's eyes slammed closed because if they hadn't, she was pretty sure they would have popped out of her head.

The word "orgasm" didn't begin to describe it. Pain and pleasure merged as every nerve in Portia's body sang. Massimo's fangs pierced her vein and for the slightest moment, she felt the edge of pressure. Then it released in wonderful blues, greens, and reds. Portia might have screamed in a foreign language she didn't know as a tsunami of sensation washed over her body. Her hands went to her sides as fire burned from her core out to the tips of her fingers. Fisting the sheets kept her in place as her hips came off the bed, her body pulling in tight before it all went completely limp. Massimo kissed her as she rode out the waves, leaving her a wet noodle on the mattress. When she opened her eyes again, it was to find the vampire, one hand laced through her hair and the other pushing himself off the mattress to observe her, wearing the smuggest smile in the history of smiles.

"His Serenity requests Her Lady's assessment on the proceedings."

"My assessment?" She spoke through racing breaths. "Holy shit; that's my assessment."

He laughed into her neck as he leaned down to mend her wound. She had to wonder how that worked, but her thoughts were set on serene, and curiosity was too sharp an emotion to break through.

"So, that *does* work on you." Massimo collapsed to the bed beside her, pulling Portia into his embrace. "Perhaps a little too well."

"Too well? What does that mean?"

"Do you remember when I told you if we ever made love, I'd probably ruin you for other men?"

"Yeah, and post-fact, that *may* be true."

Massimo kissed her forehead. "I think after tasting your blood laced with your climax, I'm ruined for all veins. See, now, you *must* stay. If you leave Venice, I'll starve to death."

He just had to take this wonderful moment and crush it under the heels of reality, didn't he? But then again, maybe Massimo had been trapped in his station for so long, he forgot there was a whole world outside of his palace walls. "Or... you could just follow me back to Victoria."

Portia caught his eyes and saw the complement to every emotion that had just run through her: longing, regret, hopelessness.

She propped herself up beside him. "What, don't Doges ever get to retire?"

"Doges, yes." Massimo stroked her cheek. "Vampires, no. I love you, Portia, and I would love to be with you anywhere, but I'm not something you can just fit into your old life, as much as I would love to be a part of it. Remember what we discussed? There's no cure for vampirism, and it's a condition not easily concealed in casual huey society. That's why you'd have to stay here."

"Oh, and you think my huey life is so simple that I can just be an accessory to yours?" She weaseled out of his grip and took to her feet. "I need to get something to eat, and I'd prefer to do it alone, if you don't mind. You, *after all,* already ate."

"Portia, please, can we—"

Talk about it? Hardly. She needed space. She needed to focus. She needed to stop letting him pleasure her in ways that shouldn't be possible this side of heaven and confuse all her emotions. Without saying a word, she went for the door that led to Massimo's office, swiped her index finger across the security device, and pulled it open. Before she was able to take a single step into the hall beyond, however, she faceplanted into the svelte, youthful chest of another vampire.

"Pavlos?" Portia looked up as her eyes adjusted to the dim light of the hall. She needed to talk to Massimo about getting some more lamps for her to be able to…

Nope, she didn't. Because she *wasn't* staying in Venice.

"Signora." He nodded before his eyes immediately went over her shoulder, looking into the inner sanctum of the Doge's suite. "I need to see Massimo immediately."

The Doge was behind her in an instant, his hands on her arms protectively. "I know, Pavlos. I just saw your text."

"Sire, the Ravens…"

A lump worked its way down Portia's throat. The evil vampires both Massimo and Patria had been worried about? "Did we get lucky and they decided they're not showing after all?"

Pavlos shook his head. "No, Dogaressa, they're already here. They arrived in secret last night..." The Greek vampire's eyes settled on Portia, wide with fret. "While you were in Florence."

TWENTY-THREE

Portia sat in one of the guest chairs in Massimo's office as he and Pavlos spun messages from their phones with the speed of gods.

"Remind me why you're so scared of the Ravens?"

"We're not *scared* of them." Massimo managed to keep typing as he spoke. "We're nervous about them. Their leader is, after all, the most infamous member of our kind ever to walk the earth."

"Blade, Stefan, or Edward?"

Massimo cocked his head to the side. "I do not know any vampires with these names."

"Then you weren't a teenage girl anytime in the last twenty-five years." Portia crossed one leg over the other. "I'd guess you were talking about Dracula, but everyone knows he's just a historical figure twisted into a villain by Bram Stoker's imagination."

Massimo's flat expression when he looked up from his phone made her do a double-take.

She sat up on the edge of her chair. "Okay, you've got to be joking."

Pavlos lowered his cell and sat down next to Portia. "Unfortunately, no. Vlad Tepeș is real and he's alive. Stoker's book may have been mostly fantasy, but the inspiration behind it hardly is."

"Of all the members of my court who would ally with them behind my back: Cara di Nali," Massimo grumbled the name, more to himself than anyone else. "All because I refused to allow her chosen consort to crèche in my city." He shook his head as his device buzzed. Another message, adding to the dozens he'd received in the last few minutes. "I thought I solved all this, or has everything I've done been for nothing?"

The question had been rhetorical in tone, but Portia couldn't help chasing after it. "Wait, what do you mean? Massimo, what happened centuries ago?"

He came back to himself in a flutter of blinks, suddenly realizing he wasn't alone. "Nothing, love."

"Massimo, don't." Portia stood, effecting the look she'd learned in her years of teaching unruly students. One of her colleagues had called it 'the look that Satan's mother gave her son when he said he was going to fight God.' "We promised each other: honesty."

Pavlos made an act of clearing his throat. "Sire, if you expect Portia to consider staying with us in Venice, she needs to know all, especially since we're still unclear what the Ravens' intentions are."

The Doge sighed, dropping his phone on his desk and running a hand through his hair. "You're right. Would you mind giving us a moment?"

The Greek vampire stood, dipped his head, and... turned into a pillar of smoke which exited in a stream through a vent in the wall. *Okay, the door would have been just as easy...* In for a penny, in for a pound, Portia guessed. Now that she was part of their truth, the vampires didn't need to modify their routines to keep her in the dark. She had to wonder, then, why Massimo had insisted the truth about her slayer heritage needed to be kept on the down-low.

A question for another time. "Massimo?"

He turned, worry written in the tightness of his eyes. "I never told you how I became Doge of Venice."

"You said you were getting revenge on the woman who killed Catalina."

His head bobbed. "But that's the *why*, not the *how*. The truth is... complex. The previous Doge was a woman who, at that time, went by the name of Luciana, though names mean little in our world. Most of us take them on and off like changing shirts. Pavlos knows the same woman as Inga, but that also is a pseudonym. When she was human, her name was Maria Ilinca Tepeş, the only daughter born to the Prince of Wallachia."

"Wait, are you telling me that Dracula—*the* Dracula, had a daughter who also became a vampire? And somehow that daughter became the Vampiric leader of Venice?"

"Yes. Luciana was intended to be their foothold in the Italian courts. Back in the seventeenth century, Venice's role in the European economy and power structure was much stronger, and Vlad had ambitions that would have made subjugating, if not directly ruling the entire peninsula, necessary."

Portia wasn't psychic, but she could see where this was headed. "And then, you came along."

Massimo nodded. "My original plan for revenge was simple. I would infiltrate the Venetian court, find a way to get close to Luciana, then kill her. Of course, I didn't expect I'd survive the endeavor, but I was at peace with that. My perspective began to change, however, when I realized two things: One, Luciana was a victim of her father's ambitions. And two: to assassinate the sovereign with no thought to the consequences for both the vampires and citizens of the city was utterly self-serving. So I changed goals and found a conspirator: the only vampire who at that time had any sort of power over the Ravens, Vlad's maker, Igor. He in turn recruited a talented hood to our cause."

"Hood?" Portia pressed her finger to her chin. "Remind me again?"

"They're another supernatural creature, one who balances werewolves. Huey fairy tales have echoes of them: Robin Hood, Peter and the Wolf, and of course, Little Red…" He looked away then, as though into memory, before shaking away the cobwebs. "Silver is deadly to wolves, and hoods have the ability to wield it."

"That hardly sounds supernatural. Anyone who can hold something can wield it."

Massimo's face screwed up. "No, I don't mean hold. I mean,

like…" His hands made a swirling motion in the air. "Magically. They can make silver take on any shape. You see, Igor only agreed to help me rid Venice of the Ravens if I promised not to kill them. Instead, the hood entombed them in silver urns, and Luciana, without their backing, lost her base. In the power vacuum, I became Doge and Igor escorted a banished Luciana from the city. I saved Venice from the Ravens and their puppet ruler, but I never avenged Catalina's death."

"I see." Portia stood, walking slowly to where Massimo sat, his eyes trained on the floor, and laid a hand on his shoulder. "Massimo, I'm so sorry. But you know that's not true, right?"

He turned shining eyes up at her. "Of course, it's true."

Portia cupped his cheek. "I know you Italians have this history of *vendetta*, but where I come from, we have another saying: The best revenge is a life well-lived."

"But I let her killer go free."

"And then you sacrificed your heart for four hundred years. You told me yourself: you've had other lovers, but you've never had a consort, a partner. You gave your life away to Venice, and you kept another woman from being a victim of evil men." Portia crossed her arms over her chest, jutting out a defiant chin. "Frankly, as a woman whose ex was an evil man, I can appreciate that."

The vampire huffed a laugh. With a smile, he invited Portia to sit on his lap, wrapping his arms around her. When she did, he let his forehead fall against her chest. "I never meant to drag you into this, but I promise I'll protect you, no matter what happens. But please, understand that this isn't merely a visit by an unsavory lot. If the Ravens have discovered I was involved in the conspiracy that had them locked away in silver urns for three hundred years, they won't be so easily distracted. They will kill me. And if they find out you're a legacy slayer, they may do far worse to you."

"But they don't know, do they?"

He shook his head. "I don't see how they could. Everyone involved in the conspiracy is dead. Or at least… I think they are."

"All right, so… You need to deal with this in a way that's best, and I'm trusting you to know what that is." Portia kissed his forehead and smoothed back his hair as she slid off his lap. "What do you need from me?"

"Only to understand that the façade I'll need to take on while they're here isn't about *us*, it's about *them*. And to forgive me that I didn't tell you this until now."

She tried to ignore the flurry of butterflies in her stomach at the thought that she and Massimo were an *us*. "I get it. It's a big, dangerous secret, and I'm only a huey. Well, *mostly* a huey. They're vampires. They could still enthrall me and get at the truth."

"Not only about my role in the conspiracy, but about the fact that you're a slayer descendant." Massimo pulled a decanter from inside his desk and two glasses, measuring a finger of alcohol for each of them. He handed Portia her glass. "I've sent word to Cara di Nali that she will host me tomorrow night. I didn't give a reason, but of course, she will understand that I've discovered her secret. I have to placate some truly loathsome vampires while keeping them at arm's length. Politics is balancing the needs of the many and the desires of a few on the tip of a greased pin."

"That… sounds tricky." Portia tipped back the alcohol before putting the glass back on the desk. "I'll make myself scarce until they're gone. And once they are, you and I can try and make this thing between us work."

Massimo exploded into smiles. "*Bella*, I've not heard any words so wonderful in a hundred years."

Oh, dear. "I'm not saying I'm staying, Massimo. I'm just saying I won't leave without giving it a try."

"I can ask no more than this, but I will hope for everything."

TWENTY-FOUR

Massimo solidified just beyond the wrought iron gate of Cara di Nali's residence on Lido. On the outer edge of the Venetian chain, the island's streets held a much more contemporary feel. Cars were permitted here. Homes tended to be more modern, and more had garden areas. Cara had lived here since the late 1800s, shortly after becoming a member of Massimo's court. Her villa couldn't compare to the palaces that dotted the Grand Canal, but it was certainly large enough to hold secrets.

The tap of Massimo's cane ricocheted off the surrounding walls as he walked. *Tick... Tick... Tick...* Pavlos took shape behind him just as the front door opened.

"Your Serenity." Cara genuflected, making little effort to hide a... what had he heard tourists call it? Oh, yes, a shit-eating grin. "What an honor to have you in my home."

Massimo came to a stop a step before her. "I know they're here, Cara."

Formalities aside, Cara crossed her arms over her chest. "And what if they are? Is it any crime to welcome old friends into my home?"

Old friends. "Of course not, but it *is* a breach of protocol for a foreign dignitary to arrive in my city without making an appearance first at *my* court. One might question their intentions. One might question *yours*."

"Let's not have any incidents, Signora." Pavlos pulled himself nearly equal to Massimo on the stoop. "Stand aside and let us pass."

Cara bowed, one arm strapped across her stomach and the other struck out at the side. "My Doge, Honorable Vicedoge... by all means."

Fairytales painted fantasies onto the frames of infamous men, giving them a presence of person that would seem unnecessary to ones whose story loomed so large.

In truth, Vlad Tepeş was not a man of significant beauty or stature. Nor was he comely-shaped, possessing some boyish charm, or predisposed to make maidens swoon. Sallow cheeks, shoulder-length black hair that curled at the end, pale skin reflecting his Balkan roots. Dead, cold, empty black eyes mounted above a sharp jut of a nose. Plainly put, he *was* plain, but he had about him the cloud of legend and legacy, a moving filter powered by lifetimes of war, cruelty, focus, and yes, leadership. Even if his ambitions and goals lay in opposition to Massimo's, the Doge would be a fool to dismiss his appeal. Vlad Tepeş was a man with a vision, albeit an evil one, and such men could always find support among those who lacked a vision of their own.

Vlad sat alone in Cara's second-floor lounge, a space updated with modern furniture, a bearskin rug, and a bar cart against one wall. Flames danced in the hearth even as a sea breeze floated in through an open pair of French doors. Perhaps the other Ravens had been here moments ago and smoked out through that door. Perhaps it was merely coincidence.

The Wallachian prince, dressed in faded jeans and a white cotton shirt buttoned down halfway, raised his glass but kept his seat. "If it isn't my old friend, Massimo Barozzi."

Massimo took a chair opposite the man he'd help imprison as Cara appeared, giving him a glass of wine. "I've gone by Bruneli since the time I was admitted to the Venetian court, but, understandably, you might not remember. Our correspondence suffered from your... *indisposition*."

"Is that what you call my being imprisoned inside a silver jar for three hundred years? Indisposition? Well, yes, I suppose I can't argue the truth of it. Bruneli, you say?" Vlad tapped his forehead with two fingers and let out an airy laugh. "Memories... even for me, with so many years and even more enemies, it can be difficult sometimes to recall... *nuances*. For example, you're looking very... flush with life for a man tipping towards stone."

And you're looking very much alive for a man who should have been *stone decades ago.*

Massimo bit his tongue, lifting his glass in salute instead. "To our health."

Vlad returned the gesture in kind, finishing off his drink. When he set down the glass on a white marble table between them, Cara rushed in with the bottle to refill it.

Vlad took her by the hair, pulling her back. "Leave us."

Massimo painted over his emotions. On the one hand, Cara was vampire and the pain would pass the moment Vlad let go. On the other hand, as errant as her actions were, this was still Venice and Massimo was still Doge. Who was Vlad to order around his citizens?

Cara fell to the ground with a whimper the moment she was free, a splash of red leaping from the bottle and staining the rug underneath. With an insistent snap from Vlad, she righted herself, left the bottle on the table next to the empty glass, and scattered.

Vlad leaned forward, taking the bottle into his hands before pressing it to his lips. A single drop escaped his mouth, chasing down his chin, as his dead eyes stayed focused on Massimo. When he finished, he pulled away the bottle to reveal his fangs, long and wine-stained.

Massimo left his glass on the table and leaned forward. "Much time has passed since the last time you and I were in a room together, Tepeș. Let's act in accordance with the times, shall we?"

"Meaning?"

"Meaning..." Massimo leaned back and crossed one leg over the other. "Let's dismiss etiquette and diplomatic dialog and speak frankly, shall we? What the fuck are you doing here?"

"Oh, Massimo. I remember now how much I liked you once, even if you did obviously worm your way into my daughter's heart to see out your own aspirations."

Massimo ignored the bait. "You come back from the dead, take over Constantinople, then turn your bloodline from members of a peaceful community to vampire-first radicals, and on top of that, you have the nerve to show up here in my city and sneak in under my nose. Your actions have the Eight Courts ready to erupt."

"Ah, the Eight Courts..." Vlad stuck up his index finger, taking on a contemplative mask. "I'm curious why you still call them that, when there are only five that still exist in any real way and the population of your communities decreases from decade to decade? Some might question your leadership."

Massimo's jaw worked. "What is your end game here? Do tell—I'm not as patient as I used to be, and even when I was married to your daughter, it was no secret that I didn't like you."

The infamous Bloody Prince took in the Doge's loosening control with ever-growing amusement, his eyes dancing, his smile stretched wide. "You've been waiting centuries to say that, haven't you?"

"Vlad, I swear to the saints, I'll—"

"No need." Vlad stood, inviting Massimo with a tip of his chin to join him. "Come and I will show you. I, too, have learned not to treat time as flippantly as I once did. Forever isn't as long as it used to be."

Cara's villa stood in a part of Lido where eighteenth-century affluence rammed into seventeenth-century military facilities. Villa di Nali appeared to the untrained eye to be just another midsize residence typical of its period but updated with modern amenities. Massimo, however, remembered when a naval barracks and prison had sat on this same piece of land.

The prison was still intact, even if it had been given a cosmetic upgrade. Cara had plastered over stone walls, but rose-colored brick still peeked out in places from behind swipes of beige stucco. Red-tiled floors played host to plush, baroque-style furniture, the wooden frames carved with intricate swirls and cushioned over in fabrics rich with soft detail. Off against a far wall, any true Italian's treasure: wine of every classic variety, no doubt also of refined vintages. It would have appeared as a wealthy woman's wine cellar, if not for the silver chains affixed to an iron ring on one wall, and the beaten-bloody bearded young man secured in place by them.

He looked up through greasy brown locks, catching the Doge's eye, sending Massimo back through centuries of regret. It had to be chance, that this creature resembled another who had once visited his court, centuries before when Massimo had still been vicedoge.

The Wallachian vampire stayed quiet, motionless, inviting the Doge by default to address his inquiries to the prisoner himself. Some answers didn't need questions, though. For example, Massimo didn't need to ask if the young man was a werewolf. What other creature required restraint in silver?

Massimo cleared his throat and straightened his back. "For what crime is the Sultan holding you?"

Vlad stepped forward when the lupine gave no response. "It's no use speaking Italian to him. He doesn't know a word."

"Turkish then?" A reasonable assumption for a vampire who made his home in the former Ottoman capital.

Vlad clicked his tongue. "And to answer your question, his crime is insurrection."

"How could a werewolf revolt against you? He isn't your subject. You're not his master. If he's committed some crime, refer him to the House of Night, assuming that order of hood still holds dominion over your city."

"I'm not his master?" The Blood Prince's smile fell. "I am master of all supernaturals in Constantinople. If they come to my city, they are my subjects. This one here was part of a team that recently raided my palace and attempted to kill me."

A shame they didn't succeed. Massimo bit his tongue and turned his attention to a cylindrical wooden object a half meter high and laced over with metal restraints.

"A traveling barrel? I haven't seen one of those in a dog's age."

In the days before specialty sunlight-filtering glass and the ability to fly on planes great distances at night, any vampire wishing to travel by boat risked exposure to sunlight. A popular solution was to take on one's smoke form and voluntarily be entombed in a sealed barrel. Such devices looked like mere cargo to the huey crew, but they also required the vampire to trust his servant would free him when the destination was reached. "Is there someone in there, or did you revert to old practices on the way to Venice?"

"I find yachts so much more agreeable than the schooners and caravels of ole. If you weren't so adverse to being on the water, as I've heard tell, I'd highly suggest it," Vlad said. "And yes, someone is in there."

Massimo arched an eyebrow. Did Vlad expect him to know who?

"Surely you don't think I could trust my father not to flee."

The Doge's heart leaped to his throat, then dropped into the pit of his stomach. The Raven's maker, the father of the most lethal vampire ever... And a man who most had believed dead for at least two hundred years. Vlad's sire might not be a legend in the huey world like his progeny, but when *vampires* spoke of Dracula, *they* spoke of Igor Karahan.

"Igor is alive?"

"Yes, and wouldn't you, a vampire creeping into his last century, love to know how?"

Massimo tried to speak past a mouth gone dry. "It's impossible. Igor Karahan met the sun long ago. If he was alive, he'd be—"

"More than seven centuries, if you take truth from his lips." Vlad hooked his hands behind his back, jerking his head in the prisoner's direction. "And it's all because of creatures like that."

"A werewolf?" The answer to never meeting the sun couldn't be so simple.

At that, the poor creature stirred. His voice held evidence of pain and fatigue, but his words flowed freely. "If you're going to bloody talk about me, do have the decency to do it in a language I can understand, leech bastards."

His tongue revealed his home. Northern England, if Massimo were to place a hopeful wager. He thought about looking to Vlad for guidance on how to proceed, but to his horror, he did so just in time to see the backside of the Sultan's hand fly.

The werewolf flew back, his form leaving an impression in the wall as his body collapsed into the ground. "I told you not to speak, cur!" Vlad growled. "Or would you like me to—"

Massimo caged Vlad, pulling him back, surprised that it proved so easy. A fact, he knew, that would reveal his understanding. Pavlos had been right; Vlad was weakening. As a vampire two centuries his senior, the Impaler should be able to toss Massimo over his body and through several walls.

"I demand you tell me why you've come to Venice." He kept his words in English now. This wolf could be a true enemy, or just someone caught in the Ravens' conspiracies. In any event, Massimo saw no advantage in keeping him out of the loop. "We both know if you were only seeking refuge, Marco di Serpente would have been all too eager to host you in Florence."

"I've come here because I need help recapturing an illustrian."

"An illustrian?" Massimo took a step back, but the blow of the statement still hit him with full force, his own words to Portia echoing in his thoughts.

Are you stuck like this forever? Is there a way to reverse vampirism? You said maybe. What's the maybe?

Just a fairy tale I heard once when I was young, and then never again. And if there's one thing I've learned in my many years, it's that fairy tales aren't true.

"They don't exist." Was he telling Vlad that, or reminding himself? "They *can't*. The product of a werewolf and a slayer? How would that happen when all the slayers are dead?"

Vlad rolled over a hand. "Let's say, for the sake of argument, they aren't. Then it's not so impossible, is it? Even if it was, impossible things are happening all the time. Take Tobias here..."

Tobias groaned as Vlad's foot swung, connecting with his

gut, and Massimo warred with his feelings to intervene. He would without restraint, but for the words, *they aren't all dead.* He needed to know what the hell that meant. Were there other slayers?

"You've noticed the silver chains?"

Massimo tamped down his rage and attempted to stay focused. "Necessary for securing a werewolf."

"Yes, indeed. Only, he isn't a werewolf. Mostly, true, but in fact, Tobias here is an asenaic. You and I both know that happens every so often. Some hood oppressed by a merciless mother rebels by rolling around on the forest floor with her sworn enemy and nine months later, an asenaic is born. They're uncommon, but not unheard of. So finding Tobias isn't all that surprising, except... *his* mate, a descendant of Gerwalta Faust, no less, is an *inceptor*."

Massimo's throat bobbed as he tried to swallow the statement. *Red Riding Hood...* That's how history knew her. But in the Supernatural world, she had an entirely different moniker: the Betrayer. Faust had done the unforgiveable for one her kind by mating a werewolf and having their child. Only, she *couldn't* have a descendant, because both she and the child had been burned at the stake for her crime.

Before that, however, she had been the hood Igor Karahan had brought to Venice in 1687 to help them overthrow the court. It was because of Faust that Massimo was Doge.

"Now I know you're lying."

"Am I?" Vlad stuck a finger in the air. "Remind me, Massimo. Who is the maker in your bloodline? Oh, that's right." His hand dropped, but his sneer widened. "There isn't one. Meaning your bloodline will die."

"I don't care about that. Families die out all the time." *Species died out.* The slayers did. Or at least, he thought they had.

"Know what the best part is?" Vlad dragged on. "She doesn't even know what she is. Very few vampires today even know about inceptors, creatures born of sky, earth, and star, whose blood could create new vampire lines. And illustrians—"

"Whose blood could cure it." The fight left him. Massimo turned slowly to the werewolf—no, not a werewolf. Asenaic. "They have a child?"

For the first time, Vlad managed to look sheepish. "No, but the inceptor is currently in possession of the slayer carrying the illustrian. She is a product of my stable."

"Your stable?" Massimo swung around.

And then it all clicked.

The way Portia's blood, laced with sun and traces of power, had healed him so quickly. He'd always known slayer blood was powerful; all supernatural blood packed a bigger punch than huey blood. But was it more than restorative? Could it allow a vampire to endure beyond their immortal lifespan?

If so, and if there were still slayers in the world, could their blood allow a vampire to endure beyond five centuries? It would hold a value far greater than diamonds. But if you wanted more than more years in your life, if you wanted the power to create and imbue vampire life and to kill one as well without consequence?

"You have slayers, and you're going to use them to breed inceptors and illustrians."

Vlad grinned. "I'm building an army, Massimo. New bloodlines, their foundations firmly among those most loyal." He hesitated. "But I cannot do it alone."

The Doge's head snapped up. "I have no interest in conquering supernatural existence and bringing world domination."

"No, all you ever wanted was Venice. So much so, that you overthrew my daughter and conspired with other supes to have me and my generals trapped for centuries."

Any other time, Massimo would have denied the charge. He *had* denied it, in fact, since the coup was still fresh and the participants living. So few remained from those days now. In his own court, Giuliano had been the last. But with the truth staring him in the face with ramifications, he refused to pull out the thread any longer.

"You would have used Venice to seize control of the Eight Courts."

"Oh, no, Massimo, I would have used Venice to seize control of *Europe*. What I lacked then was the ground power. But with an inceptor in my stables—" He turned a dubious eye to the werewolf. "—not to mention, an illustrian. Do you know that the smallest amount of illustrian blood, mixed with any other, even huey, can destroy vampirism in moments? All we need do is lace our enemies' prey!"

Massimo crossed the room faster than even a vampire should be able to. He had Vlad's collar in his hands and the infamous vampire pressed to the wall in moments. "Karahan tried for years to breed a werewolf and a slayer. It couldn't be done."

"And yet, it has." If anything, Vlad looked amused by Massimo's effort. He gave a sideways glance to the wolf before becoming smoke, leaving the Doge fisting empty space. He rematerialized a moment later, seated in one of the plush wingback chairs, and invited Massimo to resume civility, motioning to the twin seat across from him.

"Only two people have ever defeated me in my supernatural life. One of them is in that cask. The other is you. My father refused to see the light. I'm hoping you will prove wiser."

"And if I don't?"

Vlad shrugged. "I know you won't threaten my plans. You care only for Venice and I have pressing matters in Spain requiring my attention that cannot be delayed in an attempt to woo you to my side. But think about it." He jerked his head in Tobias's direction. "Once I have its lover, then the plan will all be in place, Massimo. It will give us the tools we need to be both masters of life and death."

Death to their enemies.

Massimo clutched the top of his cane. What he'd give to pull off the silver tip, expose the sharpened wood, and ram it through Vlad Tepeş's evil heart. But he was right: Massimo had no interest outside Venice. Vlad had enough of a following that destroying him without any thought to what that would do among his followers would be foolish at an apocalyptic level.

"You assume, *Vlad*, that we all want such things."

Vlad blinked. "Are you saying you *want* to die?"

"I am saying that I have very little left for which to live."

Venice would be safe in Pavlos's hands. If he could win Portia over, they would have forty, perhaps fifty years together. Beyond that…

Massimo shook his head, casting a sympathetic gaze to the werewolf before turning back. "Why live forever without purpose, when you can die happy with pride and with love?"

He rose, but unfortunately, Vlad did too. Fine, then, he'd end this without any confusion.

"You and yours may take shelter in my clutch, as requested, but I suggest you depart for Spain as soon as you've made arrangements. In the meantime, you *will* observe my edicts while in Venice. We adhere to modernity, Vlad. No drinking to excess, and erase the memories of those from whom you do imbibe. Tourists work well, especially those who themselves have had a little too much to drink."

The fingers on Vlad's hand flexed. "You presume to lecture me on remaining discreet?"

Massimo's eyes shifted to the werewolf once more. He hated leaving him here, knowing what tortures would be in store. Such disrespect for werewolves, how could he ever honor vampires? "You travel with both your sire bound by oak and an asenaic in bondage, Dracule. Such acts in our world draw attention. I bid you good evening."

Massimo could take no more. He smoked away, out of the dungeon, back to the front garden, where he became solid once more, where he found Pavlos sitting under a nettle tree.

The Greek vampire put down his phone and looked up. "Sire?"

The Doge shook his head. He didn't want to talk about particulars, especially not when he was so close to turning around and accepting Vlad's offer. It had taken four hundred years, but it had finally happened: Vlad had found something he loved more than his city.

With an illustrian's blood, he could be human again. With an illustrian's blood, he could give Portia the one thing she wanted outside of his power: a normal life.

They were halfway up the walk leading from the gate to the pier where they'd moored their boat when reality caught up to Massimo. "Cara..."

Massimo made to turn, but Pavlos's hand gripped his shoulder. "Sire, I've already spoken to her."

"And?"

"And..." Pavlos's voice trailed off, his eyes traced the sky. How unlike the vicedoge to be nervous. "Ultimately, sire, it is your decision, and if I've overstepped my bounds, I will understand if you feel the need to punish me as well. I've told her that she has until sunrise to leave Venice forever for disobeying you."

For a moment, Massimo considered congratulating his vicedoge on a fair decision, until he realized the words that were used. "She didn't disobey me, though, did she? I can barely even call it conspiracy with a foreign power, given that the Ravens themselves were meant to be here at my invitation."

"Yes, sire, and you're right on both accounts. But after you proceeded upstairs, I took it upon myself to have a look about the premises."

Foreboding rooted in his gut. "And what did you discover?"

"A man chained up Signore di Nali's bedroom, naked as the day he was born, covered in the blood of the two huey bodies dead on the floor." Pavlos dipped his head. "He was of my bloodline, sire; I could smell it. He was made Dracule."

The rage roared within.

As quick as thunder, Massimo turned on his heel. The road

here was open, and any number of hueys, while not close, were close enough. He didn't care. This insurrection could not stand. This open flaunting of his edict, unforgivable.

Pavlos didn't follow; Massimo knew he wouldn't. His vicedoge lingered, making sure that any human who happened to see a man become a pillar of smoke before zipping a half kilometer up the lane in seconds wouldn't remember the sight.

Good. One less thing to worry about. And there were, after all, oh, so many.

Cara sat on the couch in her second-floor lounge, drinking her wine. She didn't get up when he rematerialized behind her. Didn't give any indication that she knew he was there. Massimo seethed, waiting until, at last, he could wait no more.

"Have you nothing to say in your defense?"

Cara took a long, languid draw from her glass and swallowed with leisure. "I've done nothing I need to defend."

Massimo slammed the tip of his cane against the floor. "I gave you permission for your consort to receive the maker's bite *only* if he was weened in a crèche outside of the city. Pavlos says there are two bodies upstairs. Two!"

"They are only hueys, Massimo."

The sound of his own name, so informal on her tongue, roiled his insides. "I am your Doge, and you will address me as such."

Her gray eyes sharpened, turning back over her shoulder to glower at him. "Why, because you're Doge? You, who value hueys over your own kind, limit our hunting when the city is rife with blood? You, who force us to act within their society's rules, when ours is eternal and superior? You, who killed one of your own kind because he was a threat to the huey whore you have at your palace this very minute? You bring shame to all vampires, and I renounce my loyalty to—"

The button on the handle of his can clicked, the silver endcap falling off and revealing the sharpened wooden tip below.

A stream of blood and wine rolled from the side of Cara's mouth as the stake pierced her heart, the half-empty glass falling from her hands and staining the white fabric red. For one brief second, his subject struggled, pushed back against the cushions like she could get up, even tried to become smoke, her edges fraying. The ill-timed attempt only spread the damage. Purple blood drained from her fingertips, her nose, the corners of her eyes. Cara di Nali's fangs dropped into sight as she fell forward, the last moment of fight left in her.

And then it was over. She was dead.

When footfalls echoed in the room behind him, Massimo didn't have to wonder who it was.

"My, my," Vlad said. "We'll have a hard time getting invites accepted in the future if our hosts end up dead."

Cara's body slumped forward when Massimo retracted his weapon revealing a punctured back cushion with a distinct purple corona behind. "Her lover upstairs? You made him?"

"Actually, one of my generals did."

"He's still of your bloodline then." Massimo turned. "Take him with you when you go."

"A newborn in my company?" Vlad chuckled lowly. "I'm sorry, but no. We haven't the ability to accommodate the young these days."

It was at that moment that a third pillar of smoke took shape beside them.

Pavlos gave Vlad a passing glance before bowing his head at Massimo. "My liege, all witnesses have been traced and enthralled. They'll remember nothing." He turned to take in a quick glance at Cara's body. "I'll arrange to have her exposed to the dawn."

"So, this is the great Pavlos Katsaros." Vlad held out a hand to the vampire in question. Not to shake, but with the backside held out, positioned to solicit a kiss. "Vicedoge of Venice. You bring our bloodline honor."

"I'm only a Dracule by consequence of others' choices, not my own. I see little to be proud of." The Greek vampire spoke past his tight jaw. "What I choose to do is bring honor to my *Doge*."

Massimo forced himself to separate from his lingering anger, riding waves of pride in his protégé. "We need a solution for the initiate upstairs."

Pavlos's chin swept down. "Won't we dispose of him, Sire?"

Vlad turned, talking to himself as he made his way to the bar cart. "And he says he's not a Dracule."

Massimo shook his head. "Even if he was turned willingly, Cara was the one who disobeyed my orders to take him away from Venice. The two hueys would have been brought to the room and killed there. Our intelligence network would have alerted us if there'd been a double murder with the markings of vampire death." He laid a hand on Pavlos's shoulder. "Contact Alessandro in Rome. I believe he still keeps a crèche outside of the city. Ask if they will accept him and tell Sandro that I'd consider it a great personal favor, then find a way to dispose of the bodies inconspicuously."

"Yes, Your Serenity."

Pavlos nodded before turning on his heel and walking away, leaving Massimo and Vlad alone.

The Doge let his fangs drop. "I want you and the rest of the Ravens gone. You've created enough commotion here."

"And as I've said, I need to get to Spain, so we won't linger. But I do wish you'd reconsider and join us. Cara was so positive you would."

Massimo's finger jutted in the corpse's direction. "Apparently, Cara was a poor predictor of my behavior."

Vlad frowned as his head bobbed. "Obviously. I will admit, however, I never thought you'd actually carry out the deed of killing her yourself. And with a wooden stake through the heart? So brutal a death. Excruciatingly painful, I hear."

It was a philosophical trap set by an expert. The Impaler, getting someone else to argue the virtues of impaling. Massimo refused to be drawn in. "Leave, Tepeș, and never visit Venice again as long as I rule. You are not welcome in my court."

"I will be when it's mine."

Massimo's steps froze in place, his departure stalled. "You'll never have Venice."

"I will when it's Pavlos's. And when I have the illustrian's blood that I can feed to my father. Once he's human again, I'm going to enjoy torturing him through a slow and painful death. Most Dracule have forgotten what it's like to have a strong paterfamilias to our bloodline and I intend to remedy that. My father has spent much of the last century hiding from his own progeny, wasting his prospects for power. He did keep himself busy though. Genetics research mostly but turns out he did have another passion. Would you like to know what?"

"Damn you, do you ever stop talking?"

"History."

The Impaler's hand lifted as he stretched out the gun before him. When he'd gotten it, from where, and what harm he thought it would do, Massimo couldn't say. He could say, however, that when the bullet fired and lodged into his chest, everything inside him revolted.

Agony went through him, pulsing torment, liquid fire lighting his nerves, making his blood burst. Massimo gasped, stumbling backward. He couldn't remember backing out on to the balcony, but soon, Massimo looked up, saw a patchwork of stars overhead, and then down to the canal flowing below.

Vlad stepped into his chest, gripping his shirt in his empty hands. "Whoever thought it would be the hueys who thought of wooden bullets?"

Vlad pushed, Massimo tumbled, and the water rose to claim him.

TWENTY-FIVE

She sat in the courtyard, watching the first rays of sunlight angle their way down the walls and kiss the top of the unfinished mural, the whole reason she'd come to Palazzo Oscuro to begin with.

Two days. For two days, no one had seen or heard from Massimo. For two days, Portia hadn't eaten, slept, or lost faith.

The sun was rising on the third day, and the night, setting on hope. He was gone. There was no other way to say it. Massimo was dead.

Pavlos approached her from behind with slow measured steps, taking care to let his feet drag ever so slightly. A kindness, as vampires rushing to give her reports popped up from pillars of smoke or ran to her with such speed on foot, she'd been frightened into shock.

"Dogaressa, you need to sleep."

Portia sat on a bench on the side of the courtyard with her knees pulled into her chest. Lifting her head was a feat almost beyond her. "I'm not Dogaressa, Pavlos."

The vampire sat down behind her. To give her a foundation to lean back against? Maybe. "You would have been."

Would have been. Past tense. So, she wasn't alone in presuming the worst.

At the same moment she had the realization, Pavlos tried to correct himself. "That is, you *will* be, assuming you accept His Serenity's proposal. Truly accept it, not just for the sake of providing grounds in a challenge."

Three days ago, there was no way Portia could imagine herself married again, not even to the dashing vampire she'd fallen in love with. Yes, she *loved* Massimo. It was pointless to deny it, painful even. If he were here right now, she'd tell him so. She'd marry him without a second thought, and live anywhere he was, in any kind of circumstance, for as long as fortune gave them.

She untwisted herself from the bench and labored to take her feet. "Any word from Rome?"

The vicedoge granted her request for normalcy, following in her wake as she crossed the courtyard toward the stairs. "King Alessandro's minister confirms that Mr. Tebriz has been welcomed to the crèche and is adjusting well. It seems he has no memory of killing the hueys we found in the di Nali Villa. It must have been newborn bloodlust; he barely would have been conscious of it."

She nodded, pausing as a wave of dizziness forced her still. "And Patria?"

Pavlos shook his head. "She hasn't heard from him, but her spies in Spain have confirmed that Vlad Tepeș is now in residence in Navarre. She also shared an unrelated piece of news."

One of her eyebrows arched.

"Inga Rosethorn is dead."

When Portia returned only a blank stare, Pavlos continued.

"You might have heard of her by one of her other names. She was Doge of Venice before Massimo, but she was called Luciana then."

Ah, yes... Now she knew who he was talking about. Only, the context for that event was beyond her reach. Surely it meant something, but Portia was either too clueless or too tired to know what.

But then, that was true of this whole thing, wasn't it? Portia wasn't clear on the bigger picture of her own life, unable to zoom out or zoom in in just the right measure to gain scope and clarity. Pavlos had taken to calling her Dogaressa the moment he came back from Lido with the news that Massimo was missing, but in most measures, assuming the running of the court himself. At the same time, he deferred to her on anything directly related to the Doge. Pavlos was a great diplomat, Portia had concluded. No doubt he'd have a harried woman mad with grief on his hands if he hadn't included her in the process. By yielding a little power, he gained back so much more.

Massimo would have been proud.

She clutched her stomach as her own words echoed in her head. *Would have been.*

"Dogaressa, I'm taking you to your room. You *must* sleep."

"I can't sleep."

Pavlos braced her as she lost her footing before sweeping her up on her feet and making for the stairs. "I can enthrall you and make you. With your permission, of course."

That did sound... well, not good. Nothing without Massimo sounded *good*. But letting her mind disconnect for a while would *feel* nice at least.

Soon enough, her eyes opened to find that they'd entered Massimo's office. Portia lifted her gaze. "No, not in our bed. I can't stand to be there without him."

"Then where would you like me to put you, Your Serenity?"

Where indeed? "There was a bedroom I slept in for a few hours before, one that had a painting of Catalina over the fireplace."

"Ah, that one." Pavlos smiled. "Yes, I'll take you there, and Santa Catalina will watch over you, as she does all separated lovers."

She wasn't sure the exact time when she awoke, but instinct told Portia the sun was still in the sky. She rose and passed to the window, pulling back the heaviest curtains she'd ever seen, and confirmed it. Late afternoon by the look of things. From this vantage point, she could see the people passing in the lane outside the palace gate. Locals, it looked like. Men carrying cases. Women talking on their phones as they examined the daily offering from the florist shop. Children with school satchels over their wrists.

Satchels.

Portia darted to the closet, where the things taken from her holiday rental had been moved the night Giuliano died. Her suitcase was in Massimo's room, but her computer, carryon bag, and yellow satchel had stayed here since. Wallet, passport, a bag of charcoals, and regular pencils… Damn it, where was it? Only then, she remembered. She'd left her sketchbook down in the courtyard, where she'd been using her rough sketch of the mural for reference.

The floor of the courtyard was a landscape of wet brick and shallow puddles. The rain fell gently, almost like an apology from a reticent child. Luckily, one of the human staff must have seen her work cart and moved it to the portico, protecting it from the weather. Her sketchpad sat there, underneath a folded smock. Portia ripped through the pages, looking for *it. The portrait.* The one that started everything.

And then, there he was. Massimo. Only, it wasn't Massimo. The man in her work was a faint impression of the vampire she loved. The eyes were wrong still. The jaw was off. Of course, she hadn't accounted for fangs. Back then, how could she? She clutched the sketchpad to her chest as the tears came unbidden.

It wasn't gold and it certainly wasn't silver, but it was the most valuable possession she had. She only hoped it would do.

The rain kept most of the usual visitors to the well away. *Fair-weather lovers,* she thought. Portia emerged into the street to find only one man passing through, and him hurriedly so, using a shopping bag as an impromptu umbrella. Clutching her sketchpad to her chest, under the folds of her coat for protection, she stood before Catalina's Well and began to spill her heart.

"Um… Hi, Catalina. Um, *Signora Barozzi,* I guess, because you guys like formality and stuff. Anyway… I know this is weird because it's Massimo we're talking about, but please… I don't know what else to do. You loved him, I'm sure, and if you could see the way he looked when he told me your story… That man was crazy over you. Still is, frankly. And, that's cool. I'm not the kind of woman who needs her man to forget the lovers he had before. Frankly, I'd be scared if he did. If he could love you so deeply that he became a vampire just to avenge you and then forget about it, he could do the same thing to me. Well, he couldn't do the vampire thing again, of course. I mean. Shit, what do I mean?"

Portia stepped up on the edge of the well. *Focus. The quicker you finish this, the quicker dead pseudo-saints can intervene with fate on your behalf.*

After all, if she believed in vampires, why couldn't she believe in miracles?

"I don't have any gold or silver. I spent every last penny I had to come and live in Venice for a while. But what I do have is this sketch that I made of Massimo. It's the most precious thing I possess, and I'm hoping, Catalina, if I toss this down the well, you'll accept it instead of coins. Pavlos has been pampering my hope, but I've heard the whispers around the court. They say Massimo's dead, and that because a vampire turns to dust in the sunlight, we would never find a body. I don't believe he's dead, but I can't tell you why. And so..."

Rain splotched the sketchpad cover, the edges of the pages soaking up the water falling from above in a preview of what lay below.

"If I give this to you, can you bring him back to me? I never even got a chance to tell him I love him. And I do, Catalina. I love him *so much.*"

Portia extended her arm and her hopes in the same swift movement. The hesitation was brief, but just like with her heart, once she loosened her grip, everything fell into place.

She lingered there a moment, shocked at her own boldness, throwing away the only thing she had of Massimo. Until, that was, she heard a voice from the well.

"Portia, is that you?"

She leaned over the edge and peered down so quickly, she almost lost her footing and fell in. When her gaze connected with his, Massimo's gray eyes dull but full of tears, she knew she wasn't seeing things.

Damn, Catalina works fast.

"Did you just say you love me?"

As her eyes began to adjust to the darkness, she could see him more distinctly. Ten, perhaps twelve feet down, standing in a waist-high pool of oily, fetid water, Massimo was a big man for so small a space, his shoulders rubbing the well walls on either side.

"You're alive!"

Massimo nodded. "I am."

"And you're at the bottom of a well."

"It appears so." He looked around, as though realizing his own situation, before pointing up a passage to his left that she couldn't see but, based on how his arm disappeared, must be there. "It connects with a drainage pipe to the canal."

"How did you… *When* did… Where have you…"

"*Amore*, I will answer all your questions. But first, can you say it again?"

"You're at the bottom of a well."

Massimo laughed. So did Portia. She knew what he wanted to hear. She also knew she'd never hesitate to say it again.

"I love you, Massimo Bruneli, and I'm not going anywhere."

The Doge grinned. "No, you're not."

TWENTY-SIX

It was positively something out of a gothic romance. The villain shoots his pistol at the hero and hits. The hero falls, and the villain assumes he's clutched a victory. Only, the hero is wise, and knows if this bullet missed, the next one might not.

"Not that he did miss," Massimo said as he sat before the burning hearth in his suite, Portia toweling off hair still left wet after his shower. "Vlad got me, but the wooden bullet missed my heart. I intentionally fell off Cara's balcony and crashed in the water, putting on a show of floating as though I were dead. Honestly, I didn't think it would work, but Vlad was vain enough to assume he'd gotten a direct hit and so certain my revulsion to water would mean I'd never linger in it. A minute later, the Ravens hauled me onto their boat and sped away from the villa."

Pavlos, seated in a chair beside the fire, bobbed his head. "And you just let them take you?"

Massimo shrugged. "I wanted to make sure they were actually leaving Venice. After I was certain they'd traveled far enough, I waited for the boat to hit a large enough wave and *allowed* my body to be thrown overboard by the force. Then I just bobbed there in the water for a while in case they circled back. I learned quickly that it is a great advantage to be mistakenly thought dead."

Portia folded the wet towel and hung it on a hook by the fire to dry. "But then how did you get back to Venice, and why did it take you so long?"

"By the time I fled their boat, it was the edge of dawn," Massimo said. "I dove as deep as I needed to avoid the sun, but the whole time the currents were pulling and pushing me. I was the sea's toy. When the sun set, I emerged and began to swim. By that time, I must have been thirty, forty miles from shore. Every time a boat came within sight, I had to dive and hide once more. Finally, last night right before sunrise, I came into the canals. I considered walking the streets, but I didn't know if Vlad had left spies behind. I decided to hold out in Catalina's well until I could be certain no one was watching. Then," his eyes turned to Portia. "And then she said she loved me, and I knew I was safe."

Locking eyes led them to unlock their hearts. Massimo held out a hand to Portia, and she curled her fingers around his. The Doge used the touch to pull her to him, maneuvering her on to his lap. Portia wove her hands around Massimo's neck, leaning down to kiss him.

Pavlos cleared his throat. "I'll take my leave then. Your Serenities."

"Pavlos, wait."

The vicedoge stopped halfway between the fireplace and the door, turning at Portia's request. "*Principessa*?"

Portia stood, shaking off the feeling of becoming someone she wasn't. But then she understood, that wasn't what was happening at all. The nerves were because she was becoming someone she had always been but kept hidden.

"Can I ask you a favor?"

Pavlos bent at the waist. "It is my honor to serve, Signora."

"I have a friend back in Victoria. Her name is Mae. Would you mind… Can you somehow *get her* to Venice? I promise, I'll pay you back and stuff, I just don't have much money right now, and I—"

Massimo was behind her in a moment, his hands circling her hips, his lips pressed against her cheek. "*Mi amore*, you have more money than you could ever need. What's mine is yours. Only, you must know that you have to be cautious about who you let into this world. Most hueys don't adjust well to knowing we exist."

"I know, but I know Mae. She'll be shocked, but she'll understand. And besides…" Portia turned in his arms, her own anchoring on his shoulders. "…she'll need to be here if she's going to be my maid of honor."

The Doge's face exploded into a smile. "*Tesoro*…"

As they kissed, Pavlos made a quick exit, sealing the door behind him. Massimo's hands trailed down Portia's sides. His hands gripped her ass and lifted her. Portia's legs hooked behind him as he walked them back to the bed. At the edge, he paused, and she pulled back.

"Enjoy it all now, Your Serenity," Portia said. "This human body ain't going to hold out too much longer."

Massimo pressed his lips again to hers, drawing out a moan. "I don't care what age does to your body. My love for you will never die, and I will show it to you in whatever way you want me to."

Portia crooned. "Oh, that's so sweet."

A moment later, her mouth was hot on his, her tongue demanding entrance. Massimo gave it without hesitation, his grip on her backside tight and his control waning.

"All I want right now is you. But later: gelato. And gnocchi. Lots of gnocchi. And then, well… we'll just have to see what happens from there. It might involve gelato again, but we won't need a spoon."

Massimo laid her out on the bed and lifted his hand to the belt of his robe, undoing the knot. This woman was going to be the death of him, but before that, she would be his life.

"*Mia vita, si.*"

EPILOGUE

Massimo looked at the envelope a second time, tracing a finger over the impression of a dragon set into red wax. No, it wasn't an illusion. It was the official seal of his old friend and former co-conspirator, Igor Karahan. Had he escaped from the traveling barrel and learned that the Doge of Venice had forgone an opportunity to set him free? Few things could reacquaint Massimo with guilt, but that red seal had him squirming in his seat.

Massimo still questioned if, in fact, Vlad had been telling the truth, that he'd had Igor trapped in the traveling barrel when he'd passed through Venice a few months before. At the time, he'd had no suspicion, but perhaps it had been his own need to rationalize his inaction which had introduced doubt. In ancient times, the Macedonian generals had competed for custodianship of the corpse of Alexander the Great. The right corpse commanded more men than a thousand live kings. By claiming he had Igor in his possession, Vlad became the de facto paterfamilias of his line, if only by proxy until actually by the deed, and who would have the courage to call Vlad Tepeș on his bluff?

"When was this given to you again?"

Pavlos tapped steepled index fingers against the tip of his nose. "An hour ago. The messenger claimed to be representing the Varanasi paterfamilias."

It didn't matter that the seal was no longer intact. If this missive had been in the care of the Varanasi, none would have betrayed the trust afforded them to carry it.

"The messenger said that it was deposited in their archives two years ago by Igor Karmarov. Sorry, sire, by Igor *Karahan...*"

"I know all his names, Pavlos. There's no need for clarification."

"To be delivered to you," the vicedoge continued, "if he failed to advise them at some prescribed interval that he was, indeed, still alive. As of last week, that interval came and went without any word.."

Igor *was* dead then. *My friend, my mentor...*

"That makes Vlad Tepeş the father of his bloodline." His eyes roved to meet Pavlos's. "The father of *your* bloodline."

The vicedoge paled, a feat for any vampire. "And he's wasted no time in flexing the muscle of his new position. I received word from one of my brothers this morning: he's calling on us all to swarm just outside London."

"London?" That didn't make any sense. "Why would he be in London?"

"To set a trap, I'm told."

Massimo didn't need to ask the next question for Pavlos to infer. A good thing, as he'd slipped the letter open and was digesting its content.

"I don't know whom," the Greek vampire said. "But if the other news we've heard is true, that there has indeed been an illustrian born and she is in the care of Hoods at their fortress in Germany, that there is also a cadre of slayers there under their protection as well..."

"The trap is for a hood named Gerwalta Kline."

Pavlos's jaw snapped shut. He blinked his confusion. "Sorry?"

Massimo held up the letter for a moment before pulling it back and reading the core lines. "'*That, in fact, the child born to Gerwalta and Andreas in 1657 did not die, but was smuggled by a sympathetic benefactor into my care, and that one of the ancestors of their progeny, a Miss Gerwalta Kline, is now under my advisement in Chicago. In a recent mishap, however, I was given an opportunity to examine her genetic makeup and I have determined that she is, indeed, an inceptor.*' The son of a bitch knew. He knew and he didn't tell me."

"I'm certain he had his reasons," Pavlos countered. "Karahan wasn't given to irrational behavior. What I don't understand is why he'd share such a dangerous secret with you, a man who until recently didn't even know he was still alive."

"Because I owe a debt to the House of Red that I have never repaid. It was Gerwalta Faust who entombed the Ravens in silver all those years ago, whose ouster brought me to the throne. Igor's telling me this is how I pay my debt. I save Kline."

The truth fell like snow. Pavlos nodded. "You wish me to go to London then?"

"And let me know when the trap is about to spring. I'm there to save her, so in turn, she can save me."

The vicedoge's head quirked to the side. "Sire?"

"Vlad told me himself that the inceptor was the one protecting the slayer carrying the illustrian. By now, the child must have been born. So, I'm going to save her, just like Igor implied I should. And when I do, she'll owe me. What's she's going to pay me in blood. Illustrian blood."

Pavlos's throat bobbed as he swallowed down the statement. "But that will turn you human, if the stories are true."

"Yes, it will. And then I'll be able to give Portia the one thing currently outside my ability. I'll get to grow old with the woman I love."

A note from Kendrai:

If you have a good meal at a nice restaurant, you wouldn't think twice about tipping the server. Why not tip your author, too?

No, wait! I'm not asking you to send me money. You already paid for this book, and for that, I'm grateful. But I would be tickled pink if you tip me with a few moments of your time and a few words. by leaving an online review on the platform where you got this book, your generosity will help other readers discover the works I've written, and help me to pay my bills at the same time . Such acts are one of the greatest factors determining a book's success, and of making sure the author can afford basic living expenses, a factor which has proven to be essential in the writing of more books 95.6% of the time.

Many thanks.

k.

ABOUT THE AUTHOR"S"

Kendrai Meeks (aka Killian McRae) was deported from the American Midwest after graduating college and held against her will since in California. She really hates sarcasm. She first published in 2011 and has since put out books in romance and science fiction. In 2017, she decided to return to her first love, urban fantasy. She is the founder of the Bay Area Allied Indie Authors group. She has also been a featured speaker on a number of conference and industry panels on topics ranging from Fanfiction, to Audiobooks, to Serialized Fiction. She is a world music devotee and loves to travel (just hates to fly – a conflict, for certain). She enjoys twisting the extant into the exceptional, often basing her work on historical themes or legendary folk tales and mythology.

As Killian McRae, she's written several shades of romance, including historical, contemporary, thriller, and paranormal. Her Pure Souls series would make a great read for lovers of the Vampire Sovereigns.

ACKNOWLEDGMENTS

A special thank you to Chantell Reid, who helps by finding uncrossed t's and undotted i's before releases. To the pre-readers: who devote time with kindness, and suffer through enough typos to fill a book, literally and literarily. To my friends who keep me going in difficult times, and to my daughters. To Rebecca, who always helps me choose the right jello mold to make my rough outlines jiggle. Thank you to Irene Potocorvo for assistance in Italian idioms and translations. Thanks to Elizabeth Hunter and Jasmine Walt, for allowing me to share this book with their readers leading up to the release.

© 2020 Tulipe Noire Press

Kendrai Meeks, Killian McRae

Venice Dusk (Vampire Sovereigns #1)

978-1-953073-00-6

All rights reserved. No part of this publication may be reproduced, stored in a retrieval system or transmitted in any form or by any means, electronic, mechanical, photocopying, recording or otherwise without the prior permission of the publisher or in accordance with the provisions of the Copyright, Designs and Patents Act 1988 or under the terms of any license permitting limited copying issued by the Copyright Licensing Agency.

Published by: Kendrai Meeks

Text Design by: The Last TK, with compliments to the resources made available from Draft2Digital.

Cover Design by: The Last TK

Edited by: Rebecca Hodgkins and Chantell Ried

Milton Keynes UK
Ingram Content Group UK Ltd.
UKHW010443050324
438776UK00005BA/550